THE
FAIR-WEATHER
FRIEND

THE
FAIR-WEATHER
FRIEND

JESSIE GARCIA

ST. MARTIN'S PRESS
NEW YORK

First published in the United States by St. Martin's Press, an imprint of St. Martin's Publishing Group

EU Representative: Macmillan Publishers Ireland Ltd, 1st Floor, The Liffey Trust Centre, 117–126 Sheriff Street Upper, Dublin 1, DO1 YC43

www.stmartins.com

The Library of Congress Cataloging-in-Publication Data is available upon request.

ISBN 978-1-250-36445-6 (hardcover)
ISBN 978-1-250-36446-3 (ebook)

Our books may be purchased in bulk for specialty retail/wholesale, literacy, corporate/ premium, educational, and subscription box use. Please contact MacmillanSpecialMarkets@macmillan.com.

First Edition: 2026

10 9 8 7 6 5 4 3 2 1

PART ONE

FAITH

——

CHAPTER ONE

Carol

June 1 and 2

When television viewers in Detroit sat down to watch the eleven o'clock news on Channel 9 that Friday, they expected to see the usual: crime, a few tragic accidents, a community event or two, a press conference with a politician, perhaps even a cute story about animals or kids if they were lucky. Tom and Veronica would be the news anchors, with Roger doing sports and the ever-popular meteorologist Faith delivering the weather.

Faith Richards was Detroit's favorite. A mainstay at the station for five years, she was also a native of a nearby suburb, and that made her all the more endearing. Faith had left Michigan for college in a neighboring state, worked her way through small television markets ranging from Peoria to Cincinnati, and finally returned triumphantly.

The station made a huge deal of it. *SHE'S COMING HOME!* promos blasted when they hired her. That was soon followed by a new advertising campaign: *HAVE FAITH—WE DELIVER THE BEST FORECASTS!* But station management received criticism from both religious people and agnostics for using the word *faith* so cavalierly, and it was short-lived. Channel 9 settled on another phrase that finally stuck: FAITH, YOUR FAIR-WEATHER FRIEND.

The tagline became a staple every time Faith ended her weathercasts. ("And that's a look at our weather. I'm your fair-weather friend, Faith, now back to you, Tom and Veronica . . .") The "Fair-Weather Friend" slogan was so popular it was plastered, along with Faith's smiling face, on buses and billboards all across the metro.

Faith had tens of thousands of followers on social media and scored extremely high in the "Q ratings" the station used to measure popularity. She was featured prominently in several local magazines and was always a huge hit when she was out at community events, shaking hands and handing out free umbrellas with COURTESY OF YOUR FAIR-WEATHER FRIENDS AT CHANNEL 9 stamped on the handle.

Despite having never met Faith nor had the pleasure of receiving a free umbrella, Carol Henning considered herself one of Faith's biggest fans. Carol was a loyal Channel 9 viewer and had been for decades, ever since her own father preferred that station over all others. Carol had high respect for Jack, the previous main meteorologist at Channel 9, and when he retired she thought no one could fully replace him, but then along came Faith, whom Carol quickly learned to adore. Carol had always had a bit of a fascination for famous people. She couldn't wait to read her magazines: *People, Us,* and the *National Enquirer,* all delivered to the house and kept in a basket by her favorite chair.

In Carol's eyes, Faith was both beautiful and knowledgeable. Like many, Carol was especially enamored with Faith's famous "earring forecast." Faith had a collection of earrings in all colors and hues and in the shapes of clouds, lightning bolts, suns, and stars. Faith would tell viewers that they could always look at her earrings and know something about the weather.

It was like a game of I spy for Carol, and she would poke her husband, Jim, in the side as they sat in their two easy chairs each night, so close they could hold hands if they wanted to, although they rarely did anymore.

"Honey, she's got light blue earrings on, it's going to be a clear sky tomorrow!" Carol would say with a giggle, or "Uh-oh, she's wearing the *big* lightning bolts tonight!"

Jim would usually mumble something in return. It wasn't that he disliked Faith. Quite the contrary; Jim enjoyed watching her forecasts so he would know whether to bring a raincoat to work. But he was not a member of the Fair-Weather Friends Fan Club as Carol was. Those viewers got access via a password to a special spot on the station's website where they could watch the videos Faith would record each weekday teaching them about weather—different cloud formations or how a tornado starts, for example. Faith would also talk about vacations she was going on, what she did on her days off, or new earrings she was adding to the collection, and give makeup or styling tips. Occasionally she would even offer behind-the-scenes peeks at the station.

Carol relished the videos. They were so popular that local stores reported a surge in sales for earrings Faith showed off. Carol had a pair of cloud earrings that she had asked Jim to get her for Christmas, and she sometimes saw other women around town with ones Faith had worn on TV. The "blizzard" pair, made out of something resembling fancy cotton balls covered in glitter, were especially popular, as was the "heavy rain" pair of cascading crystals. Carol would always say "Fair-Weather Friends Fan Club?" to the women sporting these earrings, and they would smile hugely and nod, bonded by their mutual respect for

Channel 9's meteorologist. It made Carol feel a sense of community, something she felt was lacking in their quiet suburb, where most people just kept to themselves, driving to the closest Target, Costco, or Home Depot for their errands or walking their dogs but barely acknowledging the presence of a passerby. You'd be lucky if you got a nod.

This particular Friday Carol had even more reason to feel connected to Faith. Carol and Jim's niece, Olivia, had just started interning at Channel 9. Olivia wanted to work in television news one day and was majoring in journalism at Wayne State University. Olivia had landed this coveted internship that would have her shadowing various people in the newsroom. Although unpaid, it was still something Olivia told her aunt and uncle was highly competitive. Carol and Jim had whooped with joy and taken Olivia out to dinner to celebrate when they found out she was in.

This was the end of Olivia's first week as an intern, and although Carol had pressed her for a few details after nights one and two, she couldn't wait to chat over the weekend and get *all* of the juicy tidbits: What were Tom and Veronica *really* like? Was the sports guy, Roger, as tall as he looked on TV? How did Faith get her hair so silky and shiny? What did Faith eat for dinner? She had to be a size 6 or less. Carol could hardly remember being less than a 12 in her own life. She was a solid 16 now but chalked it up to getting older and the fact that her back hurt too much for strenuous exercise. Plus, she and Jim enjoyed comfort food and weren't about to go on some fad diet, and they had been married so long Carol didn't feel the need to impress anyone with her looks.

Faith had been on the six PM news that Friday wearing bright yellow sun earrings, so Carol already knew the forecast, but she was still ready to settle in and watch the late news top to tail to end her day. Jim was dozing off in his chair next to her.

Carol had a glass of cranberry juice and a bowl of microwave popcorn on the TV tray, the way she liked to end most evenings. They were in the den, Carol's favorite room. She considered it the epitome of cozy. Thick carpet went wall to wall, and a heavy wood hutch handed down from Jim's mother sat in the corner filled with knickknacks that appealed to Carol. She favored porcelain statuettes of angels and baby animals as well as souvenirs from trips, her favorite being a rubber Mickey Mouse figurine waving his gloved white hand. There was also a collection of scented candles on the hutch that had been on discount from the Kohl's department store where Carol worked. She would often light one at night. Right now, Spiced Apple Pie was burning and the whole room smelled like a synthetic version of her grandma's famous pies.

The rest of the den had a fireplace for winter, a ceiling fan for summer, a wood coffee table in the shape of a giant fish that Jim had made years ago in his basement workshop, and framed prints of generic impressionist art on the walls. They had been on discount when one of those big department stores was closing.

On the hutch were also a few framed photos of their nieces and nephews. Olivia's picture was pulled several inches closer to the front than the others, a nod to Carol's feelings. But if relatives other than Olivia ever came by, which they rarely did, Carol would slide the pictures to all be even before they arrived.

The space felt safe, like their own little corner of the universe, and it was from here that Carol and Jim watched so many things unfold across the world on the large TV they had splurged on.

Carol and Jim had never had kids of their own. It just hadn't been in the cards. They had tried casually for years, never following an ovulation plan or anything, just seeing if the universe handed them a baby, and when it didn't happen they turned their attention to work, nieces and nephews, and the freedom of a childless life.

Although Carol would never say this to the others, Olivia had always been her favorite. So smart and capable, with a wickedly mischievous side that Carol admired. Carol and Olivia grew closer as Olivia got older, especially when Olivia's mother, Evelyn, Carol's sister, took off for Europe after her divorce, saying she needed a deep and long soul search. She had been gone for over a year.

In contrast, Carol and Jim felt they got most of the travel they desired by watching reality shows. *The Amazing Race* always had exotic locales, and wherever *The Bachelor* and *The Bachelorette* were filmed. Why spend money to see places like Barcelona or Rio de Janeiro when television did such a good job of taking you there? That was their motto.

Carol's favorite type of show was true crime, such as *48 Hours*. If her life had gone another way she might have wanted to be a detective; it seemed so exciting. Instead, she read mysteries voraciously and tuned in to *20/20*.

She also watched the news every night, usually both the early and late shows, but sometimes she wondered why she did. Often, local news just made her feel sad, and if it weren't for the fact that she liked to be informed, and felt close to the TV anchors because they were in her den every night, she wouldn't be compelled to take in the nightly dose of bad news.

As the Friday eleven o'clock newscast started and the typical dose of crime stories unfolded one after the other, Carol shook her head and clucked her tongue. The depressing stories all included reporters delivering grim-faced reports in front of crime-tape. What a mess America was, she thought, and promised herself never to drive in certain neighborhoods lest she become the next victim of a carjacking, reckless-driving accident, or even shooting.

After the anchors made it through what seemed to be the nightly police blotter of stories, the next story was the blathering of the mayor about some new program he was unveiling to help lower-income families. Carol wasn't even fully understanding what it was about. It didn't matter; it didn't affect her anyway. She was in the suburbs. Even if they had lived in the city, they likely wouldn't qualify for any such program. While she and Jim weren't rich by any means, they were firmly entrenched in what she considered the lower edge of the middle class, a simple ranch home in a working-class suburb, never a worry about paying for groceries but always a calculation when it came to eating out or taking a vacation anywhere farther than a drive or longer than a few nights.

Now the news turned to a Detroit Ballet fundraiser that a famous ballerina had come to town for. A reporter interviewed the dancer and tried to stand on her tippy-toes to emulate ballerinas during her live report. She lost her balance and tumbled to the side as she and the anchors laughed.

"Don't quit your day job, Ashley!" Tom guffawed. "All right, up next, weather with Matthew, who's in for Faith tonight. . . . Will you need to crank up the AC this weekend? Stay tuned. . . ."

The show went to commercial break.

Matthew? Carol frowned. Matthew was the weekend weather guy. He was OK, but he was not Faith. Where was her favorite weather gal tonight? Faith had been on the six PM show and not said anything about leaving for the evening, as she sometimes did when she was going to be off.

Carol glanced at Jim, fully asleep and lightly snoring. She looked at her phone, resting between the cranberry juice and a lamp. She thought of Olivia. Maybe Olivia would know where Faith was. After all, she was working the night shift at Channel 9 and would be there now.

Carol picked up her phone and texted.

> Hi Liv, where's Faith tonight?
> I see Matthew is coming on.
> Did Faith skip out? Maybe
> she has a hot date!

Carol knew that Faith was unmarried and had no children. Could it be a date? It titillated Carol to have inside access to the station like this, and she stared eagerly as the typing bubbles were going. The bubbles seemed to be taking a long time. The commercial ended and the anchors were chatting with Matthew in that fake-banter way.

"So Matthew, I have friends coming in from out of town and I need some good weather for them. Can you deliver for us?" asked Veronica, with the huge, toothy smile that Carol always considered way too over-the-top.

"And I'm going to the Tigers game tomorrow," added Tom. "So we need that sunshine to stick around—but not too hot, please."

Tom was handsome, with silver hair, but it was extremely hairsprayed and he always looked overtanned, in Carol's opinion. In fact, Carol believed that Faith was the only one of the four anchors who was fully authentic and genuine. The sports guy, Roger, tried too hard and his puns fell flat.

"I would definitely bring some sunscreen with you to the game, Tom," replied Matthew, and started his forecast. He looked a little disheveled, his hair sticking up on one side and his tie not fully straight. Carol took a bite of popcorn followed by a sip of juice, feeling the tang of the cranberries collide with the saltiness of the popcorn. It was the perfect combination.

Her phone buzzed with a text from Olivia, and Carol picked it up.

I don't know where Faith is but something weird is going on. Matthew got called in at the last minute. Faith never returned from her dinner break. A few managers were running around whispering and went behind closed doors. Matthew seemed really mad. I heard him say he was having dinner with his fiancée when they made him come in to do the show.

Carol had to read the text twice. Never returned from dinner break? What the . . . ? That wasn't the Faith she knew and loved.

Looking back at the TV, she felt she could now see an anger in Matthew's eyes, his jaw firmly set, as he stood in front of the map talking about humidity levels. Carol frowned and glanced back down at her phone. What was going on? Curiosity mixed with just a touch of unease as she texted Olivia back:

Never returned from dinner break?

The response came quickly.

> That's what everyone is saying.
> I guess people tried to call
> and text her and she never
> responded. When it got to be late
> they had to call Matthew to fill in.

Managers behind closed doors? Faith not responding to phone calls? A prickle started in Carol's tailbone and began to traverse at a rapid pace up her spine.

The typing bubbles were going again. Carol waited impatiently, thoughts of the popcorn and cranberry juice suddenly gone.

Olivia texted again:

> You know what's even weirder? I
> might have been the last one to
> see her. I was going to my car to
> get something I forgot and she
> was out there. She handed me
> a folded-up note and asked if I
> would do her a favor and give it
> to Tom.

Carol thought immediately of an episode of *20/20* she had seen recently where a note handed to a neighbor had broken open the case. Too bad they didn't know what Faith had said in her note to Tom. Maybe if they did, Carol and Olivia could figure out what was going on. But before Carol could reply, Olivia texted one more time.

> I have to run. Laura, the
> executive producer, is waving

me over. I think she needs
something. Talk soon.

> OK, Liv. I'm so sorry you had
> this strange thing happen in
> your first week.

Olivia hearted it, and Carol knew the conversation was over for now. But what could be happening with Faith and what did Faith say in that note? Carol twisted her hands together as she watched Matthew finish his forecast. His endings were so boring, not ". . . I'm your fair-weather friend . . ." like Faith; he just always said stupid things like "So stay cool tomorrow. . . ."

"Jim?" Carol prodded at her husband with a finger.

"I'm sleeping," he muttered. Carol felt bad waking him up, she really did. Jim worked long days at his roofing job, but she needed to talk to someone.

"Jim, something is wrong with Faith."

"Carol, *I'm sleeping,*" he mumbled again.

"Well, wake up. Something is really wrong with Faith. I was just texting with Olivia."

Heaving a deep breath, Jim opened one eye.

"Who and what are you talking about?"

Carol told him everything, and Jim's other eye popped open. She was grateful that he recognized that this was more intrigue than they had seen on a Friday night in a long time.

"So what in the world do you think could have happened?" Carol asked. "I'm a little nervous."

"I'm sure she's fine. Maybe a misunderstanding, or she forgot her phone somewhere and got a flat tire. Isn't Channel 9 out on Metropolitan Road? It's kind of the middle of nowhere. If you got a flat out there and didn't have a phone it could take a bit to get to a gas station and call a tow truck."

"So she'd be walking on some dark road by herself at night?" Carol asked, shuddering at the image.

"I don't know, hon, but I'm sure she'll be back Monday."

Carol chewed at her fingernail. What if Faith was *not* back Monday? Where *could she be*?

They turned their attention to the newscast and sat through Roger's sportscast. Roger was doing a story on a swimming team, and he had all kinds of terrible water puns: "They really dunked their opponent," "They made a splash," "They dove right in . . ." Carol would have normally made fun of him, but she just didn't have it in her. Instead, she stared at the screen in numb silence.

The eleven o'clock show always had a final short segment on an uplifting subject; tonight Tom and Veronica read a story about a squirrel who would actually stand on little water skis and zip around a pool at a county fair. Carol tried to remember the TV term Olivia had taught them for this kind of silly story to end the newscast—a sticker? A flicker? No, it was a kicker, that's right. Now she recalled because it had seemed like such an odd word to her and Jim.

"A kicker? A kicker is a player in the NFL," Jim had said as they sat at the table eating dinner one night during Olivia's spring break. "And the Lions haven't had a good one in way too long."

"Yeah, Uncle Jim, but in TV it's called a 'kicker' too. My professor explained it to us like they kick out the show with something. The professor used to be a producer and she said she was always running around asking, 'What are we going to run as a kicker tonight? Who has a kicker idea?'"

So the water-skiing squirrel was a "kicker." Carol wanted to feel proud of her newfound TV knowledge and excited by her in-sider access, but the major emotion engulfing her was still worry.

All four of the on-air personalities laughed as the squirrel zipped around, a tiny red bandana around its neck. Jim even chuckled, but Carol remained silent. As the broadcast ended, Jim reached for the remote.

"Ready for bed, hon?"

She wasn't tired—she could actually feel the adrenaline in her body from the Faith mystery—but she didn't want to sit there any longer either.

"I guess so. I'm not really in the mood for any late-night com-edy shows tonight."

"Me neither, let's hit the hay."

Carol blew out the Spiced Apple Pie candle as Jim began turning off lights. He walked to the front and side doors to check the locks and stopped at the thermostat to lower the air-conditioning down to sleeping levels.

They did their usual bedtime routine, changing into paja-mas next to each other, brushing their teeth at side-by-side sinks while spitting nearly at the same time, washing hands and faces. Carol brushed her hair, while Jim merely ran his hands through his. She put on specialized face cream and used a more standard lotion for her hands and forearms.

They climbed into bed, their spots well worn and each smell-ing like them, Jim's the Bearglove brand of Old Spice deodor-ant and aftershave he wore and Carol's a body wash in a peach scent from Kohl's. They each had a favorite pillow, his flat and firm and hers large and fluffy. She always wrapped herself up in the majority of the floral comforter without any complaint from him; he usually kicked off any bedding during the night anyway.

Jim rolled to his side facing her back and put one hand on her waist in the sort of loose spoon position he favored. The heaviness of his hand through the blanket felt comforting. Normally she would fall asleep fast, but she couldn't stop her mind from going topsy-turvy about Faith, and she stared at the wall, even as Jim began to snore.

Strange how she could feel so viscerally about someone she had never even seen in person, she thought. It probably went back to her youth, when she started being interested in celebrities; they always seemed to have these amazing, glamorous lives, so different from her own humdrum existence. She had plastered her bedroom with posters of cute actors and beautiful actresses and read all about them in teen magazines. Celebrities just seemed like aspirational people, so gorgeous.

After an hour of lying in bed, Carol thought she might not sleep at all that night and debated moving Jim's arm and getting up, but somewhere after one AM she finally must have drifted off, because the next thing she knew sunlight was peeking around the edges of the curtains.

Her first thought was that she couldn't wait to speak with Olivia for more details. Trivial things like how tall Roger was or if Tom and Veronica were nice had gone by the wayside. Carol wanted answers regarding her favorite meteorologist.

But it was only 7:30 AM and Olivia might not be up. Olivia was heading into her senior year of college, and Carol remembered how college students liked to sleep. Forcing herself to wait until 9:30 to be respectful, Carol finally was unable to go a minute longer, and she called.

"I don't know anything more," said Olivia, her voice still thick with sleep. "But I guess it must have leaked out that they couldn't reach her, and Matthew had to be called in, because someone started a Reddit thread already called 'Where's Faith?'

and people on X are speculating everything from she quit or was fired to she has some incurable disease or even . . . I hate to say this, that she was abducted."

Carol sucked in her breath. "Abducted?" She could hardly say the word.

"It's just wild speculation, Aunt C. Don't believe everything you read on the internet."

"Of course not but . . . if she just left on her own, why didn't she tell the station she wasn't coming back after dinner?"

"I don't know," said Olivia.

"Other than the parking lot last night . . . did you get to talk to Faith much during your first week?" Carol asked.

"Yeah, a little. She seemed nice," Olivia replied. "She showed me the weather center and I actually told her about you, that my aunt Carol Henning was a huge fan and that you watch her videos. She thought that was cool. I even asked her to autograph a picture for you."

"You told her about *me*? She knows my name? I'm getting her *autograph*?" Carol felt a warm glow come into her cheeks, and her eyes began to glisten.

"Yeah, I told her we're super close, you're like a mom to me, that I tell you everything and that you and Uncle Jim were excited I had the internship."

"That is amazing, honey, simply amazing that you're conversing with *Faith Richards*!"

"It's neat. She's so popular. I did overhear one of the producers complaining about her, though."

"Complaining? What do you mean?" Carol's tone shifted. How could anyone do that about Faith?

"Yeah, the producer said to an editor 'Here comes the diva' when Faith was walking in one night. Then they started talking about how she always goes way longer in her forecasts than she's supposed to and doesn't care if it means they have to cut time on Roger's sports segment or anything else."

"Well," said Carol, immediately disliking this producer. "Her forecasts *deserve* more time. No one cares about sports anyway."

"Right," replied Olivia. "Listen, I'm sure she's fine, Aunt Carol. I'll let you know if I hear anything more."

They hung up, and Carol futzed around the rest of the morning, drinking two cups of coffee and sitting in the backyard listening to the birds. She put on her sun hat and pulled some weeds, but it was getting too humid, so she went back inside to the comfort of the air-conditioning and decided to do a deep clean of the cabinets in the kitchen, pulling out dishes and wiping shelves. Jim mowed the lawn and worked on fixing a slat in the wooden fence.

Carol began listening to an audiobook to distract herself. The novel was a complicated mystery that normally would have required her full attention, but she kept losing track of the characters and plot because her mind was flitting about thinking of Faith. After wiping the final shelf with a sponge, she ran a dry towel over it to soak up any wet spots and decided to turn off the audiobook and give in to the fact that she just couldn't concentrate. One thought kept repeating in her mind, and she whispered it aloud as a mantra:

"Faith is fine. Faith is fine."

She wanted so badly to believe it to be true, but somehow she had a gut feeling it was not.

CHAPTER TWO

Olivia

June 2

After hanging up with Aunt Carol, Olivia put her head back on the pillow and pulled the covers up around her shoulders. It was still very early by Olivia's standards, and she would have liked to have slept in more. Given how early she had to get up for classes this past semester—taking that 8:30 AM psych class to fulfill her humanities requirement had been a massive mistake from a schedule standpoint—she felt she now deserved sleep in the summer. Yet she had enjoyed the content of the class, particularly a section on how childhood traumas can affect us our entire lives. Olivia hadn't experienced the kinds of traumas the professor talked about, but she felt a tremendous amount of empathy for anyone who did. Plus, Olivia's parents' divorce followed by the absence of her mother was traumatic in its own way.

The internship at Channel 9 was the night shift, and she didn't have to be there until 2:30 PM, which was perfect. She could sleep late, get a run, stop at the corner coffee shop, and make a leisurely lunch all before work. But getting to sleep after her intern shift had been hard. She was usually jacked up from the excitement of the TV station and would scroll her phone endlessly or flip around on Netflix until at least two AM, sometimes later.

Last night was particularly difficult. How could Olivia sleep? She kept replaying in her head the whole scene in the parking lot and what happened after.

Olivia had gone to her car to grab a cardigan sweater. The newsroom was cold, and most people wore some kind of wrap or long-sleeved shirt, even though it was summer. Olivia had forgotten to bring the cardigan in at the start of her shift, and by dinner break she was freezing in her short-sleeved blouse.

She was just closing the car door, the cardigan in her hand, when a familiar voice startled her.

"Excuse me, intern? What's your name again?"

Olivia whipped her head around to see Faith standing there with a makeup mirror in one hand and a teddy bear in the other. A giant purse was slung over one of her shoulders with a couple of curling irons sticking out of the top.

"Oh hi, Faith. My name is Olivia." Olivia added a big, eager smile, hoping to strike that just-right intern look of *I'm here to learn, grow, and help.*

"Yes, Olivia, that's right. We met earlier this week. Sorry, we have tons of interns coming and going and I forget names."

"It's OK." Olivia kept the smile on her face. It really was OK. She didn't expect the main talent to know her name now, or even ever. They had bigger things to worry about.

"Olivia, can you do me a favor?"

"Sure!" Olivia felt the word perhaps came out sounding a little too puppy-dog-like, so she softened her tone a bit. "Yes, how can I help?"

"Are you going back inside? Can you give something to Tom? You know him, right? The anchor with the silver hair?"

"Of course."

Faith set her purse, makeup mirror, and teddy bear on the hood of Olivia's car and reached into her giant bag, pulling something out. It was a piece of paper, folded over many times into a small square as if very deliberately done. For a moment, it reminded Olivia of the origami she and her mom used to enjoy doing together, before Evelyn went to Europe and now was saying she wasn't sure when she was going to come back. A mom pang passed through Olivia's stomach, but she suppressed it.

"Here," said Faith, handing the tiny paper to Olivia. "Just tell him it's from me. Thanks."

"No problem."

Olivia placed the little square in her pocket and put her cardigan on as Faith was walking toward her car. Olivia noted Faith's walk. It was so delicate, like a ballerina's, like she was floating on air. Olivia wished she walked like that, but she felt she had been born heavy-footed.

Faith stopped, turned her head, and called out, "Hey, Olivia, good luck at Channel 9."

"Thank you," Olivia replied. "Have a nice dinner break."

"I will," said Faith breezily.

Faith seemed kindhearted, and Olivia considered herself a good judge of character. She had noticed, for instance, that Tom was gregarious and pleasant to all of the interns. Veronica was a little more standoffish but would warm up if you complimented her in any way. Roger, the sports guy, seemed sincere but a little like a buffoon. Laura, the executive producer, always had bags under her eyes—someone said she had a baby at home and her husband was gone a lot—and Matthew, the weekend weather guy, had an edge to him, like a chip on his shoulder. It was hard to believe any of them had ever been young interns like her, though. They were all so adult and confident in their place in society and in the newsroom.

One thing had shocked Olivia in her short time at Channel 9. She heard producers and others complain about Faith. Maybe they were all just jealous of Faith, Olivia decided, because she was beautiful and popular.

Olivia used her key card to get back in through the employee entrance. Having a key card to the station still felt thrilling. She was a part of the team and it was amazing. This was definitely the career she wanted. She still wasn't sure if on-camera or behind-the-scenes was the route for her, but she would figure that out.

On the way back to the newsroom was a women's restroom, and Olivia stopped to use the facilities. She was just washing her hands and looking at herself in the mirror when the thought of the little square in her pocket came into her head. She would walk down to the newsroom, find Tom, hand it to him, and tell him it was from Faith. Then she would look for Laura and see what she could help with tonight. Maybe they would let her write a short script that might make it to air. How amazing would it be to have an anchor read her words on TV!

One thing that had really surprised Olivia was that anchors did not write all of their own stuff; in fact, they wrote next to none of it. Executive producers, producers, and associate producers did the writing, with reporters writing their own stories and the anchor intros that went with them. Anchors took long dinner breaks, then came back and looked over the show, making some small tweaks but not researching or writing much of anything at all.

TV was a giant production, a dance of many people almost

like a Broadway play. You had your boatload of behind-the-scenes people all working to make the people onstage look and perform their best. It was a fascinating first week of the internship to see how it all came together.

Olivia started drying her hands with the hand dryer (a sign on the wall touted Channel 9's no-paper-towels environmentalism) but resorted to wiping them on her slacks when she couldn't get them fully dry. Was there a hand dryer anywhere in the world that fully got your hands dry, she wondered, as she looked at herself in the mirror. Olivia had been unsure how dressy to be for this internship and had opted for dressy, so she had on nice black pants with her blouse, but most everyone else had worn jeans on what she now knew was "casual Friday," and she had already decided she would do the same next week.

She was just about to leave the restroom when a thought came to her out of nowhere, so fast it was like an electric current.

That little square of paper in her pocket. What did it say? How did anchors talk to each other? What would Faith have to share with Tom? The square wasn't in an envelope, Olivia could easily open it and fold it back up and no one would be the wiser.

It might be fun to take a peek, right? The side of Olivia that her mom called "wicked" started to come out. Olivia liked to play little jokes and be sly. April Fool's Day had always been one of her favorites, and she loved testing out pranks on her family. Around Christmas they would do the "Elf on a Shelf" tradition where a small elf the size of a Barbie doll moved around to do impish things every night. When Olivia was old enough, she took command and would put the elf in ridiculous scenes every night, making her parents laugh in the morning. The elf hung from the ceiling fan, hid in the toaster oven, was found passed out next to a plate of milk and cookies, even showed up in bed next to her mom and dad once (Olivia had to stay up late for that one).

These types of things gave her a rush of adrenaline and were perfectly harmless, so why not peek at the paper burning a hole in her pocket? She glanced around the bathroom nervously even though it was completely empty. Quickly, before she could lose her nerve, she stepped into a stall and pulled the paper out, unfolding it rapidly. Her eyes scanned it over.

"Weird," she whispered aloud.

It just had a list of names on it, that was all.

Matthew (met) and Tara
Laura (executive producer) and Elliott
Steve the stalker (see PC drawer)
Kelly (college roommate) and Joel

She recognized two of the names: Matthew and Laura, the meteorologist and the executive producer, respectively. She had overheard Matthew talking about Tara and things they did together, so she assumed that was his girlfriend or fiancée. The others she didn't have a clue.

Completely unsure what this meant, she folded it back exactly as it had been, took a breath, and stepped out of the stall, scolding herself for even looking. Clearly she had now violated an intern code of ethics. Someone asks you to do something and you betray them? What kind of a person was Olivia? She lashed herself mentally as she walked back to the newsroom.

Tom was at his desk talking to his Apple Watch on a phone call. She waited a good distance away until he was done and she saw him grabbing his car keys for dinner break, then she walked quickly to intercept him.

"Excuse me, Tom?" It still wowed her to be talking to such a TV icon in her city. He turned to her with a big smile.

"Yes, Olivia?" He had told her and the other interns that he made it a point to learn all of the new names by day two.

"Sorry to bother you. I . . . uh . . . I just saw Faith in the parking lot and she asked me to give this to you. I don't know what it says." Olivia immediately regretted saying the last part. Why would she know what it said? She bit her lip as she pushed the little square at him.

He looked at the paper quizzically.

"Thank you. You're a dear for delivering it." He put it in his breast pocket. Olivia didn't even mind that he called her a "dear." In the mouth of someone else it might have sounded off-putting, sexist even, but she got the feeling he was like her grandpa and referred to women as "dears" in a well-meaning way all the time.

"You're welcome," she said, and turned to find Laura.

Olivia was able to focus on her intern work for the next few hours. She had brought her own dinner and ate at her desk while trying to work on writing a "bump" that Laura had assigned her. This was a tease to the next segment, along the lines of "Coming up next . . . ," but Olivia found it extremely difficult to summarize a story without giving it away.

"Remember, it's a tease," Laura had said. "You can't tell the audience the whole story in the bump or they won't tune in. So instead of 'Delta Airlines is giving away two-hundred-dollar travel vouchers to every American to get you to book with them' you might say 'What airline is offering a massive incentive that just might make you jump sky-high?' Get it? Don't say the airline, don't say the incentive, and use a fun play on words like 'sky-high.'"

So Olivia was laboring over how to write a bump teasing a new social media app called Picture Me that preteens were flocking to but parents found extremely dangerous. "What app could be killing your kids?" seemed a bit harsh, so she was playing around with the wording.

Suddenly it was after nine PM, and Laura seemed flustered by something. Then Laura pulled some others into a conference room. Olivia was trying to pretend she wasn't looking through the glass walls into the room, but she saw Laura gesturing and others nodding and appearing solemn.

A short time later Olivia overheard the assignment-desk manager calling Matthew and imploring him that he had to come in, saying Faith had not returned from dinner break.

Everything seemed to move very quickly from there. The producer, Kyle, asked Olivia if she was finally done with the bump. She showed him what she had written, something long and bulky that tried to play on the word *picture,* and he said, "Here's a simpler way," and changed it to "A warning all parents MUST hear about a popular but potentially dangerous new social media app . . ." She nodded and made a note to write in a more straightforward manner.

It was almost showtime. Laura was still on the phone in the conference room. Matthew showed up complaining loudly to the entire newsroom that he had been out to dinner and had to drop off his fiancée and come in to fill in for Faith; other people were whispering and wondering what was going on with Faith.

The show went on the air and no one at home would have been the wiser about the meteorologist switch, except for Aunt Carol, who texted Olivia right away asking why Faith wasn't on the eleven o'clock broadcast and wondering if Faith had a hot date.

After the show, the night crew was clearly still flustered by Faith's absence and talked about it as they walked to their cars in the parking lot. Some people were mad, saying it was typical Faith behavior, while others expressed worry. Olivia remained very quiet.

Checking social media when she got back to her apartment and seeing the Reddit thread and speculation on X, she tossed about in bed until at least four AM. Now Aunt Carol was waking her up wanting more answers than Olivia knew.

She shut her eyes again, willing darkness and slumber back into her body. She needed it. As she fell back asleep, she was dreaming of Faith. In the dream, Faith was on vacation, sipping wine overlooking the sea in Italy, when Olivia's mother, Evelyn, walked up to her and asked if they could talk. Evelyn started telling Faith that Olivia had looked at the note she was specifically asked to just give to Tom. Olivia jerked awake, her heart hammering.

Just a dream, she told herself, *just a dream. No one can possibly know. You were alone in the bathroom.* She looked at her clock: 11:30 AM Gizmo jumped on the bed and started meowing, giving her a stare-down. It was late for his breakfast.

"OK, fine, Giz." She pushed the covers off as her heart started to stabilize from the dream. Olivia lived alone. Well, she should have been living with Mom in the condo, but Mom was gone.

"I'll just be a few months, maybe a teensy bit more," Evelyn had said when she first took off. "You don't know the freedom I feel right now, with you deep into college and Dad and I no longer together. It's like I'm twenty years old myself. I need to harness this energy and do things I never thought I could do."

One year later she had returned once for Christmas but said that the nomadic European lifestyle suited her and that Olivia should just fly over to visit when she could. But how was Olivia supposed to have time to do that?

At least her mom still paid for the condo. With a full-time, unpaid internship, Olivia could not deal with mortgage payments. Mom sent money for food—she was financing all of this from cashing in stock options from her longtime corporate job. Olivia looked after the condo and the cat in exchange for the free housing, food, and a Netflix subscription.

Olivia got up and fed Gizmo, then started coffee for herself. She took a frying pan down from its hook above the stove and cracked open some eggs. While she waited for them to cook, she scrolled her phone, looking for more Reddit posts about Faith, but there was nothing startling, just more of the same. As she used a wooden spoon to whisk the eggs, she thought about why she hadn't told her aunt Carol that she had read the note Faith gave her.

Guilt. That was why. Olivia felt terrible about being a bad intern and disobeying orders to deliver the note straight to Tom. As for the content of the note, it was odd but it might be absolutely nothing. Maybe people with upcoming birthdays or an invite list to a party. Yet, now Faith had disappeared for the eleven PM show.

She didn't want to lie to her aunt. Maybe after breakfast she would be more clear-minded to tell Carol everything.

After pouring a cup of coffee and adding the vanilla cream she favored, she put her eggs on a plate, shook a little salt and pepper over the top, and went to sit down.

Her phone made a sound. Glancing down, she saw it was a breaking-news alert from Channel 9.

CHAPTER THREE

Carol and Jim

June 2

Around noon, Carol was looking into the refrigerator, assessing whether there was enough sandwich meat for two for lunch, when her phone chirped on the counter.

Looking over with her hand still on the open refrigerator door, she noted that it was one of those alerts from Channel 9. Carol had downloaded their free app and signed up for the alerts years ago. Sometimes the station sent updates about severe weather, but it couldn't be that, she reasoned, glancing out the window, where the sky was a perfect blue. Maybe it had something to do with someone being shot or a big car crash or perhaps it was something the governor or president had done or said. Carol almost didn't click on it, but curiosity got her.

She closed the refrigerator and picked up the phone, opening the alert.

Words in all capital letters blared out at her:

**BREAKING: CHANNEL 9'S OWN BELOVED
METEOROLOGIST, FAITH RICHARDS, FOUND DEAD.
COMMUNITY MOURNS.**

Carol staggered backward, dropped the phone on the kitchen floor, and heard it crash. It took her a moment to gather enough air into her lungs to scream and when she did, it was long and loud.

Jim was hammering in the final nail for the fence when the yell came from the house. It was a sound he had never heard his wife make before, piercing, anguished, clearly not just an "I stubbed my toe" yelp. Dropping his tool, he took off running and burst through the back door into the kitchen. Carol was standing with her hands over her face.

"Honey? What's going on?" He was panting from the sprint across the yard.

Carol pointed at her phone on the floor, the screen cracked. "A news alert . . ."

Jim's brow furrowed. News alert? What could that mean? His first thought was maybe some big international news, but why would Carol scream like that? He knelt to pick up the phone, scanning the words quickly.

"Oh no," he whispered. "Oh my God . . ."

Carol started to cry and slithered down to the kitchen floor, placing her back against the stove. He joined her, and she buried her face in her husband's chest, smelling his familiar Old Spice scent and crying harder.

"Let's wait for more information, honey. Maybe there's been a mistake," Jim said softly. He only hoped it was true. Didn't news outlets sometimes make mistakes and have to retract their statements?

Carol's phone rang. Seeing that it was Olivia, the only person in the world Carol would have felt like talking to, Carol fought back a sob and skipped the hellos.

"Olivia, you saw the alert?" she blurted out.

"Aunt C, I'm just sick. I don't know what to do or say."

"Me neither."

There was a long silence broken only by sniffles from each of them.

"Honey," Carol said, collecting herself. "You can come over here if you want to. I'll put on some of your favorite tea, and we have leftover cookies."

Carol enjoyed taking on the motherly role with Olivia, especially with Evelyn tromping through Europe. When Evelyn left she hadn't seemed to care that Olivia would need to process her own feelings about her parents' divorce. Typical Evelyn, Carol thought, all about herself and her emotions, as she had been ever since they were children. Carol had instead been the one to hug Olivia, let her vent, and offer to stay up late watching funny movies and eating ice cream together to make Olivia feel better.

"Maybe I'll stop by later," Olivia said softly. "I just need to go for a long walk or something. I can't believe I just talked to Faith yesterday. Less than twenty-four hours ago we were standing in the parking lot together . . ."

"I know, sweetie. It's inconceivable."

When they hung up, Carol and Jim looked at each other and Jim wrapped his arms around her, gently rocking them both, but after a minute he felt the need to do something more proactive than just sit there, so he said, "Let's turn on Channel 9. Maybe they'll have an update."

There was a small TV in the kitchen that they watched while cooking. Jim flicked it on, but Channel 9 was just running golf, the usual for midday on a Saturday. He was definitely not in the mood for that and clicked it off immediately.

"I'll check the newspaper's website," he said instead. Jim subscribed to the *Detroit Free Press*'s online edition and knew they often had breaking-news alerts. Opening his laptop, he put on his reading glasses, navigated to the site, and read the top story headline aloud to Carol, who was still on the floor.

Popular meteorologist reported dead by Channel 9. The *Free Press* is working to confirm.

Carol let out a whimper.

"This is just like Princess Diana." She sniffled. "Just like how I felt that day."

Jim remembered how distraught Carol had been after Princess Diana's death, how many months—no, really years—it had taken her to get over it, and how long he had to console her. He wasn't anxious for a repeat.

"I wonder *how* she died . . ." Jim speculated, scrolling through the rest of the newspaper's online front page but not finding anything else. "I guess it could have been natural causes. Maybe she had a heart attack or a stroke. A car accident. Or you don't think she . . ."

"Don't even say it," Carol snapped. "There's no way."

The thought had crossed Carol's mind too but she wouldn't let it go there. It was simply not possible that Faith would have taken her own life.

Silence filled the kitchen. Slowly, Carol pulled herself to a standing position, holding the counter for support. She stood there for a long minute, staring at the floor.

"I think I need to go lie down," she finally said softly. "I have a pounding headache."

"Of course, honey. Come on, I'll help you there."

Jim steered her to the bedroom, getting two aspirin from the bottle in the bathroom cupboard and filling Carol's bedside glass with water. He closed the curtains.

It felt good, childlike, to have someone tuck you in, and Carol accepted it gratefully. She smiled at Jim and watched as he pulled the door with a soft click. After popping the aspirin in her mouth and washing it down with a long drink, she curled into a fetal position and shut her eyes.

Two hours later Carol awoke, her headache somewhat better, and she came into the kitchen, where Jim was still seated at the table, peering through his reading glasses at his laptop. He looked up with a solemn expression.

"What? Did you learn something new?" she asked, and her stomach clenched.

"Honey, sit down," he said softly.

"I don't want to sit down. What did you learn?"

Jim sighed. "I think it's best if you sit down."

Warily, she lowered herself into a chair opposite of Jim and looked at him. "What?"

"Channel 9 doesn't have anything new except that there will be a vigil tomorrow at eleven AM at a park near the station," he said. "But the *Free Press* has some new information. They said the medical examiner confirmed her death, and also that their sources tell them it was no accident. Carol, I hate to say this but she was found murdered in her car not far from the station. Sounds like strangulation."

The words would not penetrate Carol's brain properly. It was as if there was a wall preventing them from going in. She shook her head and said firmly, "No. That's not true."

"Honey . . ." he replied softly, reaching for her hand again. She snatched it away.

"Don't say things like that out loud, Jim. *Their sources.* What does that even mean? I don't believe the *Free Press.* I won't believe anything until Channel 9 tells me."

"Well, let's watch the five o'clock news in a bit," Jim said, glancing at the clock. "In the meantime, do you want to see what the other members of the Fair-Weather Friends Fan Club are saying? Don't they have a Facebook page?"

Carol had sort of forgotten about the Facebook page. It wasn't something she went to often, but maybe the solidarity would be good.

Jim spun his laptop around and pushed it across the table and Carol found the page. Across the top someone had already changed the group's cover photo to "RIP Faith," with a photo of her smiling surrounded by flowers. It looked like one of those photoshop or AI-generated pictures a person can make quickly. The tributes were pouring in.

> *"I will miss her for the rest of my life."*
> *"She was the kindest person. I met her at the state fair once and she told me I looked young for my age. I will never forget it."*
> *"I used the umbrella she gave me every time it rained and I always thought of her."*
> *"Faith, we love you! Who will give us the earring forecast now?"*

Carol noticed that one woman named Chloe was encouraging the whole Facebook group to attend the station's vigil the next day and to wear their "Fair-Weather earrings" as well as bright yellow shirts in a sign of unity and love for Faith. Carol decided to see if she had enough energy to attend.

As they waited for the five o'clock news to start, Carol felt compelled to add a comment of her own to the Facebook page:

You were like a dear friend, Faith, and we looked forward to your forecasts every night. We miss you already. Your loyal fans, Carol and Jim.

At 4:58, Carol and Jim moved to their easy chairs in the den and turned on Channel 9. Jim reached for her hand and Carol took it gratefully. The music started and the graphics began. The camera went to the weekend anchor, Stella, who looked red-eyed and somber.

"Good evening. We begin with tragic news about one of our own . . ."

Stella said police confirmed that Faith had been found in her car, parked in a remote area not far from the Channel 9 studio. Her body showed signs of trauma, and police were treating her death as a homicide.

The station's stories turned to remembrance and community support. There was one long piece with tributes from colleagues, then a series of interviews with tearful viewers who all seemed to be interviewed at a big downtown farmer's market (Olivia had taught Carol and Jim that when you talk to random people like that it's called MOS—man on the street), and a montage of Faith's most memorable weather forecasts. When the show finally got to normal weather with Matthew, he started with his own tribute.

"I just want to say that Faith was a role model to me. She had the biggest heart and the most creative ideas. We're all going to miss her around here so much."

Carol found herself wondering if Tom, the main anchor, had still gone to the Tigers game as he had told viewers the previous night or if he was at home mourning. She tried to picture what kind of house he might have—large, for sure—and if he was sitting in his living room crying.

It was only when the newscast was over that Carol realized she had not heard back from Olivia, who had said she might stop by. Carol texted her.

> Hey honey, did you still want
> to come over for tea and
> cookies tonight?

There was no answer. Olivia was usually so good about texting back immediately. But maybe she was resting. Hadn't she said she wanted to go on a long walk? Perhaps she was tired.

Carol leaned her head against the back of the La-Z-Boy and thought of her own fatigue, her brain trying to digest this horrible day, which she figured had to be one of the worst in her life. Sure, Faith wasn't a member of Carol's own family, but Carol *felt* like she was. After all, she was in Carol and Jim's house way more than any family ever was. And Carol grew even closer to Faith because of those videos Faith made. Carol got to hear about Faith's vacations and see her clothes and makeup. Plus, there was just the tragedy of Faith's young age. She was maybe in her mid- or possibly late thirties, Carol guessed; so vibrant, so alive. It was impossible to compute that this bright and beautiful being was not going to be on TV anymore, sharing laughs with Tom and Veronica and making the audience feel comfortable and secure with her weather knowledge.

"I'll start dinner," Jim offered.

Carol nodded, adding softly, "There's some chicken breast. I was going to sauté some vegetables to go with it, maybe a potato."

"I got it," he said, patting her hand. "Do you want me to light one of your candles and let you rest here a bit more?"

"Yes. How about Warm Honey and Vanilla?" she said, thinking the scent would be soothing. He crossed the room and used the long automatic lighter to get the candle going, then moved it closer to Carol by setting it, and the little dish it rested on, on the fish-shaped coffee table. He headed to the kitchen, and she heard the refrigerator opening, things being chopped on a cutting board, the gas stove burner firing up, and the clattering of pots and pans.

Carol let the smell of the candle and sautéed carrots and onions wash over her. It would have been a peaceful early evening if she wasn't thinking about the murder. Her headache lingered slightly in one temple, and she rubbed at it. It made her nauseous to picture Faith dead in a car, strangled, and Carol just kept having the same perplexed rumination:

Who would ever hurt Faith? Faith had no enemies; everyone loved her. There wasn't a soul on the planet who had anything against Faith Richards.

CHAPTER FOUR

Matthew

January
Five Months Earlier

"Are you fucking kidding me? She's calling in sick *again*?"

Matthew was incredulous. Faith took more sick days than anyone he had ever worked with. Not only did she use all six of the days the station gave everyone yearly, but she got a Family Medical Leave Act accommodation that allowed her to call out an extra one to two times a month, and apparently there was nothing anyone could do about it. He was told only that it was an "HR matter" and he wouldn't be privy to any more details.

"Sorry, man, she said she's sick," responded the daytime executive producer over the phone. "I have no control over it. We need you to do the four, five, six, six thirty, and eleven tonight."

"It's supposed to be my day off! Does anyone even think of that . . . or care?"

"Abby did the morning show and Chuck is on vacation so there's no one else," said the producer. "Don't shoot the messenger. You know you'll get a comp day down the road for it."

"Yeah, whatever," Matthew grumbled, thinking of the things he would have to cancel that day: a haircut, lunch with an old buddy, a night in cooking and watching a movie planned with Tara. She had been moody lately and he wanted to try and find out if everything was OK. Their wedding was still nine months away, but she was already in manic prep-mode with her mom. He chalked her moods up to that but wanted to be sure, and he planned to sweet-talk her a bit at dinner. Now that would have to wait. All because of Faith.

He gritted his teeth just thinking of his coworker. They barely spoke when they saw each other in person, only communicating in more than a few words when absolutely necessary about things like schedules or new weather graphics, yet they put on a united front for appearances and promos. If you saw the weather-team promo or saw them out in the field together, you would think they were best friends. Faith, Abby, Chuck, and him. The four amigos—yeah, right. Nothing could be further from the truth.

None of them really cared for each other that much. They certainly never hung out or asked about each other's vacations or kids anymore. They did their jobs and went home. Matthew knew very little about Faith's personal life other than that she had a sister named Hope. Faith seemed to talk to her on the phone a lot, and they went on vacation together, always some girls' get-away for something he would not have been interested in—like a shopping weekend in Manhattan. He did hear Faith complain to Abby once that Hope was perennially broke and Faith had to finance their adventures.

It used to be different between Matthew and Faith. Matthew felt he had been very kind when Faith first joined Channel 9, even inviting her out for lunch despite his anger at being passed over for the weeknight meteorologist chair. After all, it wasn't *her* fault, and he had been warned by the news director, Perry, to make sure there was team bonding. But just a few months later he overheard Faith talking in the break room when he was walking past. She was telling Veronica that Matthew was "sooo small-market" and shouldn't be in a large market like Detroit. It still made his blood boil just to think of it. He stopped being nice to Faith after that.

If they all weren't paid so goddamn much, Matthew might have quit this job years ago. He should have done it right when Faith was hired, to be honest. He had been at the station for two years already as the weekend guy. It was his turn to be promoted. He should have been next in line when Jack finally retired, but no, they gave it to the newcomer instead. Not only that but they made a huge deal about her "coming home."

Big effing deal. Matthew was from the city of Detroit itself, not even a suburb like her, yet no one had touted his homecoming when he started at Channel 9, moving from a small station in Lansing. But for her . . . the red carpet was rolled out.

Then came her stupid "earring-cast." Had anyone in the history of television ever thought of a dumber idea? He had tried wearing ties with clouds and suns on them in his first market, but the news director told him it was childish and to stop. Yet somehow her earrings were OK with management? He just didn't get it. How could she be *so* popular that the station even created a fan club just for her?

When they were forced to be at events together, why was it that people pushed past him to stand in line for her? Couldn't they see right through her? Her phony smile, her layers of makeup, her fake eyelashes. She wore glasses sometimes in real life but contacts only on TV, colored contacts. They made her eyes look bluer than they actually were.

She even wore a wig. He didn't know if anyone else at the station knew that, but one night he had forgotten his wallet in the weather center and came back between the 6:30 PM show and the 11:00 PM show to grab it. The weather center was in its own little space set away from the newsroom, with a heavy wooden door that could be locked. He used his key, and when he walked in she was sitting there with earbuds in listening to something, curling iron in hand, styling the hair of the long wig while she wore some kind of scarf over her head. She jumped at seeing him and fumbled to cover the wig with a second scarf that was on her desk.

Trying to pretend he hadn't noticed, he mumbled about getting his wallet, dashed to grab it, and scurried out, shock overcoming him at seeing her like that. Her long, flowing hair was one of her calling cards, and he was stunned to know it was a wig. He would never have guessed. She had not done her full makeup for the later show yet either, and between that and the scarf on her head she looked much older. He told Tara about the wig that night and she burst into laughter, yelling, "I knew it! A lot of women on TV wear wigs or extensions and I just knew she was one of them!"

In Matthew's and Tara's minds, "the Queen of Detroit weather" was a phony in so many other ways too. She wasn't even a *real* meteorologist, not certified from the American Meteorological Society or the National Weather Association, like Matthew was. She was more of a weather performer, an illusionist.

Stations could hire "mets" (as they were called in the industry) without the official seals, and viewers wouldn't know the difference, but those inside knew. He had the seal next to his name on the screen, a fact that he was immensely proud of. She didn't, a fact that she seemed to care very little about. She could have studied for the tests and tried to earn the seal, but she apparently had no interest. He could spout Michigan weather facts in an instant.

Average snowfall in Detroit: 40 inches.

Average snowfall in Grand Rapids: 80 inches.

Last F5 tornado close to Detroit: Flint in 1953.

Last huge flood: August 11, 2014, with tens of thousands of
basements flooded as the city took on six inches of water in a few
hours.

Had a Michigan bridge ever been shut down by winds?
Absolutely. Mackinac Bridge, five miles long, always closed when
winds were over 65 mph winds.

He liked to predict every detail of his own forecasts by analyz-
ing maps and trends, whereas he noticed she just copied whatever the National Weather Service was saying, down to the exact
temps or how many inches of snow they'd be getting. When severe weather would hit—a blizzard or tornado warning—and
they had to be on the air wall-to-wall for hours, he felt she strug-
gled, stumbling over her words and not giving the type of information he could give. Tara would record these broadcasts and
they'd play them back, laughing and making fun of Faith.

Even the body Faith presented on TV was not quite real; it
was squeezed into outfits. He heard her talking to Abby once
about the amount of girdles and Spanx they had to wear to fit
into their dresses for TV. He knew from Tara that Spanx was a
brand of women's undergarments that helped tighten up certain
areas.

In real life, Faith had a tiny gut, but you would never know it
on TV. She chomped on appetite-suppressing gum all the time,
the wrappers all over her desk. He saw her looking up tummy
tucks on her computer. Meanwhile, he never wore anything to try
and hide his true body. Yes, he was getting a little thick around the

middle, but he wasn't going to try and hide it. He would just buy bigger suits.

Worst of all, though, Matthew knew that Faith sometimes lied to her viewers. He heard her taping her videos for the fan club. At least twice she told them things that didn't really happen.

"So here's a funny behind-the-scenes Channel 9 story in case you're wondering why you saw me on X in one dress today but you'll see me on the air in another," she said once. "I took a selfie at Starbucks in my mint-green dress and was then coming into work juggling my huge purse and an iced coffee. Veronica was coming out the door at the exact same time and we bumped into each other and coffee spilled all over my outfit! She was so apologetic but it was all my fault. I'm such a klutz! Luckily I keep several spare outfits here. I changed into an electric-blue outfit and ordered another iced coffee from DoorDash. I sure do need my cup of joe!"

Matthew knew that Faith had actually spilled coffee on herself when her elbow bumped it on the desk. He had been annoyed because some of it ruined the jet stream maps he had just printed out. So why lie to viewers? He guessed it was because it made her seem slightly less clumsy to have run into someone as she walked in the door, but it bothered him to his core, so he made an appointment with Perry to tell him about it. Matthew expected Perry to be in total lock-step agreement with his views that it was unethical. Perry leaned back in his chair to listen, cupping his hands behind his head, but when Matthew finished, Perry burst out laughing.

"*This* is why you're so upset?" he asked.

Matthew felt his face start to flush.

"Well, yes sir, I believe in journalistic integrity and she's twisting the truth."

"Come on, this isn't a Woodward and Bernstein moment. Maybe she spilled coffee twice that day. I would classify this as a giant nothing burger. My advice to you, Matthew, is to keep your head down, stay in your lane, and be sure to pick your battles. What, did you expect me to suspend Faith over this?"

"I . . . guess not. I just thought you might like to know."

"Well, now I know." Perry laughed again, shaking his head, and Matthew slunk out, ashamed.

The other time Matthew caught Faith in a lie to viewers was similar—an exaggeration of a story about how hard she had worked doing remote weather forecasts from the Storm Tracker vehicle that was set up at "Jazz in the City." She told the world that she had to dash to buy food in between the five PM and six PM shows and how crazy it was getting back in time. He knew that she had in fact eaten nothing but a power bar from her purse.

This time Matthew did not bother to go to Perry, not wanting a repeat of his humiliation, so instead he socked it away in the "I hate Faith" file he kept in his head. Tara knew all about his feelings; he complained plenty to her. She empathized, and they would have fun googling things like "how to kill a coworker and get away with it." Matthew and Tara would laugh, fantasizing about an alternate universe in which they actually did something to Faith, but they knew in this universe they were maybe stuck with her.

Five long years being on weekends and playing second fiddle. He kept hoping one of two things would happen to Faith: Either she would get fired for some indiscretion or she would take her carnival act and go higher—Chicago or LA, even the network. The *Today* show would surely love her ridiculous earring forecast for its heavily female audience, he thought, and then he would be promoted. But none of it had happened yet.

Again, the money was too good for him to leave. He made well into the six figures even doing weekends. So as much as it sucked leaving Tara every Saturday and Sunday night, he did it. But he resented it. Every single minute of it. And he couldn't wait to get Faith out of there one day.

CHAPTER FIVE

Steve

January

How lucky was Steve to have found his true love? He was the most blessed guy on the damn planet. It started the first moment he and Faith had touched hands. When their fingers grazed, Steve felt a ripple of electricity in his body, and he knew she did too.

The second time they connected he told her how beautiful she was, and she looked away—he thought it was cute that she was bashful like that. As their relationship deepened Steve started advising Faith what to wear on the air. Each day he would tell her: "You look so sexy in red" or "Blue makes your eyes pop" or "That dress brings out *all* of your curves."

There were so many things Steve admired about Faith: She was sweet and funny, with a sexy TV voice. She was smart, a science nerd; he liked science nerds. They were the same age and had grown up just two towns apart, something that kept them bonded. She had a sister, so did he. Each new thing he learned about her only cemented his love and admiration. There was no one else he wanted to be with, no one else he ever even thought of. She was the only woman for him.

If only she would return his calls, emails, Facebook messages, and letters. It was starting to piss him off.

That first time they touched he had stood in line to meet her for almost an hour. She was shaking hands and kissing babies at Greekfest. He couldn't take his eyes off her. When he got close to the front of the line his heart started to race, his face flushed, and he felt a boner coming on. Quickly he thought of an ugly neighbor to make it go away. His palms were sweaty and when he was the next person in line to greet her he wiped them on his shorts.

"Hi, thanks for watching Channel 9," Faith said, extending her hand to him. He took it and felt that brilliant energy pulse between them. Yet, the phrase was also the same one she had delivered to everyone else in line. Didn't he deserve more? Couldn't she see the love shining in his eyes, feel it radiating from his chest?

He was so flustered by her looks that he could barely stammer two words together. He thinks he remembered saying, "You're welcome," but her eyes were already past him to the next person in line as she was saying, "Hi, thanks for watching Channel 9." No matter. That magical touch of their hands was all he needed.

He watched every forecast of hers to see when she might be out at another event. When she announced that she would be greeting people at the Belle Isle Art Fair, he arrived three hours before her scheduled time so that he could be first in line.

She didn't seem to recognize him from the first time, but he had more confidence to speak at this event. He told her his name, plus the thing he had wanted to say for months, if not years:

"You're beautiful."

She looked away in that bashful way and said, "Thank you." He would have said more, but there was a family behind him in line to talk to her and the kids were jostling each other and one bumped into his leg hard, pushing him slightly to the side. He glared at them. Faith knelt down to the kids' eye level and gave them a huge smile, saying, "Hi, sweeties—how old are you? Do you like watching the weather?"

She could have asked him those things, he thought. She could have called him "sweetie." He was starting to turn away but caught sight of a hint of cleavage down her station-issued polo shirt, and with her kneeling practically in front of him another hard-on started. He had to hightail it to the bathroom to tuck it up under his belt. Then he watched her from afar for the rest of her visit.

There were lots of ways to reach her—direct messages on social media, an email address on the website, old-fashioned letters sent to the station—so he started trying all of them. When she didn't respond and, in fact, blocked him on X, he knew it was time to amp up his game.

Across the street from the station's gated parking lot were a gas station and a restaurant. It was easy to act nonchalant in his car and use his binoculars to see what kind of car she drove and the direction she turned in during dinner breaks or after work. He would stay a safe distance as he followed her.

Steve had a mix of emotions as he did this: He looked at himself as her escort, for safety. He didn't want any crazy people getting ideas. He was there to protect his baby. But he also thought about the image of overpowering her himself, of forcing his body on hers until she gave in to how perfect they were together. If he could have tied her up, he would have. She just needed time to learn to love him.

Steve would follow her all the way to her apartment building in downtown Detroit. It was called Three Diamonds and looked like just the kind of place he would want to live with her. They could stroll to the coffee shops in the area, hand in hand, looking for a great breakfast spot after their marathon session of morning sex.

She had to get to know him, it was as simple as that. True, he didn't have a job and was living with his parents, but that was just a placeholder. He had so much love to give the right woman, and she was the right woman. They were connected via their minds, he knew that. He would send her mental messages about what color she should wear each day, and sometimes she listened to him. When she did, it got him so excited he would pleasure himself right during her forecast.

But he wanted a real date, wanted to touch her hand again. When she kept ignoring his letters, messages, and even calls to the weather center (it always went to voicemail, where he would leave long messages), he decided to let her know that he knew a lot about her. So he sent her a letter with a picture of three diamonds crudely drawn on it.

"You look like three diamonds. I can make you feel like five diamonds," he wrote beneath his drawing. He figured she would then get the hint that he knew where she lived, that he meant business about being her boyfriend. Maybe it would get her to return a note to him.

If not, he might have to go even a step further.

CHAPTER SIX

Kelly

January

Kelly had a tuna sandwich in one hand and was scrolling her phone with the thumb of the other. She had five new emails, four of them junk. But the last one . . . no way. She froze, the sandwich halfway to her mouth. It was from Faith Richards.

Warily, Kelly lowered the sandwich and clicked to open the email.

> Hi Kell—it's been a long time. I still feel terrible about what happened. I'm at the point in my life where I'm trying hard to make amends with people for some of my past mistakes. I think about things I did to you all the time and I feel sick about them. I would like to meet you for lunch, and I have a gift I made for you myself. Would you please accept my invitation?
> —Faith

Kelly sighed. She was on her lunch break at work, a tiny sliver of time, twenty minutes if she was lucky, in between grading and kids stopping by with questions. She was trying to wolf down the food she hastily made that morning. She had to get ready for fifth hour.

Teaching high school Spanish was exhausting, especially when you had to deal with kids who were forced to be there because it was a requirement and couldn't give two shits about Spanish. She didn't have the mental energy to deal with Faith right now. Plus, why was Faith even reaching out to make amends? Didn't she have enough friends, as loved and adored as she was in Detroit?

But the bigger question was why should Kelly go anywhere with her, given their history? Faith had two strikes, two big, giant ones, plus Kelly was busy—new house, this new teaching job, Joel—and felt she didn't need drama in her life.

After packing up her lunch box and putting the leftovers in the staff fridge, Kelly headed back to her classroom. She had to go over complicated verb conjugations with the class in prep for a test in a few weeks. This required her full attention, so she compartmentalized Faith into a closet in her brain and focused.

After the last bell rang and the nonstop banging of metal lockers in the hallway finally subsided, Kelly sat in the stillness of her classroom. It was her favorite time of day, a chance to organize her lesson plans and take a deep breath or two. In yoga they preached taking "conscious breaths," but Kelly found she only had time for a conscious breath after the school day was over.

Her thoughts drifted back to Faith. Kelly decided she would ask Joel for his opinion. He knew all about Kelly and Faith's shared history. Heck, both Joel and Kelly could have been reminded of Faith every night if they watched Channel 9, but long ago they had switched to Channel 2 to avoid seeing her. Kelly didn't need a nightly dose of her old college roomie, not after the shenanigans Faith had pulled back at the dorms and again years later.

At 5:45, Kelly was home, heating up some lasagna they had made over the weekend, when Joel came in from running errands. He worked from home but got restless by four and usually found a few things to do to get out of the house.

"*Hola, Señora,* how was your day?" He walked over for their nightly peck on the lips while simultaneously cupping one of her buttocks lightly. She didn't mind; it was comforting and sexy at the same time.

"Hi, honey. My day . . . Well, Lexi and Aidan continue to be troublemakers at every opportunity. I busted them with a bingo card they made to make fun of teachers. They have squares for everything from 'wipes nose' to 'wears ugly jeans' and they mark it throughout the day. I think they got me on 'looks tired and bored.' I had to send them to Mahaffey's office for another talk. Those two are on the road to nowhere fast."

"Or maybe they're on the road to being the next great creatives or something," Joel said with a laugh. "That's pretty funny. Anything else?"

"There was something," said Kelly. "I'm actually trying to figure out what to do."

"Oh yeah, what's that?" Joel leaned against the counter, cocking his head in a way that she had always found incredibly appealing.

"Soo . . . you won't believe who emailed me, asking for a lunch date."

She could see the wheels turning in his head, but she was impatient to get to the story, so she didn't wait for him to guess.

"OK, I'll just tell you. Get ready for this. It was my 'fair-weather friend' herself."

"Wait . . . you mean . . . not *the* Faith Richards?" His eyebrows shot up. "You're kidding me?"

"Not kidding. She said she's at a point in her life where she wants to make amends and apologize and even made me some sort of homemade gift. I don't know, Joel, I haven't responded yet. I wanted to ask your opinion."

"Well . . ." He contemplated. He had never met Faith in person, had only seen her on TV and heard the stories from Kelly. "It would just be at a restaurant, right?"

"Yes, I think so. I mean, I would make sure it is."

"Do you want to do it?"

"Curiosity sort of gets to me a bit. It's been so many years since we last spoke. Maybe she's a whole new person. And I do wonder what in the world she made me. Faith was never crafty. It's probably part of the reason why she bought so many things. The rest of us would go to 'make your own tie-dye' nights and things like that at the dorms and she would stay home and well . . . you know."

"Right, but so many years later, I guess it can't hurt to go to lunch, right? Nothing bad is going to happen."

"That's kind of what I was thinking," she said.

Later that night before bed, Kelly read the email again three times, before taking a deep breath and deciding to respond.

Faith—It's been a long time. I have a new job teaching Spanish which is keeping me busy but I can probably find time for lunch on a weekend.

She left it at that, short, simple, to the point. No use getting into anything deeper in an email.

Hovering her finger over the send button, she took a long breath. Was she opening another Pandora's box or was she instead closing a chapter? She opted for closing—why not be optimistic? people could change—and she hit send.

But right after she did, a strange feeling came into Kelly's body, a feeling like she had just made a mistake and would regret it.

CHAPTER SEVEN

Laura

January

As the executive producer of the eleven o'clock news on Channel 9, Laura knew a lot about her anchors—prided herself on it, in fact. A producer should always be in touch with the talent (the industry term used for on-air people). It helped create the best kind of show, in Laura's mind, so she made it a point to remember the names of spouses, siblings, kids, and grandkids for the main Monday–Friday talent. Tom had a wife, two children, and three grandchildren, Veronica was married with no kids, Roger and his wife had a baby, Faith was the only one unmarried. Laura also marked down the anchors' birthdays and ensured cake and flowers awaited them at their desks.

She knew their quirks and faults too—the fact that a few times each year Veronica threw up with nerves in the women's room before the show despite the many years she had been on air; the fact that Tom had once had an affair with a young reporter, or that he anchored the show in flip-flops, unseen to the public under the desk, because he felt the cool air on his toes helped to keep him mentally sharp.

Laura kept these things secret. Tom and Veronica were so well known and well connected in the community, they knew everyone and had sources and associations everywhere. If there was a scandal in DPD or DPS (the Detroit Police Department or Detroit Public Schools) or even DPW (the Department of Public Works), either Tom or Veronica or both would know who to tap for info. Heck, they probably could have convinced the mayor to do just about anything, or paid off the governor. They were that locally famous, asked to emcee countless banquets. They had images to keep up. The world didn't need to know their secrets. Tom's marriage had survived the affair, so why bring it up? That's how Laura looked at it.

Then there was the sports guy, Roger. Poor Roger, who always thought he was the least popular of the four, because, frankly, he was. Roger with such an inferiority complex that he was constantly asking Laura if upper management still liked him. Laura had to soothe him with half-truths and white lies to keep him going. Roger didn't know that Perry contemplated every six months or so whether to replace him.

And finally, the last of the four anchors: Faith.

It had all started out so well. Since Laura and Faith were both single, professional women, they bonded when Faith first came to the station, going out for drinks once per week after the show. None of the others ever wanted to extend their workday into the night.

Laura and Faith shared gossip about people at the station, men they were seeing, their families, and of course the competition, the other TV stations in town. People in newsrooms loved to rip the competition, whether it was because a competing station had misspelled a word on a graphic, had had the camera zoom in at the wrong time, had gone lower in the ratings for any reason, or simply for what the lead story had been that night.

"Can you believe they led the whole show with that stupid fluff story that came in as a press release?" Laura might ask, shocked by the decision-making at the other newsrooms. She didn't believe that anything sent out in a press release should be of importance. It was what a lot of people in TV news called "low-hanging fruit" because the story was easy to get and everyone had it—it was handed to you and to every other station in town.

Laura believed in "enterprise stories" with exclusive big-gets that no one else in the market had. Shows featuring that kind of story were her favorite. To lead off with "First at ten, a Channel 9 *exclusive* . . ." was thrilling to her. She always told the anchors to read that word with extra emphasis to hammer it home to the viewer.

"Right, what a lame lead," Faith would giggle, sipping her gin and tonic.

Laura needed someone to commiserate with, and Faith was a good partner for that. They would criticize everything they could think of about the other stations—from the sets to the talent (one station had a main female anchor who stumbled her way through the stories she read; Laura and Faith couldn't fathom how she kept her job) to the competition's live shots, music, and graphics, until they finally ran out of steam.

Laura was proud to have the top meteorologist in town on her team. True, Faith was not a fully certified met, but she was the most popular with the public and that was all that mattered. Ratings had gone up since Faith arrived, which meant advertisers would be charged more money for each commercial they bought, which subsequently meant more money for the station and the company as a whole. Laura got a bonus in her check every six months if the eleven PM ratings stayed high, so she especially liked Faith.

For a while, Laura thought she was living on cloud nine (the term she came up with for the password to Faith's fan page when Perry asked her to think of something clever). That was why what happened in Laura and Faith's friendship next was so disturbing.

It started with Faith becoming super needy. She began calling or texting Laura at all times of day, saying she was feeling blue and was Laura available to cheer her up? At first Laura was receptive. She was not that surprised to know that someone on air was not as filled with confidence as they projected to the world. Some on-air talent seemed to walk a tightrope between self-assured and riddled with worries and doubts.

So she took on the nurturer role, coming over to Faith's apartment with takeout and plans to watch Netflix together, or listening to Faith complain about any number of things: weird guys who sent her letters that creeped her out, Matthew and the other mets who gave her the cold shoulder, or Veronica, who invited some other coworkers to her house for holiday drinks but not Faith. Laura suspected that Veronica was jealous of Faith, as were most of the on-air talent, owing to Faith's ever-soaring popularity.

Then it got even deeper. Faith brought up one of her sisters, Charity, dying at a young age, and she talked about an emotionally abusive childhood. The sister part was too painful to discuss in depth, Faith said, but she went into great detail about how her father would scream at her and her other sister, Hope, if they didn't get all A's or their rooms were dirty. He also punished them in an unusual way: through clothing, making them wear ugly shirts he knew they hated and never buying them new clothes, so they were stuck in items that were too small or otherwise ill-fitting and that gave other kids plenty of fodder for mockery.

Her father blew up at her mother if dinner wasn't made and the kitchen spotless when he came home from work. Faith, her sister Hope, and their mother had so much anxiety over cooking and cleaning that they would be frantically working in the afternoons, eyes on the clock, wiping counters madly up to the second they heard his car turn in to the driveway. He tried to quell her bubbly personality, Faith said, especially after her little sister's death. Faith told Laura that she wasn't allowed to truly be herself until she left for college.

Faith cried quite literally on Laura's shoulder a few times, confessing that she had never gone to therapy about her little sister or father. Laura had to take on the role of therapist, which was something she felt she had done before with others in a newsroom filled with type A but occasionally neurotic people, so she tried to help Faith process things and talk them out. It felt good to help a friend at first, but it got to be too much rather quickly.

Faith seemed to know no boundaries. When Laura met a guy named Elliott through one of those dating apps and they started hanging out, Faith would text even during times she knew Laura was on a date, and if Laura didn't respond within a few minutes, Faith's tone would turn and she would accuse Laura of not being there for her in her time of need. Laura knew she was supposed to feel guilty, but she just became more and more pissed.

Elliott moved in. The texting and calling continued, even in the middle of the night, to the point where Elliott said, "No more. This is insane."

"I don't know what to do. I can't block her number," Laura said. "She's my met. I need her to reach me for emergencies and vice versa."

"Then talk with her and make this stop," Elliott said, a dark look flashing across his face. "Or I'll make it stop."

"What do you mean you'll make it stop?"

"I can't live like this, Laura. She ruins my workdays, interrupting my sleep. I'll march over to Channel 9 and give her a piece of my mind."

"No, I got it," Laura replied firmly. She was an executive producer. She told people what to do all the time. She could handle this.

The next day she was nervous all afternoon, but determined. After the 6:30 PM show, she asked Faith to speak with her. They went to a side conference room. At first Faith sat down with a big smile and said, "What's up?," which made Laura feel worse about what she was about to say to her friend, but an image of Elliott came into her mind and she doubled down. It had to happen.

Trying for a tone that was friendly but firm, she told Faith that texting in the middle of the night had to be for true emergencies and to please respect those boundaries. Laura said it kindly, she thought, adding that she cared about Faith and wanted to be there for her but they needed to set some limits.

Faith's jawline tightened and her eyes narrowed.

"After all I've been through, all I've told you about myself, you're going to treat me like this? Some friend you are. I thought we could lean on each other." Faith's tone was acid.

Laura didn't want to point out that Faith never asked about Laura's life, nor inquired about Elliott or how things were going, and had completely forgotten Laura's most recent birthday. "Lean on each other" was truly not accurate, but she didn't want to exacerbate the situation, so she went for tact in her response.

"And we can, but please understand what a call in the middle of the night does to Elliott . . . and to me," said Laura, noticing that her voice sounded more pleading than stern. She coughed and started again, more firmly. "I really need to set these boundaries, Faith."

There was silence. Faith stared at her. Laura tried to return the gaze in a way that she hoped was both comforting but also projected a "there is no alternative" demeanor.

"Noted, *boss,*" Faith said sarcastically. She stood up and stormed out of the room, slamming the door. Laura sighed. She oversaw the show Faith was in and could make decisions about it, but she was not technically her boss. That would be the news director and the general manager.

Laura sat there for a few extra minutes processing the conversation. She didn't want things to be awkward between the two of them but she also needed to prioritize her still-new relationship with Elliott. She couldn't allow Faith to get between them. Feelings tumbled within her like clothes in a dryer, but she realized rather quickly that relief was the primary emotion.

For a long time after that, Faith stopped texting and calling but simultaneously stopped talking to Laura in person at all. If Faith had to convey something about the evening shows, she made a big deal about going to the producer instead, who was one level below Laura's executive producer status.

"Kyle, I might need extra time for weather tonight. Storms are moving in," she'd say, not even glancing at Laura.

"OK—did you tell Laura too?" he'd ask.

"I'm telling you," she'd reply, turning on her heel and returning to the weather office while Kyle looked over at Laura and rolled his eyes. By now, most people in the newsroom thought Faith was a royal pain in the ass. She did not exude "team player" or "good newsroom citizen" (as people in the industry liked to call it).

Faith sometimes snapped at producers, directors, teleprompter operators, and people on the assignment desk if she perceived any mistake on their part. She acted like the life of the party at station-wide meetings and get-togethers but whispered behind people's backs to the point where no one trusted her. She refused to become a mentor to the younger on-air talent when they asked all of the more veteran people to do so, saying she was too busy. She somehow wormed her way out of taking part in Fourth of July and other parades like the rest of the talent, and people said she had whined to Perry and he had given in. The prevailing sentiment was that Perry would do anything for her because the public loved her.

And now here they were two years later. Laura had learned to live with Faith's iciness toward her, and they simply coexisted. Laura and Elliott were married, and Laura was pregnant. Honestly, Laura had almost forgotten about Faith's antics, or at least she had pushed the thoughts far away thanks to everything else going on in her world.

Then, out of the total blue, Faith texted. In the middle of the night.

The ping startled both Laura and Elliott and they jerked awake. Laura had been dead asleep, and that was saying something given how hard it was to sleep with her growing belly. Elliott rolled over and said, "Who in the *hell* is texting at three AM?"

"It's Faith," Laura replied, feeling a dread come into her bones. Not again. She scanned the text, then read it aloud.

Laura—I really need you. I have a stalker who won't leave me alone and I'm also having some money problems. Can we please talk? I miss our friendship.

"Fuck no," Elliott said, pulling his pillow over his head. "You're pregnant, Laura. Does she have no class texting at this time? And what does she mean by money problems? She makes a boatload and lives alone."

"I know, honey, I know. I'll talk to her tomorrow."

"Either you will or I will, Laura. I'm not going through this again. And if it's me, it's going to get ugly."

This side of Elliott didn't come out often, but when it did, it always startled Laura.

He gave a harrumph and made a big scene of bunching his pillow, readjusting the blankets, and flopping over to his side, his back to her.

Laura rolled the other way and put her hand on her stomach, mentally sending messages of calm to the baby. She couldn't turn her phone off in case the station called with a true news emergency, but she couldn't risk Faith texting again in another hour or two. It would send both her and Elliott off the edge. So she went to her phone and hit "Block" on Faith's number. She would unblock it in the morning. Closing her eyes, she thought of Elliott's words, his tone:

Either you will or I will, Laura. I'm not going through this again. And if it's me it's going to get ugly.

She didn't need some scene between her husband and her meteorologist. What if he really marched over to Channel 9 to give Faith a piece of his mind? What would that look like? How would it affect Laura's role as the executive producer to have her husband out of control? She had trouble sleeping the rest of the night.

CHAPTER EIGHT

Matthew

February

It was Tara who came with the idea to play a few tricks on Faith. The first one she proposed was small, harmless, just a little plan to get back at Faith in an anonymous way for what she had said about Matthew being "sooo small-market" and for Faith just being a plain old bitch.

"Go into Faith's makeup bag when she's out of the weather office and hide her favorite lipstick," Tara proposed. "That red color she wears every night. I know the exact brand because she talked about it on one of her videos. I'll screenshot you a picture. Put it somewhere so she can't find it for a few days. She'll be desperate before the show, flustered. A woman without her favorite lip color is like peanut butter without jelly. She'll feel naked and lost."

Wanting to both please Tara and torment Faith, Matthew agreed, although he was on edge. He had never really been a troublemaker. He liked to follow the rules. He wouldn't call in sick, for example, when he wasn't truly ill. Not like Faith.

He waited until Faith was on her dinner break the next night and walked slowly toward her desk. Faith's enormous makeup bag was overflowing with cosmetics. Next to it sat a portable mirror with lights, four different types of curling irons, cords everywhere, and three cans of hair spray, one on its side. No surprise to him that Faith's makeup area was disorganized with items absolutely everywhere; it was a perfect reflection of her, he thought.

Gingerly Matthew approached the makeup bag, and he pushed aside pencils and tubes and containers of all sorts looking for the prize he coveted. There were oddly shaped sponge things, all dirty and smeared with various colors. The makeup brushes also seemed like they needed to be cleaned, and he avoided touching the bristles.

Women's cosmetics was largely a foreign landscape for Matthew. Although he was forced to wear powder on the air himself, as all of the men did to keep the shine down, he despised doing it. Other than ordering the same MAC brand of powder the consultant had told him to wear, he had no knowledge of makeup and felt unsure he could find this one tube of lipstick, even with the picture Tara had texted.

His fingers finally reached the lipsticks at the bottom, all in smooth tubes. Consulting the picture on his phone, he looked down and rummaged through them until he identified the tube with the red color Faith favored. When he wrapped his knuckles around it, the metal against his skin was cool but felt white-hot, stolen contraband pulsing in his hand. Now that he had it he backed away from her desk quickly. Even though no one else was in the office he felt his heart going and knew he couldn't waste any time.

Tara had said to hide it but to make it seem as if Faith herself had misplaced it in case she started to look around.

Each meteorologist had their own desk, plus there was one long shared one with all of the weather computers and forecasting tools they needed next to a desk phone and a printer that had to be from the 1990s. It was huge and took forever to print.

Glancing at his coworkers' personal desks, Matthew noted how he thought each reflected the character of the person who sat there. Faith's was as messy and disorganized as her makeup bag, and the decorations she chose were all about her. There were several pictures of Faith out and about in station-issued clothing holding a microphone at events, and she had magazine covers she was on tacked to a corkboard. The only item that was more benign was a teddy bear with a red ribbon around its neck. He wondered if some fan had sent it to her or if she got it from a loved one, but he didn't care enough to ask.

Abby's desk was clean and organized, and her personal touches were all neatly framed pictures of her kids. Chuck's desk was nearly barren of any personal items at all and looked clinical and efficient. It matched Chuck's personality in Matthew's mind—vanilla. He was the type of guy to say "Great" if you asked him about his weekend. Not that Matthew was that much more forthcoming, but at least he would have more than one-word answers.

Matthew's desk had a picture of him and Tara on a cruise, hair tousled in the wind. It sat in a heart-shaped frame that said LIVE, LAUGH, LOVE on the sides. He never would have chosen that kind of cheesy frame, but Tara had given it to him for their anniversary and he felt compelled to display it, especially for the times she came in to visit.

He favored the various sports memorabilia on the desk, his favorite being a signed baseball he had gotten at a Tigers game with his dad when Matthew was so small he was still playing T-ball. He had it in a square glass display holder. It was worth some money but priceless to him.

Assessing the weather center in its entirety, Matthew knew he absolutely couldn't hide the lipstick anywhere around his own desk, and he didn't want to implicate Abby or Chuck. Glancing down at the floor, his eyes traveled to the dozen or so pairs of shoes Faith had under her desk, all scattered and haphazardly strewn about, some upside down or not even next to their partners.

There were high heels of all sorts, as well as a few pairs of what Tara called "Toms"—flats that Faith wore around the office in between shows. Behind the shoes he could see a few crumpled shopping bags and half-crushed shoeboxes Faith had just shoved back there. Maybe that area was the winner. It seemed to be as good a spot as any.

Quickly he knelt and shoved the lipstick behind the shoes next to a shopping bag. If she looked for it she would think she dropped it and it somehow got wedged back there. If she didn't look for it he could retrieve it in a day or two and put it back in her makeup bag—if he felt like it—or he could throw it away, forcing her to buy a new one. He would see.

For now, he felt sneaky and powerful in a way he wasn't used to. It gave him a surge of adrenaline.

Resuming his spot at the main weather desk, he worked on some graphics for the weekend shows and was trying to look casual going over maps when he heard a key turn in the door. Faith walked in with a Diet Coke in one hand and a salad in a plastic container in the other. He barely glanced up with a slight nod, as had become their custom. She didn't acknowledge him in any way and walked straight to her desk to eat.

The office was always uncomfortable with so little talking and he usually tried to leave as soon as he could. She did weather for the five, six, and eleven. Talent could take a decent dinner break and have plenty of time to work in between shows. That day he had done the noon, the four, and their new lifestyle show at 6:30. He had stayed a bit late working on some fun graphics (the "grilling forecast," the "pool forecast," the "dog-walking fore-cast," and the "biking forecast"). Truth be told, they were all the exact same forecast, but people liked the pop-art graphics that showed a sizzling grill, a sparkling pool, a cute dog, or a brightly colored bike, and management was always pushing them to use these types of visuals to help convey information. "More lifestyle graphics" was Perry's constant refrain. "Think of some new ones. What do people like to do outdoors? Make it a graphic."

But now Matthew was done and free to go and he stood, gathering his coat and bag from his desk.

"I'm heading out," he said.

She didn't look up from scrolling her phone as she jabbed a plastic fork into her salad, one that he noticed was almost en-tirely lettuce. He didn't see any protein on it. She nodded and mumbled, "OK, see ya."

As he strode out of the weather center, his heart was still ham-mering. What would she do when she couldn't find her lipstick that night? She had other tubes in her makeup bag, but she wore that red almost every night. Would she suspect him? Would she find it and turn him in to Perry? Maybe this was a stupid idea.

His phone vibrated with a text. It was Tara.

Did you do it?

Matthew liked to prove his manhood around her. It seemed to make her more attracted to him, so he opted not to tell her how nervous he had been and how his heart was still going faster than normal. Instead he texted back:

Hell yeah I did!

She replied:

Yes!!! I can't wait to watch the
11:00 show!

Me too

That night the weather animation started with "the voice of God" (as TV stations liked to call it) saying, "And now, your fair-weather forecast with Faith Richards . . ." The camera went to Faith, Veronica, and Tom at the anchor desk chatting before Faith walked in front of the green screen to give the full forecast. Matthew squinted, trying to see Faith's lips, but Tara sussed it out almost immediately.

"Pink! She's wearing pink! It totally clashes with that outfit and with her forecast earrings. She must be piiiisssssed! We did it!"

Tara lifted her cocktail to clink glasses, giggling.

Faith never asked about the lipstick. Matthew thought she might put a note in their shared weather chat that hardly anyone used anymore, something like, "Has anyone seen my Bobbi Brown red lipstick? I seem to have misplaced it," but she didn't.

A few days later he retrieved the tube from under her desk and put it back, way at the bottom of her makeup bag in the corner, relief washing over him.

As the weeks passed, he chuckled more and worried less about the little trick he and Tara had played. He had loved seeing how giddy it made Tara those few nights when Faith had been forced to wear pink and magenta on her lips, not her signature red. He thought the whole gig was done and over.

But then Tara suggested that they up the stakes even more.

CHAPTER NINE

Kelly

February

She was nervous about meeting up with Faith for the "make amends" lunch, even more than she'd thought she'd be. Looking at her closet, Kelly tried on and rejected three outfits before finally settling on a favorite pair of dark-washed jeans, a red sweater, nice leather boots, and a gold necklace Joel had given her that she felt almost provided her protection as if he were there.

There was a reason for the red sweater. Joel had read an article about the power of colors. He told her red was for strength and power, that's why Tiger Woods would wear it in the final round of golf tournaments. Now Kelly hoped she projected strength and something along the lines of *I am a professional, confident woman who doesn't need you in my life but I'm also a good enough person to meet you for lunch.*

Faith suggested a fancy restaurant downtown. It was not Kelly's kind of place—she would have preferred a simple café, a diner even—but she reluctantly agreed. Kelly figured Faith was paying anyway, so why not try a higher-end locale?

As she kissed Joel goodbye, he squeezed her shoulder.

"Go get 'em, lady in red. Strong, confident, you got this, just like Tiger in his heyday."

"I just hope I survive intact," she said with a laugh.

The bustling restaurant was more or less what Kelly had expected from a spot in this trendy neighborhood: tall windows, a waterfall wall, fake foliage, high-end light fixtures, and waiters scurrying about in crisp white linens.

She spotted Faith right away, seated in a corner scrolling her phone. Faith was wearing red too, a loose top, with red lipstick. Kelly wondered if this was going to be a red power showdown.

Taking a deep breath, Kelly walked over. Faith looked older, of course—it had been so many years since they had seen each other in person—but she looked good too. Her hair had gotten much longer and was a darker hue; she must have dyed it. It was styled perfectly, and her makeup was immaculately applied. She had always been pretty, although Kelly noticed that Faith's eyes seemed bluer than she remembered them. Faith used to wear glasses too.

"Kell, oh my goodness, it's been forever . . ."

"Hi, Faith . . ."

Faith stood up. They shared an awkward slight hug, barely tapping each other's shoulders.

Kelly took off her coat and hung it and her purse on the back of her chair. She sat down and took a long, deep breath before speaking, trying to steady her nerves. *Here we go,* she thought.

"It sure has been a long time," Kelly said as an opener, then waited a beat to see if Faith would take the baton in the conversation. When Faith didn't, Kelly tried to fill the void.

"So . . . how are you doing?"

"Oh, I'm OK, I'm OK, you know, just soooo insanely busy

with work. The news never stops as they say, nor does the weather!"

Faith laughed, but Kelly could manage only a slight smile. Tension rippled between them. There was too much history to just be breezy.

"And how are things going in your life?" Faith asked, but before Kelly could answer the waiter came over with menus and he poured them each ice water.

"Why don't we just figure out what we want and then we'll chat?" Faith suggested.

Kelly nodded and they both studied their menus. The place was outrageously expensive. Who would pay thirty-five dollars for a simple salad? Kelly glanced around and noticed that the portions at other diners' tables weren't even that big. She had a feeling she might still be hungry after leaving this place.

Faith was intently studying the menu. People around them were chatting away, but the air between Kelly and Faith was silent and felt heavy. Kelly pretended to keep looking at the menu even though she had already decided what she wanted. The waiter returned.

"May I take your order, ladies?"

"Yes, I'll have the beet salad and a diet Sprite, please," said Faith.

The waiter nodded and looked at Kelly.

"I think I'll try your lobster bisque with a side salad. That comes with a roll, right?" Kelly wanted to maximize her food. Kelly added an iced tea, and the waiter took their menus. With no physical barriers between them now and nothing to do, Faith and Kelly looked at each other awkwardly.

"So . . . you were asking about me?" Kelly said as an opener. Faith nodded. "Well, I met a guy and we're living together, Joel is his name. He's great. I mentioned in my email my new high school, I'm still teaching Spanish. Joel works from home. We're looking to get a dog. You know, just normal life stuff. You seem to be doing well at Channel 9."

"I am, thank you, it's such a joy to work there—absolutely terrific people, I'm so lucky—and Detroit has been *so* good welcoming me back home. What does your new man do? You said he works from home?"

"Yes, he's in tech for a bio company. They never returned after the pandemic and he loves being home. That's why we think we can get a dog."

"I'm jealous! We worked from home for a bit in Covid, even had the green screen for weather set up in our places, but of course we've all been back full-time for a long time now. Does he get to set his own schedule or is he, like, on conference calls all day?"

"Kind of a mix of both. Conference calls every Tuesday and Thursday morning, I think. He's mostly on his own for the rest of his work."

"How wonderful, how lucky he is," Faith said. "I'm so glad you found someone, Kell. I'm still looking. Perennial bachelorette, I guess. Maybe I should go on a reality show!" She laughed again and Kelly went for a mild chuckle this time.

The conversation continued in a stilted way. Faith didn't ask more about Kelly's new job or anything else about Kelly's life, instead launching into a story about her latest vacation with her sister and how she had decorated her apartment at the Three Diamonds. Kelly found herself just nodding along.

As their food arrived, Kelly kept waiting for the main event, the big talk. Finally, near the end of her beet salad, Faith carefully set her fork down.

"So Kell, I told you I wanted to apologize and I do. I've just been thinking a lot about what I did and it wasn't fair. I had some demons in my life back then but I've worked really hard. I hope you'll forgive me."

Kelly sighed, looking across at Faith. While Faith was glamorous in a well-put-together way, there was a vulnerability, almost childlike, in her eyes. She was giving Kelly a pleading look. It made Kelly feel for her, but she couldn't forget the past either. It was there, smoldering.

"I appreciate that and you inviting me to lunch," Kelly said slowly, thinking hard about what to say. She wanted to be kind, but before she could stop herself, years of resentment and anger came tumbling out across the table. "I'm not going to lie. It was hard. It hurt. Stealing cash and items from all of us in the dorms when we were out of the room. Pawning Zoe's jewelry and using our credit cards to buy yourself clothes, lying about it until you got caught . . . Then years later calling me when you were in Peoria and saying your identity was stolen and you couldn't access your credit cards until they were replaced and you were going to be kicked out of your apartment if I didn't float you some money, that I was your only hope, that your sister had medical bills to pay. And when I did lend you the money . . ."

Faith looked down and started twisting her hands in her lap. Kelly felt a pang. Maybe she had gone too far. Maybe she didn't need to say the rest, how Faith had started ghosting her when she asked, then pleaded for her money, how she finally had to track down Faith's mom and tell her the whole story and the mom sent Kelly the money and said she would get repaid from Faith. It still made Kelly so angry to think of being taken advantage of like that. She doubted Faith even really had her identity stolen.

"I'm sorry," Faith said softly. "I was in a bad place. This is really hard to say . . . but . . . I was diagnosed . . . as a shopaholic. My therapist said it's like an alcoholic, a disease, something you can't control. But I'm good now. That's why I brought you a present."

She reached into a large purse slung over the back of her chair and brought out a white box about three inches high and eight inches long.

"I made this for you."

Kelly took the box. She had absolutely no clue what could be inside. Gingerly she began to lift the lid, and something sparkly caught her eye.

"It's a jewelry box!" Faith called out, ruining any surprise. "I went to a place where you can design your own with beads and jewels and crystals and things. Isn't it pretty?"

Lifting the lid all the way, Kelly saw that it was, in a gaudy sort of way. There were buttons and beads in every color glued all over it, giving it a circus feel. A tiny mirror was wedged in between the many other things on the top. Any empty space was filled with glitter or feathers.

"Well, thank you. That's very kind of you," said Kelly, immediately wondering what to do with this thing. It was not her style at all. Maybe she could give it to the neighbor girl. It felt juvenile.

"I was thinking of that rare, expensive jewelry you got from your mom and grandma," said Faith. "I know how much that all meant to you after they . . . you know. I'm so glad I never touched that stuff in the dorms. What I did to Zoe. I won't ever live that down. Kell, I will have that shame with me, honestly, forever. But this is my way of starting to make amends. I've reached out to Zoe for lunch too but she lives in Iowa so it might be a while. You still have that special jewelry, right?"

"Yes, of course. It means the world to me."

"And do you have the right kind of jewelry box for it? Because that's why I thought of this. Precious jewels need a precious holder."

Kelly opened her mouth to answer, but before she could, a couple stopped right at their table, looking sheepish.

"Excuse me, we hate to bother you, but are you Faith Richards from Channel 9? We couldn't help but notice you from across the room."

Faith turned to them with a full-wattage smile.

"I am. Thank you so much for stopping to say hello. I love meeting viewers. This is my friend, Kelly."

"Hello," the woman said, but neither she nor the guy gave more than a micro-glance to Kelly. They were staring at Faith.

"We can't believe it's you," said the man. "We watch you every night. You do such a great job, we're just huuuuge fans."

"Thank you. That means a lot to me. I work really hard on my forecasts," Faith said. "You can join the Fair-Weather Friends Fan Club if you're not already in it."

"Oh, we're in it. We love your videos," said the man. "Sue here actually starts her day with them."

"I have three pairs of your weather earrings, I just adore them! You are so fun, the best weather girl ever!" gushed the woman.

"Well, I love weather and I love earrings so it's a match made in the cumulus clouds," Faith said with a smile, and the couple roared with laughter and told her how funny she was on top of everything else.

"Thank you for stopping by," Faith said. Kelly could sense that she was trying to shake them. The couple seemed to sense it too.

"We didn't mean to interrupt but we just had to say hello. Wait until we tell all of our friends and the whole neighborhood about this! They'll just die!" The woman giggled. "Can we get a picture with you before we leave?"

They asked Kelly to take the picture, the couple maneuvering Faith to go in the middle as they each looped their arms around her as if they were old buddies. They all had huge smiles.

"Can you take at least five or six so we have options?" the woman asked. "Zoom in on some or turn the camera the other way."

"Sure," Kelly said, feeling like a hired hand as she did what was asked of her.

When they finally left, Faith whispered, "Sorry about that. I should have worn a hat and my glasses. It happens way too often."

"No worries, I sometimes forget how famous you are," replied Kelly.

The tension between them had somewhat dissipated thanks to the couple. If there had been a red power showdown it seemed to have been a draw, but Kelly was still anxious to wrap lunch and be on her way. The meeting had accomplished what it was supposed to. Faith had apologized, and given her the item she made, and that was that. What else needed to happen? The waiter returned with the check.

"I'll take it," Faith said, holding out her hand. Kelly smiled and started to gather her coat and purse.

"Thanks for lunch, Faith, and for the jewelry box. It's really . . . one-of-a-kind."

"You're welcome, I had fun making it. I hope you might use it for that family jewelry."

Kelly knew she wouldn't but nodded and said, "Yes, I might, thanks."

"As for lunch," said Faith. "It's eighty-two dollars and forty-eight cents. Even though yours was a little more expensive than mine, I'm willing to go halfsies." Faith smiled as if she were doing Kelly a huge favor.

Kelly's eyes narrowed. She had to *pay* for her portion of lunch? Hadn't Faith invited her in order to make amends? Didn't that mean she would pick up the tab at this ridiculous place? Kelly didn't have forty-one dollars she could easily drop on lunch. That kind of money could have meant street tacos, a beer, and a movie in an actual theater. Her heart sank. What a fool she had been coming here. Faith was still Faith, cheap as hell but always trying to live above her means. But what could Kelly do? She had to pay.

"Oh, um . . . I guess if that's how you want to do it," she said, giving Faith one more opening to take the entire bill.

"Fifty-fifty works for me, I'll even get the tip," Faith said, with a "look how wonderful I am" grin.

"Yeah, OK, thanks," Kelly mumbled. Any good vibes she had felt just a few minutes prior were rapidly receding. There was no doubt in her mind now that she was giving the insane jewelry box away or selling it. She couldn't wait to get away from Faith.

Opening her wallet, Kelly took out two twenties and a five-dollar bill and pushed them roughly across the table.

"Here you go, you can add the change to the tip," she said icily. "I have to run and meet Joel for something."

It wasn't true, of course, but she wanted an excuse to get going. Killing time with more small talk while waiting for the waiter, Faith sending her credit card back with him, waiting to sign, and then walking to the door and having a big goodbye hug all seemed too much. She pushed her chair back and stood up. Faith stood up too.

"OK then, go and be with your guy. Thanks again for coming out to meet me. Friends?"

"Uh, sure . . . yeah, friends," Kelly said, but she hoped never to see Faith again. She had done her duty.

They shared one more awkward half embrace and Kelly took the white box under her arm and breathed a sigh of relief as soon as she hit the sidewalk. She texted Joel that it was over and she had, indeed, survived. He sent her back a video of Tiger Woods pumping his fist on the eighteenth hole in some tournament, wearing a red polo.

At least she wasn't as hungry as she feared she might have been. The roll and bisque had done the trick, even though the salad was nothing but arugula and bits of candied walnuts.

When she got home and recounted the entire lunch date for Joel, he rolled his eyes at various parts but didn't come down on her for frivolously spending over forty dollars of their hard-earned money, and she loved him for it. She felt bad enough for being duped.

"Well, you never have to see her again," he summed up. "Can I check out the jewelry box?"

"Sure." She pushed the white box toward him. Opening the lid, he laughed.

"It looks like a twelve-year-old girl made this." Lifting it out, he turned it over in his hands to view all sides.

He stopped when he had it upside down, and peered closely at something.

"There's a signature on this button, did you see that? It says Emilio Gonzalez."

"What? Let me see." Kelly grabbed the box and squinted at the tiny signature. "You're right. She told me she made this but did she? Or I guess that could just be on a leftover button she got at the make-your-own place?"

Joel was already reaching for his phone.

"Hold on, let me google that name and jewelry boxes . . ."

Several seconds passed.

"Kell, check it out. This dude has an Etsy site. Look . . ."

Kelly saw a page filled with jewelry boxes and earrings.

One-of-a-kind, handmade items. Crafted by Emilio, an aspiring jewelry, clothing, and interior designer. Help him get to college by supporting this site.

"It's not a twelve-year-old girl but a seventeen-year-old boy who made this!" Kelly said. "She lied to me. She bought it on Etsy. And she made me pay for lunch. What the hell was that all about then? She's as full of shit as ever."

"Does it surprise you that she lied to you?" Joel said. "Can we agree that the witch has used up her last chip? Never ever go near her again, no matter what line of BS she throws at you."

"Oh I won't, I am so done with her," Kelly replied. "I truly can't believe she lied about this one, why lie about a jewelry box?"

"You said yourself she isn't crafty, but she probably wanted you to think she had worked so hard to make something with her own hands, as if it had more meaning that way, so she bought something but I guess didn't notice the button with the signature."

"Well I'm not keeping this thing. No way. I do hate to throw away someone's hard work, though. What should we do with it?"

"I was planning to go to Goodwill with some old clothes soon. Let's just throw it in that pile. Someone will like it, maybe a twelve-year-old girl." Joel laughed. "Come here, let me give you a hug. Trust is so important and you can't trust her but we trust each other, don't we?"

Kelly let herself fall into Joel's arms and inhaled his earthy scent deeply. Then she let out a long, slow exhale. The lunch date she had dreaded was over. Faith was a confirmed liar and cheapskate but Kelly would never again have to deal with her.

She pushed it out of her mind for the rest of the day as she and Joel took a bike ride, made dinner, and went to the corner bar to meet up for a beer and darts with friends.

But that night lying in bed the lunch date came back to her. She couldn't help but replay the whole conversation in her mind. Was there something she missed? Some ulterior motive Faith had in the meeting? Now that she was back to not trusting Faith, she was wary of everything. Had Faith really wanted to apologize and to give her a fake homemade jewelry box? Was that what this was all about? Because if she lied about the box, she could be lying about her apology too. It seemed insincere now. Kelly's antennae were up. *A liar is a liar to their core,* she told herself.

Yet, Kelly had her purse with her the whole time, so Faith could not possibly have swindled anything out of her—except the forty-one dollars for lunch—and nothing else weird had happened. Still, Kelly had a gut feeling something was not quite adding up and she had better be wary moving forward.

CHAPTER TEN

Matthew

April

Matthew was alone in the office one weeknight when he noticed that his favorite baseball and his Channel 9 water bottle were both gone. The baseball was the one in the shiny glass holder that he had gotten as a child with his father at the Tigers game. The water bottle had a Detroit Pistons sticker on the side so he could differentiate it from others in the newsroom, identical water bottles all given out at the station Christmas party.

Matthew started scouring around. He looked in every drawer, under the desk, and all around it, but there was nothing. How could his favorite memento and a big metal water bottle just disappear? He began to feel frantic, rechecking the drawers he had just looked in and pushing some papers aside, although it made no sense for either to be under those papers. He would have noticed the bulging.

"This can't be happening, where's my baseball? My bottle?" he whispered to himself.

Dread started to wash over him. The water bottle, not a huge deal, he could ask for a replacement, but he couldn't lose that ball, it meant so much to him. A baseball doesn't just disappear. It had to be here somewhere . . .

And then a thought exploded in his head.

Faith. No way. Could it be? *Could it?*

Turning slowly toward her desk, he eyed it warily. Would there be any chance Faith took his stuff? As retribution for the lipstick, maybe, if she somehow was on to him. No, she couldn't possibly know about that. It had been months since it happened and she hadn't said anything or acted any more cold to him (she was cold enough as it was). But still . . .

He walked toward her desk, looking in disgust at how dirty and cluttered it was. Yet, he couldn't really start shuffling things around or it would be super obvious that someone had. Maybe he could peek in the drawers.

Putting his fingers on the handle of one, he slowly slid it open. It was jam-packed with a huge assortment of random things: Tylenol, gum, mints, more makeup, hand sanitizer, various business cards, rubber bands, tape, a pair of scissors, and other crap. No baseball. No water bottle.

She had three other drawers, and he tried all of them, but two just had stacks of papers or old magazines and one was crammed with a similar collection of junk, this one more of the food variety, protein bars and her appetite-suppressing gum and Lipton's Cup-a-Soup in a few flavors and some Red Bulls.

Matthew sighed. Nothing much to see here. He turned and looked at Abby's and Chuck's desks. No way they took his stuff. None of them were great buddies, but they wouldn't stoop this low, would they?

Just in case, he quickly inspected all of the drawers in their desks but didn't find anything of note. Theirs were way more clean and organized than Faith's, though, as he could have guessed.

Clearly the baseball and bottle were not hidden in anyone's desk drawers. If they weren't back the next day, though, he would have to report them to HR and to Perry. Anything that went missing had to be looked into. Maybe the cleaning people took his stuff when they were alone in the office at night. But he had a hard time believing that. The same Russian family had been cleaning at Channel 9 for twenty years, and while he didn't know all of their names, they would always say hello and be friendly. They were kind, hardworking people who had never stolen anything to his knowledge. Plus, there were way more valuable things to steal if you were left unsupervised at night in a TV station. Microphones and cameras and lights and Emmy statuettes and other awards that people kept on their desks or Perry lined up on a shelf for all to see.

The Russian family might not know the value of that baseball either, he reasoned. He had tried to discuss the Tigers a few times with the father and son during the height of a playoff run but the duo had just looked at him quizzically. The baseball *was* valuable, signed by Kirk Gibson, one of the Tigers' most well-known players. Matthew had once looked up the price on an auction site—not that he would ever sell it, he was just curious—and it was more than $600, especially in the pristine condition it was in, kept in that glass box for all of these years. As for the water bottle, ones with the Channel 9 logos were everywhere if someone wanted to steal one. But now both were missing. And something was fishy. Quickly he went to his phone and the weather-team text chat they all shared.

> Has anyone by chance seen my signed Kirk Gibson baseball I keep on my desk or my water bottle with the Pistons sticker? They're both missing.

The typing bubbles started going right away. Abby was first, as he could have predicted.

> No, I haven't. That's terrible though. I will keep an eye out.

Chuck was next.

> Dude, I have no idea but I'll also look for them.

It took over an hour before Faith responded. Matthew was already home when his phone buzzed. He picked it up and read her words, or rather word:

> Nope

That was it. And he knew that this was her doing. If it was revenge for the lipstick, he could not be sure. But she had taken his baseball, maybe his water bottle. He could feel it in every cell of his body. And if that's how she wanted to play, then it truly was game on.

CHAPTER ELEVEN

Kelly

April

Kelly and Joel didn't get dressed up very often. Too much work, Kelly always thought, and they were casual people. But one of Joel's coworkers was getting married, and given that it was at a country club on a lake, Kelly decided to go all out.

She got a fresh mani-pedi and booked an appointment for her hair to be styled in an updo the morning of the event. Her freshly pressed dress was a low-cut black cocktail gown that she had chosen so that some of her grandma's rare jewelry would really stand out against it. Joel was planning to wear his best suit.

It was an important night for Kelly. She kept hoping Joel would pop the question. He hadn't, which was starting to worry Kelly. Was he bored with her? They had talked of possible marriage some time ago but he had been all quiet since then and she was afraid to bring it up. If he said he didn't want to marry her anymore, her heart would be broken. She was getting older, was almost even into what they called "advanced maternal age" (over thirty-five), and she might want a child. But she desired a husband first and Joel was her guy, there was no question about that.

Kelly was hoping that being at a wedding would jolt him to action, and she planned to look like a knockout for it to happen. She fantasized about him not being able to take his eyes off her, sweeping her across the dance floor and whispering "We're next" in her ear. Or maybe she'd catch the bouquet and all of his friends would tease him and he'd blush and get down on one knee right then and there, surprising her with a sparkling ring he had hidden somewhere as the wedding guests cheered and cried.

Speaking of jewelry, Kelly couldn't wait to wear some fancy items that night. Her grandmother's and mother's jewelry was an eclectic mix of expensive brooches, necklaces, bracelets, earrings, and rings, with rare stones and intricate metalwork. She once had it all appraised, and the entire lot was worth over $100,000. Not that she would ever sell.

Kelly had her mind's eye on a necklace and earring set from her grandma and a bracelet and oversized ring or two from her mom. She kept all of the items in a velvet-lined wooden jewelry box on her dresser. The tacky jewelry box Faith had given her at the overpriced restaurant was long gone, handed to Goodwill.

When Kelly got home from the hairdresser she went straight to the mirror in the bedroom and admired the updo; the bun looked like a flower, and thin wisps hung down the sides. She would work on her makeup last so that none of it smeared when she put on the black dress.

She laid the dress across the bed and pulled her best Jimmy Choo stiletto heels out from the closet and set those next to it. Then she got out a pair of tummy-tightening underwear, some Spanx to really keep things firm, a push-up bra, and opaque black pantyhose. Finally, she walked to the dresser for the jewelry.

Opening the lid, she was excited to see the jewels for the first time in a while, but instead her body went into a state of shock.

There was nothing in there, nothing. The red velvet sat empty; there were outlines of little imprints of rings, but that was it. Her hand flew to her mouth. She staggered backward.

Joel was downstairs and she wanted to call for him but her throat felt as if it wouldn't function. It was like one of those dreams where you need to scream but can't muster more than a whimper. Her mind began to race. Where could the jewelry be?

Her first thought was that maybe she was crazy. Had she moved it somewhere and forgotten she did it? No, that was definitely not it. Joel had been urging her to get a safe-deposit box at some point, but they hadn't done it. Although Kelly rarely looked at the jewelry in the box, it comforted her knowing it was there. It was all she had left of her grandma and mom, both killed in the same car accident by a drunk driver when Kelly was in high school.

Seeing the jewelry gone, she thought she might throw up, and she swallowed down a rush of bile. Her next thought, as much as she hated it to be, was Joel. Her eyes narrowed. Had her boyfriend taken the jewelry? Pawned it off? What could be happening? It felt as if the floor beneath her suddenly tilted, like one of those crazy carnival rides she loved as a kid. Everything she thought she knew was a certainty in her life—most importantly that she was dating a moral human being—was now askew. Spots began to dance in front of her eyes, and she realized in a sharp panic that she probably wasn't breathing in enough air.

Steady, Kelly, steady. She made her way slowly to the bed and sat down next to her black cocktail dress. The thought of lying down came to mind, but she realized that would ruin the updo.

The wedding. Would they even go? How could she go anywhere

with Joel? It had to be him who took the jewelry. No one else was ever in their bedroom.

Her mind flipped back to the last time she had opened the jewelry box. It was the day after she met with Faith, the day after Joel suggested giving the Etsy box created by Emilio to Goodwill. All of the talk about the jewelry made her want to see it again, to touch it, to feel close to her mom and grandma, so she had taken some time that afternoon to let her fingers gently wander over the stones and metals, the gems and patterns. A brooch with a woman's face intricately carved into it was one of her favorites, although brooches were so old-fashioned she rarely wore it. Still, the details of the woman's face, hair, and clothing were so carefully etched in ivory, it made her smile, thinking of her grandma wearing this, perhaps to some dance. Maybe it was even the one where she met Grandpa.

But now everything was gone, 100 percent gone. She took a ragged breath and mustered the strength to call out, "Joel?"

Her voice sounded weak and thin, so she cleared her throat and tried again.

"Joel?"

A little stronger but not enough to reach him downstairs. She could hear dishes clattering in the sink and music going and she knew he was cleaning up. She stood and walked to the top of the staircase. Inhaling a deep breath, she could feel anger now starting to replace shock in her system, and her voice got stronger because of it.

"Joel?" she bellowed.

"Yeah?" he called back over the music.

"Come here right now. I need to talk to you."

Her tone must have alerted him to the serious nature of it,

because she heard the water turn off first, then the music. He walked to the stairs wiping his hands on a towel.

"Everything OK, honey?"

"No, everything is definitely not OK. Where is my jewelry?"

He looked genuinely puzzled.

"Your what?"

"My jewelry. Where is my jewelry? The good stuff from my mom and grandma."

"What do you mean?" he asked. "Don't you keep it in that jewelry box?"

"I do and I went to get some out for tonight and it's not there, Joel. The entire box is *empty.*"

"*Whaaatt?* What the hell are you talking about? It's empty?"

His face and voice registered shock, and she stared at him, trying to assess if he was doing an acting job worthy of an Oscar or not.

"Empty. Nothing there, not even one ring." Her throat caught at the reality of those words, and tears came into her eyes.

Joel bolted up the stairs and rushed past her. She heard him gasp and say, "*What the . . . ?*"

She followed him and stood in the doorframe.

"That's exactly what I want to know," she said icily. "Joel, just tell me the truth."

He turned and his eyes were wild with confusion.

"Kell—I have no idea, you don't think . . . Of course I have nothing to do with this. I would never touch your jewelry, you know that."

But did she? How well do we know anyone in our lives? Was Joel a psychopath? Was he playing her even now? She felt her palms go sweaty and the term "fight or flight" came into her head. Was Joel a threat to her safety even? If he stole the jewels he could be capable of anything. She took a step backward and the next words came out like daggers.

"How could you do this, Joel?"

"Kelly, are you kidding me? I swear on my grandmother's grave that I would never touch your items, ever."

He sounded genuine and looked stunned, so she was forced to reevaluate her hypothesis. Maybe it wasn't him. But then who?

"No one comes to our bedroom or even upstairs, Joel. Guests always use the downstairs bathroom. Our place hasn't been broken into. If someone had, they surely would have taken TVs and laptops and your crazy expensive guitar. Why would they beeline right to the jewelry? It just doesn't make sense. It had to be you."

"*It's not me.* Let me think . . ."

She could see his mind whirring. He walked to the bed and sat, putting his head in his hands. He still had the dish towel in one hand but seemed to have forgotten it.

"When did you see the actual jewelry last?" he asked without looking up.

She told him it had been a day after the ill-fated Faith lunch.

"OK, so in one month, who has been up here?" He was more asking himself, and he rocked back and forth with his head still in his hands as he spoke, the words coming out in a jumble. "We had Becky and Stefan over for dinner but they were downstairs the whole time . . . My mom stopped by for lunch and dropped off some plants, but she never came upstairs, not that she would *ever* steal anything from us . . . We had an electrician one day but I was with him the whole time . . . I can't think of anyone else . . . *oh wait* . . ."

His eyes grew big and he turned to Kelly. She felt a shiver go up her spine even though she had no idea what he was about to say.

"Do you remember one day, maybe about a week after the electrician was here, that I told you someone rang our doorbell in the middle of the day while I was working?"

Her mind flipped backward. It had been a small mention in the midst of many other things they talked about but yes, she did remember.

"A woman?" she asked.

"Yes. I had a conference call coming up and was working on some notes for it. The doorbell rang and a woman with curly hair and glasses was standing there."

"Go on . . ." Kelly could feel where this was going, and her throat tightened.

"She said she was the electrician's assistant and he had left a tool here. He had told her where it was and could she dash upstairs and grab it? She was on her way to meet him at a job-site. She had on work overalls. My conference call was about to start so I told her that was fine. She's the only person I can think of who was unsupervised upstairs. Oh my God, Kell, do you think she . . . ?"

"Did she have a bag with her?"

"Uh, I don't know, I honestly didn't pay attention."

"And you didn't notice anything else gone after she left?"

"No. She went upstairs quickly and left."

"But Joel, you said you were with the electrician the whole time. How could he have left a tool here?"

"I had to step into the hallway and take a call while he was working so he was alone in the guest bedroom fixing that light switch. We don't go into that room much so I guess when the woman was at the door, I just figured the tool was in that room somewhere. I pictured it like a screwdriver or something he set down on the bedside table."

"And you never got her name, or saw what kind of car she drove or anything?"

"No, I didn't . . . I should have. Oh no, if she did this . . ." His voice dropped. "Kelly, if she took your jewelry, I will never forgive myself, ever. I'm so . . . so sorry."

He glanced at her with eyes glistening and a pleading look on his face. She felt herself believing him, giving in to the story that he was likely not a robber but had perhaps inadvertently let one into the house. Kelly wanted to scream at him for being such an idiot but she knew deep down that she likely would have let an electrician's assistant in too.

"Our Ring cam, Joel, would it still be on there? Does it save video for that long?" Kelly wanted to see this woman herself.

"Great idea. We paid for the premium that holds the videos for sixty days."

He took off down the stairs and Kelly followed him. They went straight to his laptop and he started madly typing until he had the Ring cam backlist pulled up.

"It must have been a Tuesday," he mused. "Because that's when we have the big conference call each week. Right before ten is when she arrived . . . Aha, here it is . . ."

He hit play and they both leaned forward for a closer look. A woman appeared from the edge of the screen. She did not seem to have a car, or at least she wasn't getting out of one. She stopped at their house and looked up at the front door, then walked confidently up the steps and rang the doorbell. Kelly noticed right away that she did have a bag, kind of a larger one, like a hobo purse. She was wearing thicker glasses that made it hard to discern her eyes. The video showed her talking to Joel for a moment, then walking in.

Three minutes and thirty-seven seconds later the video had her leaving and heading in the same direction she came. Kelly tried to see if the hobo bag looked any larger than when she walked in but it was hard to tell, plus rings and necklaces and brooches wouldn't take up much space.

"Holy crap, it had to be her, she's literally the only person I can think of," said Joel. "We have to call the electrician and ask if he sent someone. I threw his business card in the kitchen drawer. Really nice guy, he even put his cell number on the card in case we had any problems with the light switch."

Joel ran to retrieve the card and punched the number into his phone. Kelly could hear someone answer.

"Hello, yes, is this Vince Ingraham? I'm sorry to bother you on a weekend," Joel said, and started explaining the whole situation while Kelly stared at her boyfriend intently. His face fell quickly and he looked at her with dread. He hung up and whispered, "He says he didn't leave a tool and he absolutely didn't send someone to retrieve it. We have to call the police *now*."

"And tell them what? We have no name and no vehicle."

"What choice do we have other than to call the cops? Are we going to sit here and do nothing?" Joel asked, his voice rising. "A woman stole from you, from us. We have to at least try. We have the Ring cam video."

Kelly thought for a moment, twisting her hands. Her stomach was a tight knot. "One thing I don't get, Joel, is how this woman would know we had an electrician if he didn't send her. Why would she tell you that at the door? Could the electrician be lying to us right now? Maybe he did see the jewelry and then sent someone back for it."

"But Kell, he never went into our bedroom, and you keep the box closed anyway. He wouldn't have seen your things walking past. I'm telling you, we went straight to the guest bedroom and he started working on the light switch. I was with him except for that brief time I had to take a call and went into the hallway."

"Then it all makes no sense," Kelly said. Sadness and anger settled into her bones in equal parts. "You're right. Let's call the police. Joel, honestly, I don't even know if I can go to the wedding now."

"Wait, what? Can't you wear something else? Some other jewelry? We're going to blow off the wedding?"

"It's not that, I just don't know if I'm in the mood."

Joel gave her a look she couldn't place. It wasn't a glare, it wasn't a confused stare, it was more like . . . he was assessing her. She didn't like the look. He spoke slowly.

"Kell . . . this wedding is important to me. Hank is a good friend and an important coworker. And honey, can I say something else? The fact that you thought it was me who stole from you . . . that really hurt."

Her stomach clenched and the next words came flying out of her mouth too quickly.

"So now *I'm* the bad guy? What else was I supposed to think? I go to my jewelry box and everything is gone. And when I say I'm not sure if I'm in the mood for a wedding you don't listen to my feelings at all. You just say that Hank is a good friend. Well, I'm your *girlfriend,* Joel. Can you think about my feelings for once?"

Immediately she regretted adding "for once." Really it wasn't true. Joel was very attentive. She just needed to dump her seething rage and profound loss over the jewelry on someone, and he was the only target.

"That's it," he said, standing up with a harsh scrape of the chair on the floor. "I'm going for a walk. Call the police if you want . . . or don't. I'm just trying to help, you know? A robber came into our house, Kelly, and took things."

He grabbed his coat and stormed out the front door, slamming it. Kelly felt tears well up. Her priceless jewelry was gone, her boyfriend was mad at her, their day and night were ruined, and, somehow, a woman posing as the electrician's assistant had outsmarted them. Kelly kept turning the scene from the Ring cam over and over in her mind.

Something began to dance at the tiny corners of her brain.

That lunch with Faith. Faith asking about Joel working from home, even inquiring about his conference calls, Faith knowing about the jewels from college and asking Kelly if she still had them. The jewelry box Faith gave her. Was it possible Faith was hoping Kelly would use the gaudy box so Faith could send a woman into the house and direct her there? But Kelly couldn't figure out how Faith would have known an electrician did work at their home. Kelly had never mentioned that during lunch. Maybe this was a common ruse the police knew all about, the "electrician's assistant scam" or some such, and this woman went to every house until she found one that matched her story. No matter what, Kelly and Joel had been duped.

She picked up her cell phone and called the police. They said they'd be there within thirty minutes, and she texted Joel to please come home, then paced the kitchen until he arrived, followed shortly by the chime of the doorbell and a cop standing there.

She and Joel told the officer everything and showed him the Ring cam video. He took notes and asked them to forward the video to his email while he went upstairs and looked at the jewelry box. Then he sat back at the kitchen table across from the two of them.

"This is the first I've heard of this sort of thing happening. There's no scam going around like this in the city, and we get scam reports every day. It looks from the video and from what you're telling me that you were targeted and that this person perhaps knew what they were looking for. I'm very sorry. There's little for us to go on but we'll still open an investigation. It might be helpful if you can think of anyone who knew anything, like the fact that you had rare jewels or that one of you worked from home. We'll also check the local pawnshops. You might want to fish around online and see if someone is selling your stuff. The problem is there's a big black market too."

Kelly gulped back tears and glanced at Joel. He looked serious and sad. She turned her gaze back to the officer.

"Officer, I actually can think of one person who both knew about the jewelry and that Joel worked from home."

The policeman's eyebrows went up and he opened a little notebook.

"Yes . . ."

"Well, I know this sounds crazy . . . but . . . it's Faith Richards at Channel 9."

Joel's head whipped her way.

"Oh my God," Joel whispered.

The officer tilted his chin and looked at her like she was crazy.

"You mean that weather gal? The one with the earrings? My wife loves her," the officer said. "How would *she* know?"

Kelly told him about the freshman-year heists, followed by

Faith being suspended from school, how Faith had later lied to Kelly when asking for money because her "identity was stolen," and then about the recent lunch and what appeared to be a lie about the jewelry box. The officer clucked his tongue a few times and wrote some things down, but he had a disbelieving look on his face.

"We'll look into it," he summed up, closing his notebook and standing up. "But remember—there needs to be motivation, not just coincidence. What would motivate Faith Richards to send someone over here to steal your items?"

"Isn't money enough of a motivation?" Joel asked.

"Sure, lots of times," said the officer. "But I would think Faith Richards has plenty of that and wouldn't want to risk her career and reputation on this, but like I said, we'll look into it. Good day now."

He let himself out of the front door as Kelly and Joel looked at each other.

"It's Faith, isn't it?" Joel asked. "She's somehow behind this."

"I think so," Kelly replied. "I have a gut feeling, and sadly I know her too well."

"But how would she have gotten our address? You didn't tell her, did you?" Joel asked.

"No, but there are all kinds of people finders. If you google my name I bet it comes up. Let's try."

They did, and there it was in seconds. Name, address, the amount they paid for the house. Kelly moaned. Joel reached over and took her hand.

"As for the electrician part, could she have cased our house and seen one come in and out?" Joel asked.

"I mean, I guess she could have. Maybe she saw the truck in the driveway."

They were both lost in thought for a full minute.

"Listen, Kell, this day has been the absolute worst but we have to get ready for this wedding, if we're going. Are we going?"

She thought of her updo, her clothes still sitting on the bed. She thought of the idea of sending Joel and staying home herself, but honestly, what would she do all night, watch TV while he was dancing and having a good time? It might further drive a wedge between them. If this was Faith's work—and Kelly strongly believed it was—then she couldn't let Faith also ruin her relationship.

She nodded and said, "Yes, we can go."

But the whole time at the wedding her mind was distracted, her smile vacant, and she lost her train of thought in small-talk situations and had to excuse herself for the bathroom too often, dabbing at her eyes and trying not to smudge her makeup. The jewelry, that rare, expensive, precious jewelry, was gone. It was as if her mom and grandma had been ripped from her arms without her consent again. Joel was distracted too, his eyes constantly checking on her, his laugh with his friends not genuine.

Kelly was acutely aware of the absence of the pieces she had planned to wear. Her collarbone and neck felt empty without the stunning necklace she had in mind, even though she substituted a much more plain one from her collection. Her wrists and ears had the wrong items too.

She did not catch the bouquet, did not even try, standing in the back of the group of bachelorettes instead, not even raising her arms as the flowers flew their way. Joel did not whisper in her ear "We're next" when they were dancing, and the night did not end with him on one knee. Far from it. They made an excuse and left early, and when they got home he said he had a headache and went to sleep right away. She lay there in the dark trying not to weep too loudly, the empty jewelry box gaping at her from across the room. But as each minute passed, with Joel's legs kicking involuntarily as they always did when he was falling asleep, her sadness morphed further and further into anger, white-hot anger.

CHAPTER TWELVE

Steve

April

Steve was at the end of the driveway getting the mail. Taking a pile out of the box and riffling through bills and junk, he suddenly froze.

There was a manila envelope with the sender's name of "Faith Richards" and the address of Channel 9. His hands started shaking and several beads of sweat popped out on his forehead. Could this be real? No way, really?!

He looked at the envelope multiple times, blinking to be sure he wasn't imagining it. But no, it was all true. His breath was shallow, and a ringing started in his ears. He didn't bother to walk back to the house; he couldn't wait that long. Instead he ripped open the top of the manila envelope right there, nearly tearing the contents inside. He forced himself to slow down lest he ruin the two things he saw: an autographed photo of Faith and a piece of paper with a handwritten note. He scanned the photo eagerly: It was a studio photo with the Channel 9 logo. Faith looked amazing, wearing that red lipstick he adored. She had autographed it in a curly, right-leaning signature.

To Steve, thanks for making me feel special.

His hands began to shake so much he wasn't sure he could read the letter. He took a rattled breath and slowly did so.

Dear Steve,

I apologize for ignoring some of your calls and emails. I hope this will be the start of something new between us. You asked in one of your letters if I remembered you from the Belle Isle Art Fair. Of course I do, how could I forget? Please don't reach out to me though. I will contact you. Station management wouldn't like me talking to a viewer like this but I make an exception for you.

XO Faith

He almost fainted right there, putting one hand on the mailbox to keep himself from falling over. She was *finally* coming through, finally getting back to him after so many months. She did remember him! And she was flirty in her correspondence. He felt a surge of love and wondered if he should just get into the car right now and drive to Channel 9.

"Stevie?" came a shrill voice from the house. "Can you hurry up with the mail?"

His mother was the last person he needed right now to break this magic spell.

"In a minute," he snapped back, wanting to revel in this moment, this bubble of love. Faith knew his name, remembered him, wanted to start something new, acknowledged that he made her feel special, and she was even making an exception for him.

He started to get excited and knew he'd have to find a private place soon. His Faith, his Faith was on the path to loving him. It was all finally coming true. Just as he knew it would. He wanted to write her back so badly, to profess his love and suggest some places they could meet up. He couldn't really afford a fancy place, but something like Applebee's would be great for a first date. There were three within driving distance of his house.

Yet the words of warning not to contact her came back to him and he didn't want to risk her being fired. They would both need her income to live the kind of lifestyle they wanted. He would have to wait, and trust that she would reach out to him again. He just knew she would now that the floodgates were open.

And since she did remember him, he also felt maybe he could be a little more brazen about in-person contact with her, away from the prying eyes of management, of course.

CHAPTER THIRTEEN

Carol

June 2 and 3

Between the six PM and eleven PM news, Carol decided that she would, indeed, attend the vigil Channel 9 was planning at the park near the station. How could she not?

Naturally she assumed Jim would accompany her, but he reminded her that things like funerals and memorials always made him uncomfortable. He had walked out of his own mother's service to stand in the church parking lot because the whole thing was giving him so much anxiety, so she didn't push it, knowing she could represent the two of them. Jim offered to drive her instead.

"Traffic is probably going to be a nightmare, what with how popular Faith is . . . err, I mean, was," he said. "If I drop you off you won't have to worry about parking."

Carol nodded. She would ask Olivia to go with her instead.

It was late evening when she sent another text to Olivia, who hadn't been in touch since they spoke at noon and said she might stop by after taking a walk. Carol explained that she was planning to attend the vigil and assumed Olivia wanted to go too and that Jim could give them both a ride.

There was no response. Carol waited twenty minutes, checking her phone often. Then she started to worry and tried calling several times. Olivia didn't pick up.

"Jim, why is she not writing me back or answering?"

"Honey, she's a college kid. It's a Saturday night. She's probably out with friends. Leave her be. If she wants to go to the vigil I'm sure she'll text you back before it starts tomorrow and we can swing by to pick her up. Maybe she doesn't want to go. Give her some space to deal with what happened. It's a lot for a new intern."

"You're right, you're right, I shouldn't expect her to text me back. She probably needs a night out with friends."

Carol shifted her mind instead to what she was going to wear the next day. She wanted to stand in solidarity with the Fair-Weather Friends Fan Club and dress in yellow along with donning some of the famous earrings. Carol only owned the cloud pair Jim had gotten her for Christmas, so that choice was easy.

Her brain sifted through the yellow item options in her closet and dresser drawers, and she finally decided on a simple mustard top plus light cotton white capri pants. It was going to be warm again, but Carol didn't like wearing shorts in public, the varicose veins in her legs always felt too ugly for anyone but Jim to see.

Carol and Jim watched the late news, which like the five PM show featured a very long segment devoted just to Faith with lots of tearful comments. This time Tom, Veronica, and Roger were each in the tributes, interviewed at their respective homes.

Carol had to admit that in addition to listening to their wonderful words about Faith, she was also curious about the tiny bit of the personal things she could see over their shoulders in the interviews: Veronica's all-white kitchen, Roger's office space with walls dotted with sports pennants, and Tom's living room, a massive stone fireplace behind him with framed family photos on the mantel. These people were celebrities, and celebrity homes were endlessly fascinating to her.

The newscast featured another touching tribute from Matthew and interview clips with Abby and Chuck too. Carol was feeling a little less shocked and a little more as if her mind was starting—just barely starting—to process the information. There was nothing she could do to bring Faith back, but she would honor her memory in any way possible. She was looking forward to the vigil.

Before bed Carol looked at her phone several times more to see if there was anything from Olivia.

But there was still no response. Jim reminded her that Olivia might be out at a bar or a movie or something.

It was not a great night of sleep, but it was enough to get by and attend the vigil. In the morning she almost texted Olivia again but decided to heed Jim's advice. Olivia was a college student and was not even her own daughter. Carol had to remember that and give her some breathing room. If Olivia wanted to attend the vigil she would let Carol know. Carol decided to take some pictures of the event to share with Olivia instead for when they did get together.

Jim and Carol planned carefully for Carol's trip. Sunglasses, sunscreen, water, a protein bar, and lots of tissues for the sure-to-come emotions. They didn't know how long the vigil would last or what the seating at the park might be like so Jim got out a camping chair in a bag with a strap Carol could carry. She placed everything else into a large fanny pack, and they drove the thirty minutes to the park.

The parking lot was packed, and Carol saw a good number of women in various shades of yellow getting out of their respective cars.

"Just drop me here and I'll walk," she directed as their vehicle inched along in the line behind others. Jim stopped, threw his blinkers on, gave her a peck on the cheek, and promised to come back whenever she texted him. He would find a place to get a coffee and read an actual old-fashioned newspaper in the meantime.

Carol followed the other mourners down a path from the parking lot to a spot where a gazebo sat in a large grassy area flanked by trees. Rows of folding chairs had been set up, but they were all taken and many people were standing. Carol was grateful for her camping chair.

A woman in a Channel 9 polo was walking around with name tags and markers, and Carol took one and wrote her name, sticking it to her shirt. Those in yellow tops and dresses—presumably all from the Facebook group—seemed to be congregating to one side, and Carol drifted that way, nodding at a few others who were also wearing forecast earrings.

Finding a spot partially under a tree for a sliver of shade, she opened her camping chair, sat down, and looked around. The crowd was a huge mix of ages, races, and what looked like economic status. There were families with strollers and babies, older couples leaning into each other as they slowly walked, professional-looking folks talking on cell phones or into watches, and a group from a local college with METEOROLOGIST CLUB stamped on their shirts. Faith had truly touched every part of Detroit, Carol thought, and she nodded approvingly.

A woman about Carol's age and holding a similar chair came up on one side of Carol and plopped down, giving Carol a nod and a smile. Carol returned the greeting. A microphone was set up in the gazebo, and some official-looking people were milling about near it. Several TV cameramen were walking around with cameras on their shoulders, and others had cameras on tripods at the edges of the vigil. She heard a slight buzzing overhead and looked up to see a drone above them all. She guessed this would all be a story on the later news.

A woman stepped to the microphone and tapped it.

"Good morning, can you all hear me?"

The crowd murmured yes.

"OK, wonderful. Thank you so much for coming to this Channel 9 remembrance for Faith Richards. You can see how many lives she touched just by looking at the size of this incredible crowd. Faith was a special person to all of us. I'm Hilary Sanfilipo, director of human resources for Channel 9. I will be your emcee today. We have several guest speakers lined up, we'll also play some of Faith's favorite music, and we have a nondenominational prayer for those who wish to take part. Our first guest speaker is our news director, Perry Schofield. Perry?"

There was polite clapping, and a man stepped forward and started to talk about how he had recognized that Faith had that special TV magic the very first time he saw her on the air, how he followed her career and just knew he had to get her back to her hometown one day, how thrilled he was when she returned to Detroit and how she transformed local TV news with her videos and earring forecasts. He kept his composure until the very end, when he choked up saying how much he would miss her and that he couldn't believe this was really happening. Coughing, he looked down and wiped at his left eye as the crowd sniffled along with him.

Hilary then brought up some other people from the behind-the-scenes part of Channel 9: the general manager, who said he had never worked with a more popular meteorologist; the creative services director, who said he was in charge of making promotional videos and commercials about the weather team and loved the bonding of the meteorologists; the eleven o'clock executive producer, a woman named Laura, who had a baby strapped to her chest in one of those carrier things and said that Faith was exactly like what you saw on TV—warm, genuine, and kind to everyone.

At first there didn't seem to be any on-air people, and Carol was disappointed. Who really cared about the GM anyhow? But as Laura wrapped up, she said, "And now we'll bring out Tom, Veronica, and Roger as well as the weather team."

There was a gasp from the crowd as the anchors started walking from behind a makeshift curtained area behind the gazebo. People began to murmur and crane their necks. Carol heard a woman a few chairs over hiss, "Tom is even more handsome in person!" Somebody else was wondering if these celebrities would be giving autographs. Carol thought this talk was a bit inappropriate at a vigil for someone's life, but she also couldn't help noting herself that Roger was indeed taller than she had thought and Veronica was a little shorter and was getting a bit of middle-aged thickness around her waist.

Tom stepped to the microphone.

"Channel 9 viewers are the most loyal viewers in Detroit, and I think we can all safely say that Faith had the biggest following of any of us."

The crowd applauded. Carol's eyes shot to the members of the weather team, who were all looking down at the stage. Matthew shifted back and forth on his feet and kept scratching at his cheek. He looked tired again.

"I'm going to speak first today and then we will all share some thoughts," said Tom. "We are broken to pieces, shattered, and still in a deep state of shock. But the warmth you are showing our Channel 9 family is lifting us all up."

He proceeded to share a few memories of Faith and silly things they had talked about on and off the air, plus how she was so nice to his grandchildren when they visited. Taking the mic off its holder when he was done, he handed it to Veronica, who talked of Faith's wonderful sense of style and how kind she was to every coworker. Roger was next and he said she made the show better every night and pushed them all to be their best. Roger passed the microphone to Matthew. He coughed and stepped forward, looking uncomfortable.

"I, uh, I said this on the air before my weathercast last night but she was creative and had a big heart and we're all going to miss her . . . so much."

He handed the microphone to Abby, who spoke for a few minutes but got so choked up she had to pass it to Chuck. He only said a few words and passed it back to Tom.

"So there you have it," said Tom. "To equate it to weather terms, Faith was a lightning bolt who came into all of our lives, the best kind of lightning bolt, because then she filled our lives with sun. Faith, wherever you are . . . this isn't fair, we vow justice on your behalf, and we miss you."

He passed the microphone back to Hilary and looked up to the sky as a collective sob came from the crowd. Carol took out a tissue from her fanny pack and wiped at the tears now rolling down her cheeks.

"We'll play one of Faith's favorite songs now," Hilary said. "As Tom so eloquently put it, she was always looking for fair weather and the sunny side of life."

Hilary nodded at someone offstage and the Beatles' "Here

Comes the Sun" began. The Channel 9 group onstage put their arms around each other and started swaying. People in the audience seemed to have a variety of emotions: Some were singing along, even smiling; others were crying harder than ever. Carol felt a lump in her throat too big to allow her to sing, but she tapped her hand on her knee slowly to the beat and thought, *What a perfect song for Faith. She was an absolute ray of sunshine.*

When the song ended, Hilary stepped to the microphone again.

"Faith's sister, Hope, told me that Faith also liked Barry Manilow's music. So I chose this next song and I think it's extremely fitting."

She motioned again to the person cuing the music, and "Can't Smile Without You" started playing. This one evoked even more emotion than "Here Comes the Sun," and a sob rippled around the vigil. The lump in Carol's throat turned back into a flow of tears on her cheeks, and she pulled out another tissue and wiped at her face. Barry Manilow was one of her favorites too, and she felt even closer to Faith knowing they had this in common.

The TV cameramen around the park were getting right into people's faces at this key moment, really looking for that emotional reaction shot to things, Carol guessed. When the camera came near her, she turned her head so the producer or whoever it was who picked the shots would not choose her. She did not want to be on TV looking like she did, a little sweaty from another warm day and also wearing mustard yellow, not her best color.

The song ended and there was an awkward moment of silence with nothing but the sounds of sniffling and nose-blowing. Hilary walked back to the mic.

"We're going to close this vigil with a prayer now. Some of you have asked about a funeral. Faith's sister tells me it will be very small, family only, and completely private. Others have inquired if there will be a balloon release. At Channel 9 we don't condone balloon releases because they are documented as unhealthy for the environment, but we do have several doves in a cruelty-free extra-large cage with a professional animal handler. You'll see that to my left. The handler will release the doves into the air immediately after the prayer. If you are physically able, please stand; if you are so inclined, please bow your head; and if you are also so inclined, please take the hand of the person next to you. We're all family today, all members of Faith's Fair-Weather Friends Fan Club. Faith has brought us all together, just as she would have wanted."

Most people stood, including Carol. The woman next to her reached for Carol's hand, and Carol took it. Holding a stranger's hand always felt odd and a little uncomfortable, but she pushed the thought away and focused on Faith. Hilary invited a Lutheran pastor to the microphone. The pastor led them in a prayer about missing the ones we love but how we're better for knowing and loving them in the first place. He added that we must persevere through adversity and help each other and that sadness is a part of the human experience but so is comfort and joy and we can eventually find both in the memories we share.

Closing her eyes, Carol pictured Faith as she wanted to remember her: onscreen in front of the seven-day forecast, smiling with red lipstick, her hair flowing and perfectly curled, her tiny waist in some fashionable outfit, those bright blue eyes that always popped so beautifully, her long lashes, and of course some fun earrings.

Even though it was nondenominational, a good number of people said "Amen" when it was over. All eyes went to the animal handler, who slowly opened a very large white cage to release the chalk-gray doves into the air. The fluttering of their wings was the only noise apart from some sniffling. Carol took her phone out and managed to quickly grab a photo of the doves before they got too far away, for Olivia.

Hilary told them that the doves going to the sky was a fitting tribute for Faith's love of Mother Nature and weather. The vigil was over, Hilary added, but they were welcome to stay as long as they wanted. Channel 9 was providing coffee, lemonade, water, and cookies on several long tables to the side of the gazebo, and there were free umbrellas for everyone to remember Faith by.

Carol texted Jim to start heading back. She was folding up her camping chair and contemplating getting a cookie and a cup of lemonade when the woman who had been holding her hand during the prayer struck up a conversation.

"Hello," she said in a sort of nasally voice, glancing down at Carol's name tag. "Are you a Fair-Weather Friends Fan Club member, Carol? I am too."

The woman seemed younger than Carol, but not by too much. She was holding a teddy bear with a red ribbon around its neck, which Carol thought a bit odd. Something about the curve of the woman's jawbone and the way her eyes were set actually reminded Carol of Faith. Carol smiled.

"Yes, I'm a longtime member, in fact. I adored her."

The woman pointed at her own name tag. "I'm Heather, I adored her too. Have you ever met Faith in person?" Carol noticed that the woman had poor posture and hunched shoulders. Her voice was annoying, but Carol tried to be polite.

"No, I just saw her on TV every night. My husband, Jim, and I watch Channel 9. Have you ever met her?"

"Two times at festivals. She was amazing. Oh—you might be wondering about this bear. This is Mr. Bojangles. He's my emotional-support bear. I take him places when I need something to hold on to. He helps me through hard times. I need him for grief."

Before Carol could respond, another woman in yellow nearby started yelling, her hands cupped around her mouth to create a makeshift megaphone.

"FAIR-WEATHER FRIENDS FAN CLUB MEMBERS, WE ARE GOING TO GATHER UNDER THE LARGE OAK TREE OVER HERE TO HAVE OUR OWN PRIVATE MOMENT. PLEASE JOIN US."

Carol and Heather looked at each other and shrugged in a "why not?" way. Everyone in yellow and a few not in the color started walking over. It was almost entirely women, and the few men seemed to be paired with a female partner, all except one. He stood nervously, shifting from one foot to the next. His name tag read STEVE. The woman in charge had a name tag that read CHLOE and she had drawn little lightning bolts, clouds, and a sun next to her name. Carol realized that this was likely the organizer she had seen on the Facebook page.

"Hi, everyone, and thank you for being here on this absolutely devastating but moving day. I'm Chloe. I started the Facebook page and I'm the admin. Thank you all for wearing yellow and your special earrings today. I have twelve pairs but these are my favorite . . ."

She touched her earrings, happy snowmen that Faith wore for school snow days. They looked odd on such a sunny and warm afternoon.

"I thought we'd take a moment to have our own vigil since clearly no one is a bigger fan of Faith than any of us." Chloe stopped to wipe her eyes and sniff. "She changed my life. I know more about science now than I ever did, and I got makeup and fashion tips from her too. I was absolutely gutted yesterday, gutted. It was one of, if not the, worst days of my entire life. I'm sure many of you would agree. Whoever did this . . ."

Her voice turned to anger, but she shook her head and continued.

"As Tom said, we will get justice. For now, all we can do now is honor her memory. So, who would like to share a thought about Faith?"

They all glanced at each other. Who was going to speak first in front of strangers?

"I guess me," said a man's voice somewhat shakily, and Carol saw it was "Steve." He stepped forward, but his eyes kept darting from the grass to the crowd. He was wringing his hands. Despite his apparent unease, Carol gave him credit for being brave enough to speak before anyone else.

"Go on," Chloe encouraged. "Please tell us your Faith memories."

"Well, some I can't share," Steve said with a nervous laugh. "Because . . . when you say biggest fan, there was no one, not one single person on this earth, a bigger fan than me. You see, Faith was my girlfriend and we were in love. I'm heartbroken. I don't think I'll ever get over it, ever."

There was a gasp in the crowd and some murmuring. Carol had a feeling a lot of people were thinking what she was thinking: *This guy* was Faith's boyfriend? He just didn't look the part. He was out of shape, his hair was kind of greasy, he had bad teeth, and he was wearing cheap-looking and outdated clothing: a yellow T-shirt with the branding of a local pizza place, jean shorts that were too long, and white tennis shoes with white socks that came three-quarters of the way up his calves.

Perhaps Steve sensed disbelief in the crowd. He seemed to take a defensive tone.

"We *were* in love, madly, deeply in love. We were soulmates, we were going to get married. Here is the last picture we took together."

He opened a string bag that was over his shoulder, took out an eight-by-ten piece of paper that looked like it came off a home color printer, and started passing it around. Carol leaned in for a look, as did many others. There was Steve and there, indeed, was Faith. She had on a green bikini, while he was wearing Hawaiian swim trunks. They were standing on a beach somewhere, arms around each other, smiling.

Carol noticed that the Steve in the picture seemed to have a better body than the Steve in real life. The picture Steve's stomach was flatter and his arms were more muscular. It was not like he was a bodybuilder in the photo by any means, but he was definitely more fit. His teeth looked better too, but the rest of the face was definitely him, and Faith was absolutely Faith, down to her perfect figure and ironing-board-flat stomach.

"We went to Florida on vacation just a few weeks ago," Steve said. "Didn't you hear her talk about it in one of her videos? About finding shells on the beach? That was our trip."

Carol remembered the video he was talking about, but in her memory Faith had said something about a sister, not a fiancé or boyfriend. Heather, the woman who had held Carol's hand, leaned over and whispered:

"I think he photoshopped that image or had AI make it, that's not him. Look at the height."

Indeed, the man in the photo looked taller than Steve now. Even the way he was standing was different. The man in the photo had better posture and held his feet differently, more straight to the camera. Steve's shoulders were rounded and he stood with his toes and knees splayed out nearly at right angles.

Others seemed to be reaching the same conclusion, and Carol could feel the energy shift to an "OK, we're dealing with a slightly crazy person here, so let's appease him" mode.

"That looks like an amazing trip, Steve," Chloe said. "We're all so sorry for your loss. Now, who's next?"

"Wait! There's something else. Faith was pregnant with my child!" Steve yelled, and another gasp ripped through the crowd.

"I call BS," whispered Heather in Carol's ear.

Chloe looked uncomfortable and was clearly fishing for something to say.

"Oh my, that's just terrible, Steve. What a tragic, tragic twist. Thank you for sharing that very personal bit of information. We are pressed for time so let's keep going. Anyone else?"

Others spoke about Faith. Carol listened until she felt the phone in her pocket buzz. It was Jim.

I'm in the parking lot.

Chloe was just ramping up a story of her own but Carol didn't feel bad about leaving. Others had already done so, plus she was hungry for more than the protein bar in her bag or the Channel 9 cookie, if there were even any more left. She was turning to leave when a hand touched her forearm.

"Heading out already, Carol?"

It was Heather. She was smiling.

"Oh, yes, I have to get going," said Carol.

"I'll walk out with you. I have to go too."

"OK, uh, sure." Carol had barely talked to Heather and now she felt as if they were supposed to be bonded, but hey, a new friend who also loved Faith couldn't be a bad thing, right?

"I was going to grab an umbrella," Carol said, gesturing to the Channel 9 staffers in polos handing them out by the path to the parking lot.

"Me too! Let's go together," said Heather. They started to walk, and Carol noticed that Heather had a slight limp as if her knee or hip were bothering her. As they made their way across the grass, Heather said softly, "I hate to talk this way already but who do you think they'll replace her with? I'm hoping it's Abby. Maybe she'll start up the earring forecast again. Matthew and Chuck are both just kind of average, in my mind."

"I hadn't really thought ahead, but I guess they'll have to hire someone," replied Carol with a long sigh. "No one will measure up to Faith, though, no one. The shoes are too big."

"I couldn't agree more," Heather said.

They walked in silence for a minute, but then Carol thought of something to say.

"Do you know what's crazy? My niece was interning at Channel 9, just started last week. She got to meet Faith and all of the others."

Heather stopped and turned to Carol, her eyes big. She grabbed Carol's forearm. Heather's casual nature with touching a stranger was a little off-putting to Carol, and Carol reflexively took a step back.

"You're kidding me!" said Heather with an especially nasal squeal. "That's amazing. What did your niece think of Faith?"

"Oh, she said she was very nice and that she showed her the weather center." Carol decided not to tell her that Olivia might have been the last person to see Faith alive. Why would a stranger need to know that?

"That's incredible," said Heather. They resumed walking toward the umbrella area. A young woman reached into a cardboard box and pulled out two.

"Here you go, thank you for coming and know that we're grieving with you during this awful time," she said.

They nodded. A few steps beyond, a reporter stood with a cameraman.

"Hi, I'm interviewing people about Faith for a story for the news tonight, would you like to say a few words?" she asked.

"No thank you," said Heather with a tight smile. Carol said the same. She knew her eye makeup had smeared from the heat and crying and she also knew she'd likely freeze up on camera with fright. They both walked past the reporter, who was already asking the next people walking out the exact same thing, word for word.

"Hey, I came alone, do you need a ride?" Heather asked.

"No, no thank you, my husband is picking me up," Carol said.

"Do you live far? Honestly, I could save him the trouble," said Heather.

"Uh—no, not really far, one of the suburbs," Carol said. Why was Heather pushing this? Carol did not want to reciprocate and ask where Heather lived, because suddenly Carol's antennae were going up. Sometimes when a woman level-jumped in a friendship in this manner Carol couldn't help but wonder if the person might actually be hitting on her. Could Heather be *attracted* to her? Why was she asking how far away Carol lived? Carol would never tell Heather her address, that was for sure. She valued her privacy.

"Well, listen, Heather, it's been nice meeting you. I need to go meet my *husband* now. I hope you have a nice rest of your day."

Carol was grateful that she got to use the word *husband* again to show Heather clearly that she was heterosexual and in a relationship.

"You too," said Heather. "Maybe I'll see you around. Once a fair-weather friend, always one, right? Do you like my earrings? I don't have an official pair but I enjoy doing arts and crafts so I made these."

She flicked one of the earrings around with her fingers. They were long, bold, and odd, and they didn't look like any weather earrings Carol had ever seen. They had colored beads and buttons in all colors and a little mirror in the middle.

"Oh, um, beautiful," said Carol, and between the earrings and the emotional-support teddy bear she was starting to wonder if Heather was also a crazy person she needed to appease, like Steve.

"I know the earrings probably don't make much sense," said Heather. "But to me they represent all of the colors Faith wore and the light and brightness she brought into all of our lives. Really I feel like I've had a death in the family."

"Me too," said Carol, and she moved Heather back into the "most likely sane but I'm still done with you" category. Glancing around the emptying parking lot, she was relieved to see their car, Jim in the driver's seat.

"Oh, there's my hubby. Goodbye now," she said.

"Bye," Heather responded, lifting the bear's paw and waving it. Carol thought it was ridiculously silly but felt compelled to wave back at Heather and the bear.

As Carol walked to the car she felt as if Heather's eyes were watching her. When she got there, Jim hopped out to put the camping chair in the trunk, and they climbed back in, the air-conditioning feeling fantastic as Carol turned it up a notch.

"How was it?" Jim asked. "I saw you talking to someone else in yellow so you must have met some fellow fans. Was that woman holding a teddy bear?"

"Yeah, she was nice but maybe a bit odd," said Carol. She glanced out the window but Heather was no longer standing in the spot where they had said goodbye. Carol was relieved even though she truly had no solid reason to distrust this woman.

On the way home she told Jim every detail of the vigil and the gathering afterward of the Fair-Weather Friends Fan Club, including Steve, who had said he was Faith's boyfriend.

"I bet all TV people have a few crackpots in their lives. Overall it sounds like a nice vigil," summed up Jim. "Any word from Olivia yet?"

Carol pulled out her phone.

"Nothing," she said. "I managed to get one photo of doves being released for her, but I was so broken up for most of the vigil that I forgot to take others."

When they arrived home, Carol was tired. She made a quick lunch and took a nap. It wasn't until later that afternoon that she thought to look on the Fair-Weather Friends Fan Club page to see if anyone had posted pictures of the event. There were a decent amount, and Carol was actually in some of them. She was squinting through her reading glasses looking at the photos when she got a Facebook Messenger ping. No one really wrote to her on Facebook, so curiosity caused her to open it right away.

Hi Carol, it's Heather. We met at the vigil today. I wondered if you'd like to have coffee sometime to talk more about ways we can honor Faith? I'd like to maybe start a scholarship in her name or something like that. I'm looking for someone to brainstorm with.

What the heck? Carol didn't know how to react. This woman just kept on level-jumping. Carol had to put a stop to it. Heather could collaborate with Chloe. Quickly, Carol fired off a reply:

Thank you. I am actually too busy for a coffee but you and others can keep me posted if the group does something.

She actually wasn't too busy at all, but she needed the white lie, and she thought that by saying "and others" and "the group" she would show that she wasn't interested in anything one-on-one.

Heather replied that she would keep Carol posted, and Carol sighed. Hopefully that put an end to that. Just as she was closing the laptop, her cell phone rang. Olivia. Finally!

"Liv, where have you been? I have so much to tell you."

"Sorry, Aunt C. I was just having a hard time with all of this. I went into a little bit of a funk and needed some alone time honestly just to process what happened."

"I understand, honey. Grief takes time, you know. I was at the vigil this morning. I wish I had taken more pictures, but I did get one and there are lots on the Fair-Weather Friends Facebook page if you want to see more."

"I saw your text that you were going. I just couldn't. I mean, I saw Faith Friday night. What if I truly was the last person to see her alive other than the killer? I just . . . I just can't wrap my head around that. And then there's the note she asked me to give to Tom. That was honestly kind of the other thing I was busy processing."

"What do you mean? Why is that bugging you?"

Olivia let out a long sigh.

"How about I come over for the tea and cookies you mentioned? I have something to tell you."

"Something to tell me? Is everything all right, Liv?"

"Yes, I think so, I mean maybe . . ."

"Honey, your voice sounds weird. Come over right now. I'll start the kettle. It sounds like we definitely need to chat."

CHAPTER FOURTEEN

Laura

June 3

Laura watched as the crowd slowly dispersed. She was still onstage but off to the side sitting on a folding chair, trying to soothe baby Quinn, who was getting fussy. Laura knew attending this vigil would be a chore. She was just back from a short, six-week maternity leave. (Why oh why, she constantly asked herself, didn't she take the full three months?) She was exhausted, yet Perry had said they needed representation from managers and she was the executive producer of the show and had to be there. Since Laura was nursing and parenting alone that weekend, she didn't have much of a choice but to bring Quinn along. She had bottled pumped milk in a cooler in her massive diaper bag, nursing pads in her bra, and a headache brewing from the whole event.

What a horrid twenty-eight hours it had been since she heard the news. She had screamed when Perry had called her first thing Saturday morning to tell her that Faith was found dead, and she sobbed most of the day, upsetting baby Quinn, who cried along with her. She wished Elliott had been there to help, but he was on a camping weekend with the guys and out of cell phone reach, so she was on her own. He didn't even know the news yet.

Quite frankly, Elliott had not been the kind of husband or father she thought he would be since Quinn's birth. He was constantly complaining about his lack of sleep although she was the one to get up and nurse all night; he didn't like to give baths or even really to rock the baby. He just wanted to go golfing, fishing, and camping or watch shows about golfing, fishing, and camping. Because Laura worked nights and Elliott days, he had to be alone with Quinn after day care closed at six, but he would always try to rush Quinn to bed by seven, often neglecting bathtime and, Laura thought, causing Quinn to be up many times during the night due to the early bedtime. She wished Quinn would stay up later and sleep later to help her out. She didn't get home until after 11:45 PM and would be up multiple times during the night and then have to take care of Quinn all morning before dropping him at day care.

Elliott's attitude, in Laura's mind, was to think the baby was for her and he could mostly do as he pleased, as if both of their lives shouldn't be upended. She was perturbed by him, and they had a few more fights recently, about baby duties but also about Faith, who had continued to text during the night at least once per week recently despite Laura's pleas.

Yes, there were times she despised the way Faith was acting, but Laura was still in a deep sorrow over her death. How could any of this be real, she thought, as she pushed the nipple of the bottle gently into Quinn's open mouth and looked out again over the departing crowd.

What a crowd it had been, hundreds of viewers, maybe thousands, all pulled together in such a short time. She hadn't understood at first why Perry wanted to rush this vigil the very next day after the death, but he said he felt it was important to do it on a weekend to get more people to attend and to "strike while the iron is hot." It would be too long to wait for the following weekend, he said; mourners needed closure now. He set the time for eleven AM so churchgoers could still attend. So here they were. Yet, Laura felt she and others barely had time to process the death, so everything had a surreal and rushed feel.

Perry had instructed his assistant news director, who was good at planning things, to pull off the entire thing at warp speed: the music, the animal handler, the speakers, the umbrellas, even the free cookies and lemonade. Laura knew Perry had an ulterior motive, which was why there were so many cameras and a drone. He wanted to make a thirty-minute special out of it that they could run in prime time during sweeps to drive up ratings. She heard him telling the photographers and reporters what reaction shots to get and what questions to ask to evoke emotion—"Give me tears, lots and lots of tears."

A prime-time special would be expensive real estate for any advertisers, and she knew he was licking his lips. It disgusted her but it didn't surprise her. That was what TV stations often did, placing their big stories during sweeps or coming up with ideas for specials that would sometimes capitalize on someone's pain, yes, for their own profit.

The irony was that Faith probably would have approved of both the vigil and the special. She knew how TV worked and she would want maximum exposure even about her own death.

Perry had all kinds of plans on top of the special. His goal was to have a "Faith Richards Day" in Detroit, with a declaration from the mayor. He asked the assignment desk manager to call some of the largest corporations to see if they wanted to go in on a scholarship fund in her name, and he even talked about a night where all downtown buildings would turn yellow in her honor, the way they could light up silver and blue for the Detroit Lions or orange and blue for the Detroit Tigers.

Laura thought if Perry put half this much effort into finding Faith's killer it might be a better use of his time. She was still stunned at what had transpired Friday night. A totally normal 6:00 and 6:30 PM show followed by dinner break. Faith usually took an hour or so, which wasn't unusual. Other anchors were gone for much longer, to be honest. Producers complained often that Tom and Veronica took breaks so long that they barely read their scripts before going on the air.

At nine PM, Laura had walked back to the weather office to touch base with Faith about that night's show. No one was there, but that wasn't a big deal. She went back fifteen minutes later. Still no one. On her third visit, at 9:30, she began to really wonder what was going on and texted Faith with no response. Laura called multiple times and texted more. She was getting concerned. Faith had never been away this long and never not answered when anyone from the station needed her. For all of her jerk-like behaviors, she was a professional about stuff like the station calling her.

Laura pulled a few other newsroom leaders into a conference room so they could discuss what was happening. It was a Friday night and Perry didn't like to be bothered at the end of his week, but she had to let him and the assistant news director know what was happening. Perry told her to contact the GM and the HR manager, and she did both.

Then she texted Faith that if they didn't hear from her soon they would have to call in Matthew. They needed a met for the show. Tom, Veronica, and Roger couldn't do the weather, after all. This wasn't some tiny-market TV station where the anchor was also the producer, editor, sportscaster, and weathercaster. They were Detroit, for Christ's sake, a major market. Number thirteen in rankings of television markets in the entire US. New York was number one, followed by Los Angeles at number two and Chicago at number three, but Detroit was larger than Denver, Minneapolis, Miami, Cleveland, and Portland, just to name a few. Detroit's designated market area had over four million people in it.

Someone had to do the weather that night. Someone who knew what the heck they were talking about. That left only one choice: Matthew. She knew he would be incensed—Matthew covered for Faith a lot—but they simply had no choice. Laura would figure out Faith's sudden absence later; for now, she had a show to get on the air.

Matthew didn't arrive at the station until 10:55 PM, just five minutes before the show. He had been out to a late dinner with Tara when he got the call, he said. She could tell he had a drink or two in him, but he was good enough to go on air.

He didn't have time to refresh the graphics or double-check the forecast Faith had delivered at 6:00 and 6:30, and Laura knew that he had to go on the air with Faith's information and graphics to give viewers and that it likely bothered him to the core, but they needed someone on air, period.

Matthew stomped into the studio to get his microphone on, complaining loudly to anyone who would listen. When the show was over, he ripped the mic off and stormed out seconds after they signed off.

Laura continued to text and call Faith during this whole time with no response. She spoke on the phone to HR, the GM, and Perry again, but they all said they would deal with any discipline—if that's what it required—Monday. If Faith went home and got drunk and passed out or something like that, she would be in deep trouble. No one was in a panic. A little worried, yes, but more pissed at her than anything. She was capable of too many shenanigans, as they had all seen, and there had been instances before where she suddenly said she felt sick and had to leave halfway through her shift and things like that.

So Laura had gone home, relieving the babysitter they had due to Elliott camping; she nursed Quinn for his midnight feeding and had gotten her usual bout of two hours of sleep here, nurse, three hours of sleep there, nurse, a few more minutes of rest before getting woken up by Perry's devastating call in the morning.

He said they would do a push alert on their app around midmorning but he needed to call other people, send a note to the newsroom, and get a game plan going for the vigil. Later in the day he pulled together a conference call with all managers and main anchors to inform them of the plans—they were sending a reporter and photojournalist to the anchors' homes for comments; they needed everyone at the vigil saying nice things about Faith.

Laura pushed down any negative thoughts she had ever had about her former friend. She could not speak ill of the dead. She thought of some kind, if not entirely true, things to say and rehearsed her part over and over in her head as she cried and rocked Quinn and cried some more.

Strangled? In an area near the station? How was this even possible? Fear began to overtake her as she wondered if this was random, a robbery or something, and the perpetrator didn't even know who Faith was. What if that psycho had done this to a different woman from the station, like Laura herself? Her throat constricted, and she hugged Quinn and cried harder as they rocked in the wooden rocker her sister had gotten her for the baby shower.

But the rational part of her knew it had to be someone who actually was acquainted with Faith, not just a random act, someone who had something against her. Strangulation was a form of anger. She had covered enough trials and crimes to know that. She wasn't sure yet if there had been sexual assault; she only heard about the strangulation part from the medical examiner.

In television news, nothing was official until the medical examiner (which everyone shortened to "ME") said it was. They were often waiting for the ME's report before they would broadcast a death. Now that it had come out about Faith, she knew it was true. That, and the police report. That was also out.

She was thinking of all this as she sat on the stage with Quinn. When the final few viewers finished their lemonade and cookies, talked to Tom, Veronica, and the others (she noticed many people asking for pictures or autographs), and left, Perry came up onstage next to her. Quinn had finally fallen into what she called the "milk coma" and was breathing hard through his perfect little rosebud lips, his eyelids flickering.

"So how'd we do? Did viewers like the vigil?" Perry asked. Laura noticed that he didn't even glance at the baby, nor had he ever once asked about him since his birth.

"It was a very nice event," Laura said. "Faith would have been pleased."

"We got some great footage for the special, it's going to be kickass," Perry said. "Faith would want it that way, you know. I need to talk to you about who is going to take over as our main met. For now, Matthew will be interim and Chuck will do weekends. I'm looking for a freelancer to round out the staff until we hire someone."

"OK, sounds good," Laura replied, standing up. She started to carefully maneuver Quinn into the BabyBjörn on her front. It was strange to talk to her boss about totally normal things, as if she weren't strapping an infant to her, and it also felt jarring to be talking about Faith's replacement already, but she knew that the TV wheels kept grinding and that Perry was doing what needed to be done for the business. Picking up her diaper bag, she wiped her brow. It was hot out, even in the shade of the gazebo.

"I'll see you tomorrow, then," she said, starting to turn away.

Perry grabbed her elbow and Laura, startled, looked back. Perry's face was serious, and he stared right into her eyes in an unnerving way that he did to everyone.

"Laura, there's something else I want to tell you, something hardly anyone knows. I'm telling you this in confidence," he whispered.

Something else? Laura's throat tightened. What else could there be that was so serious? Didn't they have enough bad news?

"What is it?" she asked warily.

"The medical examiner told us something and we asked him to redact it before going public."

Laura had absolutely no idea what it could be, but her mind started to flip through guesses: A toxic level of drugs in Faith's system? An undiagnosed disease? An abnormality in some organ? Or could it be the findings of a sexual assault? She shuddered at the thought of the last one.

"Laura, none of us were aware of this . . ." Perry said, taking a deep breath. He was still staring her right in the eyes. "But Faith was six weeks pregnant."

CHAPTER FIFTEEN

Steve

June 3

He knew that people from the Fair-Weather Friends Fan Club
didn't believe that he was Faith's boyfriend. Steve could sense it
even though he brought along the picture of the two of them at
the beach as proof of their relationship.

It didn't matter what those idiots thought, he knew the truth.
Faith was his girlfriend and he got her pregnant. They had even
talked about names: Zeus for a boy and Charity for a girl. They
both liked strong boy names, and Steve knew Faith would want
to name a girl after her sister.

He remembered when Faith had shown him the pregnancy
test, how she cried with joy and how they made wild love on the
silk sheets of her king-sized bed in her fancy apartment in the
sky.

It all started when he opened that first letter from her, the day
he was getting the mail at the end of the driveway. He read and
reread the letter probably two hundred times, kissed and then
licked her eight-by-ten photo all over, and tucked both under
the pillow of the twin bed he'd had since childhood. He could

barely sleep, he was so excited. Faith was going to be his soon! He would be touching her, caressing her. His face flushed and he stayed up until five AM, masturbating more in one night than he ever had.

She said she would write to him and for him not to write to her so he waited anxiously, debating what to do if she didn't make that next move, but just three days later another letter came.

His heart soared when he saw it. She was as good as her word! When he opened it he was thrilled that she had really ramped it up: She said she had set up a private email address for the two of them to converse away from the eyes of management. And she said she was starting to fall in love with him.

His thought was *Oh my God, oh my God, oh my God.* He ran (for the first time in twenty years) as fast as he could from the mailbox to the house and straight to the laptop computer his mom and dad kept on a desk in a corner of the dining room. Panting, he frantically typed in the email address. He fired this off:

> You're the best Faith. I love you too. When should we meet?

An hour later came the response:

> Let's just flirt like this for a while. It'll be fun. I'll go first. Here's a picture of me in my bedroom. Do you like what you see?

The photo was a selfie taken in a full-length mirror. It was from the neck down and she was wearing a very short silk bathrobe that was showing cleavage. He almost fell off his chair but was conscious that his mother was in the kitchen one room over making dinner.

"Stevie," she called. "Food will be ready in twenty minutes. Did you get the mail?"

"Yeah, uh . . . I'll uh . . . I'll leave it on the table for you. I'm not hungry. I'm going to hang out in my room."

"Not hungry? But it's your favorite, meat loaf," she said, and he noted a tinge of pleading in her voice. She had been using that tone since he was a child, always with him, never with his sister who was married with kids and had a job she enjoyed as a dental hygienist.

"Maybe later, Ma."

He needed time alone with Faith, time to examine every inch of that photo and to take a selfie of his own to send back.

From there they had tons of fun sending photos. Faith said she would send two or three a week, and he checked email incessantly until they came in. He wasn't really good at this "sexy selfie" thing, so he just emulated her. If she took a picture of her bare shoulder, he took one of his. If she was standing in her underwear, so was he. If she had a hand on a hip, he did too. They agreed to never show anything above the neck because she said, "You know what my face looks like. Now it's time to get to know my body," and he thought that was a great idea.

It went on like this for more than a month. He would watch Channel 9 at night with his parents, who had no clue what was happening between him and Faith. But both his mom and dad were fans of Faith. "She's as cute as a button," his mother had said more than once. "And that earring forecast is clever."

"Yeah, I never thought no one could replace Jack but she's a good one they got over there," his dad offered.

"Do you like her forecasts?" his mom asked, turning to Steve.

"Aww, she's all right," he lied.

Meanwhile, he was having a ball emailing sexy things with Faith but he also started to get frustrated that they couldn't meet. He asked her for that first date multiple times but she always had an excuse or said she wanted to keep sending pictures.

Then one night she announced on the air that the whole weather team would be at an R&B festival Saturday with the Storm Chaser vehicle. The four meteorologists planned to greet people and sign autographs.

He decided to surprise her.

He put on his best jean shorts and clean white socks, plus he asked his mother to iron a polo shirt for him.

"Where are you going, Stevie?" she asked.

"Just out," he replied, and she looked happy. He knew his parents were always pleased to see him leaving the house.

At the festival he ignored the food and music and beelined straight to the queue of viewers waiting to see the weather team. Matthew, Abby, and Chuck were there along with Faith. The line was long plus Steve was anxious, so he pushed his way past an older couple about midway through the line, telling them he had to cut because he was in a hurry. They glared at him.

As he got closer to Faith he felt his excitement rise. She was going to be thrilled to see him! A boyfriend who comes out to show you support! A boyfriend who surprises you!

She was standing at the end of the line of the four meteorologists, next to Matthew. She looked so good, in shorts and another station-issued polo shirt. She was saying "Thank you for watching Channel 9" to each person but he knew he would get something else. He imagined her eyes widening when she saw him and her mouth opening in shock. He figured she would whisper, "Steve! Wait for me when I'm done," or something like that.

He did a perfunctory handshake with Chuck, Abby, and Matthew and he was next to get to Faith. He waited for her to finish with the woman in front of him and then to catch his eye.

Her gaze slid over to him but she showed no recognition as she put her hand out and said, "Hi, thank you for watching Channel 9."

What?! He was tongue-tied. Why was she acting like this? She must not recognize him right off the bat.

"It's me, Steve," he said. She looked blank. He tried again.

"*Steve.* Your boyfriend. We've been having fun with the pictures."

Faith looked uncomfortable. Matthew glanced over at the two of them.

"Uh, OK, hi, Steve," she said. "Thank you for watching Channel 9."

Then she was on to the couple behind him and he was being pushed to the side. He slunk away, confused and humiliated, and when he looked back he saw Matthew staring at him.

Finding a spot under a tree, Steve watched Faith until the line dwindled to nothing. He was thinking that he would talk to her again after the event and try to figure out why she was acting so aloof. Yet, as soon as it was over, Faith, Matthew, Abby, and Chuck all got into the Storm Tracker and drove away. He didn't have a chance to get close to her. Pulling out his phone, he fired off an email right there.

What's going on? You were acting like you don't know me today.

It wasn't until that night that he got a response.

> I'm sorry, honey. I just didn't want Matthew and the others
> to know about us.

Oh, OK, that made sense. He guessed he could forgive her, but if they were going to be boyfriend and girlfriend they also needed to step out in public at some point, so he tried again.

> Want to go to Applebee's tomorrow?

She didn't reply, and the next day he tried yet again, asking the same question. Still no response. He was baffled and angry and was about to tell her that when she finally wrote.

> You know what would be even better for me for now? Can
> you follow me home at night in your car and come out to
> every event I am at to be sure I'm safe? There's a weird
> dude stalking me and I would love your protection. I will
> email you my schedule of events.

He wrote back immediately:

> Of course. I can start tonight

She might not have realized that he had already followed her home plenty of times. He knew the route well. But now that she had authorized it he could be a little more public about it. He thought he would honk as she turned into her parking ramp at the Three Diamonds, or be sure she saw him at every public event.

And that's when their relationship really took off. She trusted him. He followed her home, honking each time so she knew she was safe. She emailed the list of events and he went to every one. She told him she couldn't talk to him at these but that just being there made her feel safe and protected, so he clung to that. And they fell even more deeply, madly in love, culminating with the pregnancy. She told him that the very first person she shared the good news with was her sister, Hope. Steve had read a magazine article about Faith when she first moved back to Detroit and he knew that she had two sisters: Charity, the one who died very young, and Hope, the one she was close to now.

PART TWO

HOPE

———

CHAPTER SIXTEEN

Hope

There were three of us. Hope, Faith, and Charity, born in that order. Yes, we knew the well-known phrase went a different way—"Faith, Hope, and Charity"—but Mom always said she didn't realize she'd have three girls. If she had, she claimed, she would have put them in the proper sequence.

Dad wanted boys, and said so in front of us.

"If I had that little guy I'd take him hunting with me this weekend," I recall him grunting at dinner. Faith and I looked down at our plates. Neither one of us wanted to be the tomboy who offered to go.

Dad worked as a manager at a bank and wore a suit during the day but on weekends he would change into camouflage gear and go to the shooting range or pheasant hunting while always eagerly awaiting deer-hunting season. We had three mounted deer heads in our house, and Faith and I secretly gave them names and made up stories about their lives, always with cheerful endings where they got away from the hunters and lived happily ever after, munching on berries and sleeping in the forest.

Mom volunteered at church and dragged us girls there with her every Sunday. Somehow Dad was exempt from this duty, which caused confusion for us as kids, and resentment as we got older. I remember Mom making up excuses for other parishioners: "Pete is out of town" or "Pete is not feeling well." Eventually people stopped asking.

I don't recall a time when Dad wasn't domineering toward the rest of us in some way, but it got way worse after the tragedy. He never hit us but it was always a threat, simmering just below the things he did do. I can picture his balled-up fists and red face, sweat popping on his lower lip when he was angry. Lots of things set him off. Dad was a neat freak. All the socks in his drawer were rolled carefully and laid out in rows, every tie hung in its own slot on the rack in his closet. He didn't leave a toothbrush or a shaver out on the counter in the bathroom; each had its own spot hidden from view. He liked the shower to be wiped down and spotless after anyone used it. The kitchen had to be perfectly clean almost immediately after cooking. Mom's anxieties became our anxieties and we all knew the punishments: him screaming or throwing dirty dishes on the floor and making us clean them up, or what turned into Dad's favorite form of retribution for me and Faith, forcing us to go to the "disobey box" to pick out some clothes.

Dad knew that Faith and I both liked clothing and makeup. He also thought everything we wanted, from dresses and tights as small girls to crop tops and leggings as teenagers, was expensive and not needed. So he cooked up the "disobey box" and filled a cardboard container with items he purchased at Goodwill. I don't think he even looked at the sizes. Or maybe he did and chose them to be deliberately wrong. Regardless, they were all way too small or much too large, some were men's shirts and sweatshirts, and the items that were women's were hopelessly outdated colors and patterns for stylish girls. Depending on the length of our punishment, we would have to wear things from the disobey box to school for anywhere from a day to weeks. It was torture. Truly, I sometimes wondered if I would rather just be hit. You can't imagine the feeling of walking the halls of your middle or high school in clothes that looked like they belonged to your grandma or even grandpa. The shoes were too big and Faith and I would have to put on multiple pairs of socks to make it even possible to walk. Thinking back on the girls pointing and snickering and the boys staring still brings hot shame to my face. Even teachers would do a double take.

"Wear these or wear nothing at all," Dad would say. Mom's eyes would get teary as she watched us drag ourselves to the disobey box but she never stopped it from happening.

As we got older Faith and I became craftier about clothing. We found a spot at a nearby park where we hid clothes from our own drawers in a plastic bag behind several bushes. The park was on the way to school. If we had to take things from the disobey box, we would leave early for school, claiming a club meeting or that we wanted to go to the library to study for a test, then we'd run to the park and be on the lookout for each other as we changed clothes behind the bushes. After school we'd do the reverse and make our way home. The whole time we'd whisper to each other, "Just get through it. Someday we'll be rich on our own and buy anything we want."

In high school we both found jobs at the mall—Faith at Orange Julius and me at a hip thrift store called Ragworks. Because I had a small discount, we spent hours combing the racks at Ragworks, and we would buy clothes that we loved for once. In the backs of our minds was the thought that Dad might take these away, so we kept most of them hidden in boxes we labeled "Yearbooks" or "Art Projects" in our closets. Dad never knew. Mom did, though. My senior year and Faith's sophomore year, Mom pulled us both into our shared bedroom and sat us on Faith's bed, giving us a stern look.

"Girls, I was cleaning the closet and found some boxes I didn't know you had in there. I wanted to see your old art projects and yearbooks so I opened them. Where did all of those clothes come from?"

I think she thought we had stolen them, so when we told her about how we were afraid of Dad finding out but had purchased them at Ragworks, relief flooded her face. She was quiet for a while but then said, "Keep them hidden. You can take them to college."

I do have to give Dad credit for one thing, though: I don't think Faith would have become the meteorologist that she was without him. Dad had a fascination for weather, and I think Faith saw it as the one way to connect with him. I still remember her coming home from fifth grade with a rain gauge they made in science, and Dad was excited to set it up in the backyard with her. The two of them were outside for a long time finding the perfect spot. A thunderstorm was expected that night, and at dinner they both talked about how they couldn't wait to see how much rain filled the tube.

I thought it was kind of stupid. I didn't care what quantity of rain our little suburb got, and I had zero interest in the weather, but I could see Faith beaming as Dad promised they would both get up early to check the gauge.

From that point forward Faith and Dad were the weather geeks. They watched Channel 9, Dad's favorite, where Dad liked Jack, the meteorologist who had been on the station forever.

Faith and Dad got thermometers and wind gauges, and Faith started checking books out of the library describing thunder-storms, hurricanes, and tornadoes. If a storm was coming in, Dad and Faith would set up camping chairs in the backyard and watch it. Was I envious that Faith was growing closer to Dad? Not really. Being around him for any length of time made me uneasy, so I wasn't looking for ways to get tighter with him. But Faith was clearly happy about this burgeoning part of their rela-tionship.

In the back of my mind I also couldn't help but wonder if it was her way of making up for what happened to Charity.

CHAPTER SEVENTEEN

Kelly

June 3

Kelly declined the free umbrella and the chance to talk with a reporter about Faith after the vigil, and she walked slowly to her car, sitting in the parking lot for a long time, staring out the window as she tried to make sense of her feelings. A squirrel kept running up and down a tree, and she watched it as though in a hypnotic state.

She hadn't been planning to attend the vigil at first. Her anger was still so searing toward Faith. But then she thought, *Faith is dead. Show a little respect.* Plus, Kelly couldn't be sure Faith had actually orchestrated the robbery of the jewels. It was the only thing that made sense logically, but still, she couldn't be 100 percent certain.

Joel refused to accompany her, saying she was nuts for even thinking of attending. Things between them had not been great since the night she discovered that the jewelry was stolen and accused him of doing it. They were coexisting as partners but it was a little stilted. Their hellos and goodbyes to each other had become a peck on the cheek, and he stopped putting his hand on her buttocks the way he used to. He was taking long walks and bike rides on his own.

The firm footing of their relationship seemed like it was eroding, and she bounced between sad, lonely, and angry. Her mother's and grandmother's jewelry was *gone,* a heartbreak in her life, and yet Joel seemed fixated on the fact that she had accused him of doing it, saying again that he was shocked by her lack of trust in him. He was also irate at Faith and said more than once that he would like to show Detroit's favorite meteorologist a little something-something for what she did to them. Kelly didn't know what exactly that meant.

The police had been back to their house to say they had looked into the robbery with Faith but could not find any evidence that she was involved. Kelly and Joel had scoured a few pawnshops and online sites but hadn't seen the jewelry there, so it was probably black market if it was being sold.

Kelly stopped watching the squirrel, put the car in reverse, and made her way toward home. She tried to remember the good times with Faith, the early part of college, before Faith had started stealing from all of them.

Freshman-year move-in came to mind. Kelly and her dad had arrived first to the tiny dorm room with the two single beds and chipped dressers and desks. The walls were cinder block in the blandest off-white color. Kelly had some posters and poster putty, and she and her dad decorated her side as best they could. She unpacked her clothes and put them away, then pulled out the wooden jewelry box.

"Where should I put this?" she asked as her eyes started brimming with tears. Kelly's mom and grandma had been killed in the drunk-driving accident just the year prior. Her father teared up too before saying, "Somewhere special, honey."

She slid it into the top dresser drawer behind her socks, and she and her dad shared a long hug. Kelly wiped her eyes and continued unpacking, moving to the minuscule closet to put her extra sheets, towels, and laundry detergent on the shelf.

There was a clatter in the hallway and in swooped a whirling dervish of a person. The word Kelly remembered thinking was *big*.

Big personality, big entrance, big hair at the time.

"Hey there! I'm Faith," the newcomer said, arms laden with an alarm clock, a pillow, and a lamp with a bright pink shade. Faith did a dramatic twirl in a circle, added, "Yup, I'm the new roomie . . . ta-da!" and set everything on the dorm bed.

Faith's mother and sister were there, and they all met. Kelly's father seemed as baffled by Faith as Kelly was. They both just kind of stared at her. Faith talked nonstop as she set up her side of the room. She clearly favored bubble-gum pink for decorations, and her comforter was in the same color as her lamp. She didn't have as many clothes to hang or put in drawers as Kelly did, but the ones she did have seemed like the kind of cool clothes you might find at a funky thrift store, not a standard department store.

"OK, Mom and Sis and Kelly's dad, byyyeeeee," Faith said with a big wave. "Kell and I got this."

Kelly was surprised to be called "Kell" so quickly, but it felt nice too. Her dad turned to her and raised his eyebrows in a "do you really want me to go?" look. She nodded.

"I'm ready, Dad."

They walked to the front door of the dorm and shared one more long embrace.

"Your mother and grandmother are so proud of you, honey bear," he said. "And I am too."

"I know," she said into his chest, crying. "Thank you, Daddy."

She stopped at the communal bathroom on the way back to the room and cleaned herself up, not wanting her new roommate to see her like that right off the bat.

Back in the room, Faith's mother and sister were gone and Faith was blasting rock music and hanging up Christmas lights.

"Ready for a killer year?" Faith asked with a grin.

"Uh, sure, yes, I guess," Kelly stammered.

Kelly had always been a quiet and serious person, made more so by the accident. Faith was bold, mischievous, and always looking for a party. As the weeks went on, Kelly learned more of Faith's habits. Faith didn't care what anyone else thought of how loudly she played her music or blasted the TV. She spoke to her sister, Hope, in a bellowing voice on the phone, and she hummed at such a high decibel while doing homework that Kelly actually had to ask her to tone it down so she could focus on her own work.

For the first semester they got along pretty well, though, and Kelly was fairly pleased with her roommate. They were opposites in many ways, but Kelly looked at Faith as a creature from another planet, a fascinating one to be studied. Kelly would watch Faith as Faith sat on her bed painting her toenails and singing off-key to whatever band she was into that week. They would go to the cafeteria together, and Faith would direct them to sit with new people each time.

"Hey, we're really fun and cool," she would tell whoever was at the table. "Mind if we join you?"

Her outgoing personality constantly awed Kelly, and it was how they got to know Zoe and many others. Zoe lived down the hall, and soon they were in her room as often as they were in their own.

It was just before winter break, though, that they all started to notice little things missing. Small stuff at first—a watch, a pair of earrings, a CD. Things you could explain away as being something you had misplaced. Then cash started disappearing. Zoe's roommate suspected Faith from the get-go, noting that things in their room only seemed to go missing when Faith had been there and one of them had stepped out to use the bathroom or run to get a soda, but they all pooh-poohed that idea, as Faith reported that some of her things were gone too. So Kelly stayed on Faith's side.

But not long into second semester, Zoe's entire jewelry collection disappeared on a night when the whole floor had a party and everyone's dorm door was open. No one had seen anything and no one could be sure who was in or out of what room when. The resident assistant and university security looked into it, but they had no evidence. Zoe's roommate once again pointed the finger at Faith, but to no avail.

At the weekly craft nights, most of the women from the floor would get together to do things like tie-dye shirts to wear to the next basketball game, or make sock puppets with their names on them to hang on their room handles. Faith claimed she wasn't into stuff like that and stayed back.

Credit cards started going missing. Not every week and not from the same people. In fact, a girl on a different floor altogether complained about it. The RA asked everyone to lock their doors when they left. It wasn't until people's credit card bills started coming in that the alarm bells really rang. There were charges at the mall, all for women's clothing at stores that college students liked. Every person on the floor was questioned and everyone denied it.

It was Zoe's roommate who finally broke the case open. She

followed Faith to the mall and took secret pictures of her in various stores, then waited for the credit card statements to come in showing charges at those exact same stores. University police got involved and compared exact times of the transactions to the times she was in the stores. Faith was busted. She cried and apologized, saying something about being poor and never having proper clothes. She said she was on antidepressants that made her wired, jittery, and impulsive. She was told the university was suspending her midsemester. If she attended counseling, she could return. So Kelly didn't have a roommate for the rest of freshman year.

As college continued, Kelly would see Faith occasionally, and they even had a class together during Kelly's junior year. Faith asked her to coffee one day, and Kelly, feeling in good spirits, agreed. They talked about their futures—Kelly wanting to be a Spanish teacher and starting some in-class work, and Faith working to be a meteorologist and holding down an internship at a nearby TV station. When Kelly's graduation came, Faith was there even though she still had that extra semester to make up. Faith sought out Kelly across the football field to give her a hug and wish her well. Faith said they should keep in touch, and they exchanged emails.

For years Faith would send an occasional email hello. Kelly was guarded but kind. Then came the middle-of-the-night phone call from Faith saying that she'd had her identity stolen and was desperate for help or she'd be kicked out of her apartment. Why Kelly believed her, she did not know. Trust in the goodness of human nature, she guessed. Plus, it had been years since the freshman-year debacle, with nothing else occurring. She figured Faith was mortified enough then and reformed now, so she loaned Faith the money.

Faith said she would get her half back within a month, the other half shortly after, plus a bonus $400 for helping her. But the benchmarks passed with no repayment. That was when Faith started ghosting her. Kelly's calls and emails went unanswered, and Kelly was getting desperate.

> Faith—what is going on? I need that money. I have my rent to pay too. I loaned you the money out of the goodness of my heart. You promised you'd get it right back to me when your credit was restored.

Silence. Kelly remembered Faith's mom from the times she had met her at freshman-year move-in and again when Faith was forced to move out. Kelly looked up her name and called her, crying on the phone as she explained that months had now passed with zero word from Faith. Faith's mother sounded horrified and promised she would take care of it, and she did, sending Kelly a check. Kelly and Faith both wound up in the Detroit area, and Kelly saw Faith on TV, but she didn't hear from Faith again until the email the day she was eating her tuna sandwich in the staff break room.

Faith was a troubled person, Kelly knew that. One night early in freshman year, the two of them had stayed up late whispering in the dark across the tiny room from each other.

"Tell me about your childhood," Faith had said. "Did you like your mom and dad?"

Kelly gulped back a huge sob and sputtered about her mom and grandma dying in the accident. Faith was quiet, but as Kelly finished she heard footsteps coming across the room. Faith sat down next to Kelly and said, "Oh, Kell, I am so sorry, I had no idea," and she leaned in for a hug. They embraced for a long time, both shedding tears.

When Faith went back to her own bed, she whispered, "I have some things to tell you about my childhood too." And she shared with Kelly that her younger sister, Charity, had died at the age of three, and also bemoaned all of the things her father had done, the yelling and how he shamed Faith and her sister by withholding decent clothing from them. They were the laughingstock of their suburb, Faith said, in their ill-fitting and outdated items. It was only late in high school that Faith and her sister Hope were able to buy clothes from the thrift store where Hope worked.

"I can't wait until I'm an adult and I have my own money," Faith said. "If I have a daughter I'm buying her the best clothing. He ruined my childhood, he really did. He even changed my personality. You know how I am, outgoing and fun, right? Around him I had to be quiet as a mouse. The only thing we had in common was the weather."

"The weather?" Kelly asked quizzically.

"Yeah, we both liked rain gauges and storms and lightning and stuff. I might even want to be a meteorologist. One came to our high school career fair and I thought it was the coolest thing."

All of this background helped Kelly to understand Faith more. Kelly had never heard of any parent making kids wear horrible clothes as a punishment. It also made Kelly realize why Faith did what she did with the credit cards and with the other stolen items, which they learned she had pawned. It didn't excuse it, but it allowed her to understand it just a tiny bit more.

Now Faith was dead, killed by someone near the station. It didn't feel real. Kelly's mind was having a hard time computing it and also sorting out her complicated feelings toward Faith.

As Kelly turned the corner onto their street, she was surprised to see a police car sitting in front of the house and a policeman at the door talking to Joel. Her heart rate quickened. Did they have new information on the stolen jewels?

She pulled into the driveway just as both Joel and the officer turned to look at her. She gave a little half wave and a smile but they appeared to be very serious.

As she stepped out of the car, the officer said, "Kelly Watters?"

"Yes?" It was not the same guy as before.

"Officer Nordgaard. I'd like to speak with you both inside."

"Of course. Is this about the jewelry? Do you have a new break in the case?" Her optimism surged at the possibility of getting the jewelry back.

"Let's talk inside," the officer said. Kelly glanced at Joel, who had a blank expression.

When they settled into the living room, she tried again.

"Did you find the jewels?"

"Ma'am, I am not here with any new information about your jewelry."

Her spirits plummeted.

"So what is this about, then?" Joel asked.

"I'm here to ask you some questions about the death of Faith Richards," the officer said. "Where were you both on Friday night between the hours of seven PM and eleven PM?"

"I'm sorry, what?" Kelly said. "You're asking *us* about Faith's death?"

"Ma'am, please answer the question. Where were you Friday night during the hours I just noted?"

"I was here, watching a movie," Kelly said. "I work long hours as a teacher and I like to relax on Friday nights."

"And I went for a hike," said Joel. "I work at home and need to get out for exercise. I drove myself to the Ojibway Nature Centre and hiked, then came home."

"Are you in the habit of hiking at night, sir?"

"It's summer, it stays light late, and yes, I do hike at night, I have a headlamp. I told you I need to move my legs after being home."

"Do either of you have anyone who can corroborate your whereabouts? Anyone with you?"

They looked at each other.

"Uh, no . . ." Kelly said. "I was alone."

"And I was alone too. Why would we need someone to corroborate our whereabouts?" asked Joel. "What is this about? Why are we being questioned? Do we need to get a lawyer?"

A spike of adrenaline ran through Kelly. A lawyer? What in the actual hell was happening?

The officer gave them both a long stare. There was a beat of silence before he took a deep breath.

"On the night Faith Richards was killed she handed an intern a piece of paper in the parking lot. She asked that intern to give it to Tom Archer, Channel 9's main anchor. Your names were on that list. Now, why would that be? We're looking at each of those people for connections to Faith. It turns out you two had recently told an officer that you thought she stole from you although you had no proof. And now you have no alibis?"

All of the blood drained from Kelly's face. She glanced at Joel, whose eyes were bulging.

"We're completely innocent," Kelly said. "We would never hurt anyone. This is ridiculous."

Joel said nothing. Kelly glanced at him for support, but he didn't look back at her. She had a sudden, sharp thought. Joel had been gone for a long stretch Friday. At the time she had chalked it up to him seemingly needing long breaks from her, but he hadn't returned until after ten, long after it was dark. And he had been extra cold toward Kelly when he walked in the door, mumbling about being tired and going straight to bed.

No way. No way Joel did something to Faith. *No way.* He was so angry at Faith, though. She couldn't stop the seed of doubt. And now she had to defend her own innocence and wonder about her boyfriend's, all at the same time.

CHAPTER EIGHTEEN

Matthew

June 3

The worst part of the day was not that he had to get up earlier than usual, stand in front of thousands of strangers at a vigil, and lie about how great Faith was. It was not even that he had to shake hands and give hugs to viewers, saying things like, "I know, it's horrible. We'll miss her forever at Channel 9."

No, the worst part for Matthew was that he was still expected to go in to work and be on the five and eleven Sunday broadcasts, putting in a full workday while Perry was probably home drinking a rum and Coke with his feet up.

The other talent from the weekend team—Stella, the anchor, and Emma, the sportscaster—had been given the option of attending or not attending the vigil, and both chose not to attend. But Matthew was on the weather team and Perry had required them all to be there. Thus, Matthew was the only one at the vigil who both had to play the proper grieving role *and* work that day, and he had to go straight from the event to the station, sweaty from the heat, annoyed by the day, and overwhelmed with thoughts, as his mind was still processing all that had happened.

To add final insult to injury, he didn't even have time for lunch. It would have to be one of those crappy microwavable meals from the vending machine.

Matthew used his key card to gain entry to the gated parking lot and swiped into the two doors that led to the newsroom. The air-conditioning was blasting, as it always was, protecting lots of expensive equipment. The coolness felt incredibly refreshing, and he dabbed at his brow.

Walking quickly to the weather office, he went to the small fridge in the corner for a bottle of water. After downing half of it in three giant gulps, he said, "Ahhh . . . ," wiped his upper lip, wandered to his desk, and flopped down in his chair. Closing his eyes, he tried to quiet his tired mind, but he couldn't stop thinking about Faith, about the vigil, and about the thing in this office that had plagued him for months.

Matthew's baseball and water bottle had never been returned. He looked with dismay once more at the empty space where the ball used to sit on his desk. He had reported it to Perry and HR but they couldn't find any evidence of wrongdoing and Perry just said, "Are you sure you didn't misplace it?" Of course Matthew was sure, but he didn't feel like dealing with Perry's BS toward him, so he was forced to let the whole thing go.

Still, memories of the game with his father were so strong that Matthew could almost smell the popcorn mixed with the scent of his dad's aftershave. Matthew had been sitting on Dad's lap munching down a snack for most of the game. After it was over, an autograph line formed and his father put Matthew on his shoulders as they waited. Matthew adored when his dad did that; it gave him both a bird's-eye view and a feeling of complete safety being fully supported by his dad's broad shoulders. Matthew would wrap his skinny arms around his dad's head, and his father would laugh. "Don't block my eyes, kid, or we're both going down!" he'd say, and Matthew would slide his arms higher or lower, sometimes tickling Dad as he did.

A lump started to come into Matthew's throat now. He would never get over the loss of that ball. Matthew and his dad remained close, but his dad had retired to Florida and they didn't see each other that often.

Matthew let his eyes drift to Faith's desk, and his stomach clenched at the almost inconceivable news he had learned Saturday morning. He couldn't compute that Faith was not just on vacation, but gone forever. Yes, he hated her, and yes, he was still 99 percent sure she had something to do with the baseball, and yes, he had wanted her gone, but not in *this* way, and now that she was, he didn't know how to feel. Perry had told Matthew that Matthew would be ascending to the Monday–Friday main meteorologist chair on an interim basis and they would see if it was permanent or not.

This was what he had always wanted, had dreamed of since he watched Detroit TV as a kid. He was in Jack's position now. It was the fulfillment of so many years of work and sacrifice, yet he felt somehow unsatisfied and ill at ease. A ball of sour acid was growing in his stomach, and he turned back to his desk and reached for the Tums he kept in a drawer, downing five in one handful. They said to take a max of four but he always thought one more would be for good measure and surely couldn't hurt.

OK, Matthew, focus now, you have to work.

He needed to microwave his lunch and start going over maps and trends, designing his forecast for the shows. Perry had him not only working today but all five days of the week ahead. A seven-day week, and he didn't even get overtime since he was on a salary. It was just something people on TV were expected to do when needed. In what other industry could you be asked to work any shift anytime and put in marathon weeks and not be compensated? Maybe a doctor, he didn't know, but it was one thing he had always disliked about television news.

The news never stopped: not for nights, not for weekends, not for holidays. He had worked countless holidays in this business, eating the catered-in Thanksgiving turkey on paper plates in the back hallway, or rushing to his mom's house for a quick Easter or Christmas brunch before a long workday.

He had to get going on the forecast, but first just one more minute. He closed his eyes again, thinking of Tara.

She had not wanted to attend the vigil, and Matthew couldn't blame her. He wouldn't have either if he didn't have to. He had to work a normal shift Saturday, which was hard enough. When he got home close to midnight after the show, Tara was in her flannel pajamas, the ones with little pictures of sheep on them. She was curled in the corner on the couch. The air-conditioning had been set so low it was freezing in the apartment, and he stopped at the thermostat and cranked it back to a more normal level. There was a bottle of wine next to Tara that was almost entirely empty, and she looked at him with glassy eyes.

"It was just a silly thing," Tara said, slurring more and leaning over to top off her glass. She spilled some wine on the table. "Just soooo silly, silly."

"Right, honey, right," he said, moving over and gently sliding the wineglass away from her. He would clean up the spill in a moment. "How about we go to bed early? It's been a lot. And I have the vigil in the morning."

She nodded and uncharacteristically allowed him to lead her to bed like a child; she was usually independent, feisty, and fiery. He tucked her in as she mumbled, "Just a game, a silly game . . ."

Matthew kissed her on the forehead, turned out the light, went back to the living room to clean up, and drank the glass of wine she had topped off for herself while pacing for over an hour. Now it was just thirteen hours later and he was in the weather office needing to focus.

He spun back around in his chair and looked at Faith's desk one more time. And suddenly he noticed that it wasn't quite as messy as usual. Messy, yes, but some of the shoeboxes under her desk had been removed or more carefully arranged, the teddy bear was gone, and her makeup bag was not there, nor were two of her curling irons. It was all kind of odd, he thought. Did someone take these things yesterday after they learned she was killed? He had been in the office most of the day, so he didn't think so, but maybe in the morning when he wasn't there, maybe it was Perry, and Matthew just hadn't noticed until now? Or had Faith taken these things with her on her dinner break Friday night? But that made no sense. Why would she go out for dinner with her makeup bag, a teddy bear, and two curling irons? He was just tossing this all around in his mind when his cell phone rang: Tara.

"Hey, babe," he said with a deep sigh, anticipating having to recap the vigil. She had still been sleeping when he left that morning.

"Matthew." Her voice was filled with panic. "The police are here. They said they need to talk to both of us."

A dagger seemed to stab into his throat.

"What? Honey, what are you talking about?"

"Two officers are in our living room. They asked me to call you."

Shit, shit, shit. His mind started flying through scenarios and possible lies and what the police might know or not know, or maybe they were doing this with all the mets and it was nothing. He could tell that Tara was trying to keep it together in front of the officers, but the panicky note in her voice told him she was thinking the same.

"Can I speak to them?" he asked.

"Uh, sure. I can ask."

There was some muffled talking and the exchange of the phone before a female officer's voice rang out.

"Sir, I understand you're at work?"

"Yes, I work at Channel 9 as a meteorologist and I have to be on TV." He tried to keep his voice strong but felt it waver.

"I understand, sir, but I'm sure you can see the importance of this. We're opening an investigation into the homicide of Faith Richards. We need to ask you and your fiancée some questions. How quickly can you get home?"

"Well, my issue is I still have to create the forecast. It's 2:30 and we're on the air in two and a half hours. Is this urgent?"

"I would call it urgent, absolutely. How far away do you live?"

"Twenty minutes. I can get home if you need me to." He did not want Tara to have to deal with this alone. As for the forecast . . . he shuddered but he could always pull up whatever the National Weather Service had to say; thankfully it was shaping up to be a quiet week. It made him physically ill to think of stooping to Faith's level and copying the NWS forecast, but it could be done in a pinch.

"Can I get back in time for the five o'clock news?"

"That might be possible, yes, sir," the officer replied. "We'll come back in thirty minutes and speak with you both."

Matthew grabbed his car keys and bolted for the parking lot, rushing past one of the reporter-and-photographer crews that had been at the vigil interviewing people about Faith.

"What's your hurry, Matthew?" called out the photographer, a grizzled guy who had been at the station for over thirty-five years.

"Just, umm . . . forgot something at home," Matthew yelled over his shoulder, hoping for a breezy, happy tone.

When he got to the car, he frantically dialed Tara. She answered after half a ring.

"They just left," she whispered. "They said they'd get coffee and be back. Matthew, I'm scared, I'm so scared."

"They don't know anything, don't worry, honey," he said. "Let's just chat for a minute and get our stories straight."

"No, it's bad, Matthew, really bad. There was something I couldn't say on the phone. When they first got here, they told me that Faith handed some intern a note before dinner break Friday and asked the intern to give it to Tom. On the note it had a list of names. Honey, our names were on the list. The cops said it's fishy enough that they're talking to everyone. They don't know why she made the list but the fact that it came out right before she died made them suspicious. Like it was a list of suspects or something."

"*What?*" Matthew almost veered off the road. The tires squealed and he had to jerk the wheel back to the straight and narrow. "That's not possible, how is that possible?"

"I don't know but I feel like we need to stop talking on the phone now," Tara replied, and suddenly Matthew thought of wiretapping. His fingers turned cold at the thought of what he had just said: *They don't know anything, don't worry, honey. Let's just chat for a minute and get our stories straight.*

Coughing, he made his voice sound strong, picking up on Tara's cue.

"Right, OK, we'll tell the police anything they want to know. We're completely innocent, I just work with her," Matthew said.

"And I barely know her, only met her at a few station parties," Tara replied, sounding relieved that he had figured out the message she was sending him.

"I'm heartbroken by my friend and coworker's death," said Matthew.

"Me too," added Tara.

They hung up, and Matthew noticed that his right hand was shaking uncontrollably. He tried to stop it but it wouldn't even slow down, it was like an alien had taken over his body. His armpits filled with sweat despite the air-conditioning in the car. How would Faith know anything about what they had or hadn't done? And she then gave this list to an intern the night she died? What the hell was going on? His shirt was soaked and he wondered if he could quickly change before the police got back so he wouldn't look so nervous.

Taking the elevator up to the apartment, he stopped in front of their door and put his ear to it, trying to ascertain whether the officers were already back or not. He didn't hear anything and breathed a huge sigh of relief; at least he could change his shirt.

But when he opened the door, he saw immediately that he was wrong. Two officers, a woman and a man, stood up from their seats on the couch as Tara's eyes whipped over to him, wide as Jupiter. She was perched on the edge of a side chair, and her knee kept jiggling up and down at a frantic pace.

"Matthew? Please sit down, we have some questions for you," the male officer said.

Matthew stepped in warily, conscious of his sweat-covered

shirt and Tara's jiggling knee and trying to will both of them to seem helpful and at ease. He sat down in what he hoped was a casual pose in another side chair.

"Yes, Officers, how can we assist you?"

The duo repeated what they had told Tara about their names being on a list and he feigned shock.

"I have absolutely no idea why we would be on that, how long was the list?" he asked.

"We are not at liberty to discuss any details other than the fact that you two were on it," said the male officer. "Why would she do that? Did the three of you have any kind of argument recently? Anything like that?"

"No, we got along great," Matthew lied. "Faith and I have worked together for years. We were not the kind of coworkers who hang out outside of work but we respected each other immensely."

"I only met her a few times," Tara threw in loudly—a little too loudly, Matthew thought.

"If we talked to your other coworkers, would they agree that you and Faith got along great?" the female cop asked, looking directly at Matthew.

He tried not to gulp.

"Uh, yeah, sure, I think so," he said, but he was thinking of the times he had said disparaging things about her to any number of people in the newsroom. God, he only hoped his coworkers would have his back if they were interviewed.

"And where were you both Friday night between the hours of seven PM and eleven PM?" asked the male cop, looking back and forth between them.

Oh, thank God, they at least had an alibi. A partial one anyway.

"We were at dinner," said Tara quickly. "And then Matthew got called in to the station to fill in for Faith. He was on the air at eleven. You can confirm that with anyone. We even had to skip dessert. We came back together after dinner and then I was alone until he was done."

The male cop raised his eyebrows.

"You arrived back here at what time?"

"Uh, like close to 9:45 maybe?" Tara said.

"Where did you have dinner?" asked the female cop, taking out a little notebook from her breast pocket.

They told her the name of the restaurant, what time they arrived and left, what they ate, even what the waiter looked like.

"I remember his name," said Matthew. "It was Sergio." He was relieved the guy had a name that stuck out to him. They couldn't be accused of murdering Faith if they were being served roasted duck by Sergio. Although he didn't want to think about the fact that some of their time was unaccounted for, after they left the restaurant and before he got to the station. He had been pacing in the apartment and ranting about Faith, until Tara looked at the clock and told him he had better hurry up for the eleven o'clock show.

"OK, we'll look into some things," the woman said, closing her notebook. "But I want you to think long and hard about why Faith Richards would put you on a list. Now is the time for honesty. If you think of new reasons, we need to hear them from you. Not from other people, from you. Got it?"

"Yes, of course, but there are no other reasons," Matthew said. Yet, his voice sounded weak to him and his heart was going so fast he felt like he might faint.

"Good to know," the male officer said, sounding entirely unconvinced. The two cops stood.

"We'll let ourselves out," said the woman, and Matthew and Tara watched as they walked stiffly to the front door and shut it behind them.

Matthew popped out of his chair and went over to kneel in front of Tara and give her a hug. She started to cry and was shaking.

"What is happening, Tara? This can't be real, can it?"

"What if they trace things? What then, Matthew, what then? Oh my God, I even googled 'how to kill a coworker.' Oh my God, no," she sobbed. "What do we do?"

"I don't know," he replied, but the truth was Matthew could almost feel the blood on his hands.

CHAPTER NINETEEN

Hope

There was blood on Faith's hands, and on mine, for what happened to Charity. Not literal blood, of course. We didn't hurt our little sister. Faith and I loved Charity. She was the sweetest little thing in her three years, chubby cheeked and with curly strawberry-blond hair. Mom sometimes called her "my little Shirley Temple."

Faith and I might have been jealous of Charity, but she had another quality that we found endearing: Charity was slow to learn to talk, and we all tried to help her.

"Milk," we would say, pointing at the container in the fridge.

"Gah," she would reply.

"Cat," we would say pointing at Bo, our cat.

"Bah," she would reply.

"No, cat like a *K,* ka-ka-ka-cat," we would reply.

"Fah" would be her answer.

Somehow her struggles with words made her more likable to us, more human, and although Mom fretted about it constantly, Faith and I enjoyed the fact that Charity, clearly the cutest of the three of us, was not perfect. And we liked being the teachers.

We set up a "word school" and took turns being the instructor, with an easel and markers Mom had given us for Christmas. The reward for Charity if she got close to the correct pronunciation was a lollipop, grape being her favorite flavor.

"Today we'll learn the letter *M*," we would say. "Mama, moon, milk, money. Say 'moon,' Charity."

And she might grunt out something like "Moo" if we were lucky. More often it would be completely different, like "Bubby," and we'd crack up laughing.

Mom later told me she was considering whether to get Charity a speech therapist but never got the chance.

I was ten and Faith eight when Charity died, but I still remember every detail of that day. It was sunny but windy on the beach along Lake Michigan, an area known for big sand dunes. There was the popular part of the beach, with a boardwalk and tourists and ice cream shops, and then there was the quiet part, much farther up toward the trees and state park that bordered this stretch. Dad preferred the quieter spot, even though there was no lifeguard. Sometimes other people were up there, and sometimes it felt like our own little beach.

Faith, Charity, and I would spend hours building sandcastles, all of them with moats that we'd fill with water carried in buckets from the lake. But the sand would soak up the water so quickly we were constantly sending poor little Charity back down to the water's edge for more buckets. She was our water runner. Faith and I were the architects of the elaborate castles we were creating, adding twigs and rocks for decorations. Lake Michigan had no true seashells, only tiny ones for snails and black ones for mussels. But there were plenty of smooth gray rocks, and if we ever found sea glass we thought we'd hit the jackpot.

I can still see little Charity, her swim diaper bulging under a purple one-piece, struggling with the weight of the red plastic bucket in her hand. She wanted to please her sisters, I could tell that even at my age, and we used it to our advantage, sending her back and forth so many times her tiny feet wore a rut into the sand.

Mom and Dad sat in lawn chairs back by our towels, Mom with a floppy sun hat and Dad with dark sunglasses. They even held hands at one point. I remember that clearly because it was so unusual. I never saw them have any kind of affection for each other before or after that, in public or in the privacy of our home. This was before the "disobey box" came to be, before Dad's neat-freakiness soared to a manic level, before Faith brought home the rain gauge. This was when Dad was still not the happiest person, still going to the shooting range most weekends, still on us about our grades and about keeping the house clean, but before his rage hit new heights.

Thinking back, those few hours on the beach before the incident might have been the happiest we ever were as a family.

And then Faith and I had to ruin it. Well, one of us more than the other.

CHAPTER TWENTY

Olivia

June 3

It was Olivia's guilt over looking at the note that kept her from attending the vigil or even answering her aunt's phone calls or texts. The same thought kept running through her head: Should she go to the police with what the note said? But then everyone would know how untrustworthy Olivia was and she could be fired from an internship she had just started, her future career in the toilet.

No, there was no way she could do that. After all, she gave the note to Tom. He had the same information she had and *he* could go to the police if it was important. And maybe the note was unimportant in the end, something completely innocuous. Olivia knew she had to pretend everything was normal, and yet the stress of keeping it all inside was crushing. During her long walk yesterday, she had to stop multiple times to sob or dry heave. And she had been debating whether she could trust anyone.

Channel 9's assistant news director had texted Olivia and all of the other interns en masse to see if they could hand out free umbrellas at the exit of the vigil, and most said yes right away, but Olivia faked that she was sick.

After she returned home, she had grabbed Gizmo and gone straight to bed, where she stayed for most of the day, occasionally dozing but mostly just fretting. She saw her aunt's text about attending the vigil but didn't know how to say no without sounding weird, so she acted like she hadn't seen it or had time to respond.

This would have been a great time to have a mom around to lean on, but Olivia's mom was nearly impossible to reach. You never even knew what country she was in these days, and if you did talk to her it wasn't about deep stuff. This situation would take too long to explain. Olivia's dad was definitely not the type for this either. She could only imagine going to him. "You did *what?*" he would ask, that look of pure disappointment in his eye. She didn't need that; she felt bad enough on her own.

So she settled on telling Aunt Carol.

The vigil was over and her aunt was inviting her for cookies and tea. The time was as good as it was going to get. Olivia drove over and was trying to quell the butterflies in her stomach as she pulled up at Jim and Carol's ranch house, one that felt almost as familiar to her as the house where she had grown up and the condo where she now lived. She had the autographed picture of Faith in her purse to give to Carol as a gift too.

Taking a long, slow breath, Olivia pulled the car visor down to look at herself in the mirror. She looked tired. No wonder—she had barely slept the night before despite being in bed so long the past twenty-four hours even Gizmo got bored and moved to the living room window.

You'll feel better when you talk about this with a trusted loved one, she counseled herself. Her therapist always said things like that and told Olivia that speaking about things made them less scary and more manageable.

Walking up the front walk, she noticed her shoulders were rounded forward. Her feet felt like they were shuffling. It was not her usual upright posture. As she rang the bell she tried to keep herself from looking too forlorn.

The door flew open and there stood Carol, wearing a mustard-yellow shirt and a pair of Fair-Weather Friends Fan Club earrings that Olivia recognized. Olivia imagined many women at the vigil in similar outfits.

"Liv! Come in, sweetheart," Carol gushed. "What's going on?"

"Hi, Aunt C, how was the vigil?" she said.

"Lovely, just lovely. We'll get to all of that. First, you said you had something to talk about. Your voice worried me. Is everything all right, honey?"

Just those words, *Is everything all right?*, caused the floodgates to open for Olivia. She bit her lip to fight back tears but they were coming, she could tell, and she couldn't stop them.

"Oh dear, come inside," Carol said, glancing up and down the block nervously and ushering Olivia into the foyer. Carol steered Olivia to the den, where a candle that smelled like key lime pie was burning.

"Sit in Jim's easy chair," Carol commanded. "He ran out to the store. There, there, honey, it's OK . . ." Carol grabbed a box of tissues, a glass of water, and a throw blanket all in record time and handed the water and tissues to Olivia while tucking the blanket around her. Carol sat in her own easy chair and turned her body to fully see her niece.

"What is it, Liv?"

Olivia took a ragged breath and it all came tumbling out,

starting with the parking lot and the folded-up note, the way Olivia felt compelled to look at it in the women's restroom, the way she then handed it to Tom as if nothing had happened. She spoke of the deep guilt and shame she felt looking at the note and how it kept her up all night and prevented her from taking part in the vigil, even to hand out umbrellas.

"And then there's what the note said. I just don't know what to do," Olivia summed up, sniffing.

"My goodness, what did it say?" Carol sucked in her breath.

OK, here it goes, thought Olivia. She had to tell someone, and Aunt Carol was truly the only person she trusted fully right now.

"Promise me you'll keep this between us, maybe just Uncle Jim," Olivia implored, and Carol nodded and put her hand on top of Olivia's.

"It had a list of names on it. I'm not sure why but what if she knew something bad was going to happen and these are *suspects*? I know two of them."

"*Whaaat?* What do you mean you know two of them? Who are they?"

Olivia looked down and spoke so softly that Carol had to lean in to hear her.

"Matthew, the weekend weather guy, and Laura, the executive producer. Two people I work with at Channel 9. For Matthew it also said 'and Tara,' who it turns out is his fiancée."

"Nooooo!" Carol replied, and her hand came off Olivia's and flew to her own mouth. Her eyes grew wide. "Matthew? I'm telling you I noticed something weird Friday. He looked odd during the forecast. Like his tie wasn't straight, his hair was sticking up, he seemed angry. But who is Laura and why would she be a suspect?"

"I never in a million years would have pegged her, she's one of the newsroom managers and like a new mother or something and looks tired all the time but she's also super nice. Then there were other names I didn't recognize: Steve and Kelly and Joel."

Carol was speechless for a moment before saying quietly, "I saw a guy named Steve at the vigil. He said he and Faith were boyfriend and girlfriend, but he was a really weird guy and I don't think anyone believed him. He also said Faith was pregnant. I wonder if that's the Steve she wrote about on the note? Olivia, this is terrible. Faith might have known something bad was going to happen to her from one of these people. Oh that poor thing, that poor, poor thing."

Carol started to cry and Olivia found herself consoling her aunt even though Olivia felt she herself was more in need of help. Carol took two tissues from the Kleenex box on the fish-shaped coffee table and blew her nose loudly. They looked at each other.

"What should I do, Aunt C? Should I go to the police? But then I could be fired. But how can I work with Matthew and Laura knowing this? I'm just so torn apart. I wish I'd never seen that note. It's confusing me."

"OK, let's think logically," Carol said, switching her brain into detective mode. "So Tom had the note. I'm certain he went to the police. How could you not if a friend gave you that and then wound up dead? So that part has to be taken care of. Liv, I'm usually one who thinks honesty is the best policy but in this case . . . I wonder if this stays a secret between the two of us. You don't want to lose your internship. I know you have to work with two of those people but the note could be nothing important, plus we have no idea who did this. Maybe it was a robbery or someone from her past or who knows. I mean, be careful around Matthew and Laura but I think it's OK. You work in a busy newsroom filled with lots of people, right? You're never alone with Matthew or Laura. The police will be looking into them after Tom shares the note and if they find anything, they'll be arrested. I think my vote is that you just stay the course. What do you think?"

"I think . . . I agree," Olivia said with a long sniffle. She reached for a tissue. "I'll just keep my head down and pretend it never happened."

"Yes," said Carol. "Pretend it never happened but also be glad it did in a way. Because you and I now know something that no one else on this planet does except for Tom and the police. I wonder if we can do a little sleuthing on our own. Maybe we can help break the case. What sweet justice that would be for Faith. It's the very least we can do for such a wonderful person."

Olivia knew how her aunt loved true crime shows and mystery novels. She could see Carol's eyes gleaming as she spoke of justice for Faith. Sure, Olivia would love to help solve a crime and bring a criminal to justice too, but she was still just an intern and didn't want to get too entangled in some web, especially if a killer walked among them. Her plan was to shut up and be totally normal, but she nodded to appease Carol.

"You know what, hon? I won't even tell Jim at this point. Our little secret, OK? That way you know it's just between us. You keep your eye on Matthew and this Laura. I wonder if there's a chance for me to cross paths with Steve again and scope him out more. Liv, we could be the difference makers here."

Olivia nodded again. Carol seemed filled with adrenaline and plans, but Olivia's own chest was still heavy, and a lump sat in her throat.

"Come on, let's get tea and cookies," Carol said. "I'll text Jim and send him on to another store for a few more things so we can have girl time. OK, Liv? You good now?"

"Not exactly good but I'm a little better," Olivia said, forcing a smile. She didn't feel good at all, but she was slightly improved from when she had arrived. At least she told someone.

"Oh, I do have your autographed picture of Faith with me too," Olivia said, reaching into her bag. "Did you realize this might be the last autograph she ever did?"

Carol sucked in her breath and her eyes started to tear up as she looked at it. She read the inscription aloud.

"'To Carol and Jim Henning, thank you for being Fair-Weather Friends. Stay on the sunny side of life! Best always, Faith.'

"I'm going to frame this and put it in a very special spot in the den," Carol said with a sad smile. It was instantly the most treasured item she owned.

CHAPTER TWENTY-ONE

Carol

June 4

Carol had always enjoyed her job. It wasn't what most people would call glamorous but she didn't care what others thought. It was something she had been doing for decades and it fit her. She first walked in the door as an employee at Kohl's when she was in her thirties, getting a job as a cashier and working her way up, all the way to being one of the daytime assistant managers.

Kohl's was your classic department store, sectioned out for women, men, kids, and toddlers/babies. There was a home goods area, where you could buy everything from sheets to towels to saucepans; a section for makeup, jewelry, perfume, and luggage; places to purchase vacuums, blenders, shoes, and wrapping paper. About the only thing they didn't sell was food. Carol knew the layout of the store so well she could tell you down to the square inch where everything was located.

It was Monday morning and Carol was scheduled to do some inventory in the back, then help design several carousels of sundresses. In the afternoon she would be interviewing a prospective cashier as well as helping out on the registers.

Her favorite part was the setting up of the clothing. There was an artistry to it, and it was both creative and meditative deciding what dresses would go on what rack to catch the eye of the customers. She was looking forward to the meditative part, especially. It would give her time to think and reflect on her conversation with Olivia. What a crazy thing for poor Liv to get wrapped up in. Carol hadn't wanted to scold her niece for looking at the note; she could tell how bad Olivia felt about it. Carol herself might not have peeked at a note that someone gave her and asked to give to someone else, but Carol wasn't Olivia. Olivia had always been what Evelyn called "a rabble-rouser." Carol actually thought it was exciting to be related to a young, strong, independent-minded woman who pushed conventional norms to the side. And now Carol knew more information about Faith's final night than almost anyone else. It was a weird thing to think about. In some ways Carol was glad to have this bonus knowledge, and in others, it made her uneasy. She needed time to process.

Walking into the employee room at Kohl's, Carol went to her locker and hung up her purse, turning the combination lock to keep it safe. She poured herself a cup of coffee from the shared pot on the counter and added two creams and one sugar, just the way she liked it. Glancing at the clock she saw she had four minutes until her shift officially started. She was sipping the coffee when two other employees walked in.

"Good morning, Carol," said Simone. "We were just talking about that big news from Channel 9. Did you hear what happened Friday night?"

"Yes," Carol said with a sigh. "It's sickening, just awful."

"I heard they had a massive vigil yesterday," piped in Rita. "I thought about going but we had other plans. Did either of you go?"

"Not me," said Simone. "I never really watch the news. I mean, I know who Faith Richards is but I don't watch hardly ever. The news is too depressing. My doctor told me it's not good for my heart."

"I actually attended the vigil," offered Carol.

"You did? How was it?" said Rita.

"Extremely touching. So many fans there as well as people from Channel 9."

"You have some of her earrings, right?" asked Rita. "Didn't you get some for Christmas?"

"Yes, good memory," Carol said.

"Well, I can't stop thinking about it," said Rita. "I didn't have any earrings but I was a fan of hers. I watched some of her videos. She was so good. I just can't believe the never-ending violence in our community."

They all nodded solemnly. There didn't seem to be much else to say, and they each futzed with their own things before drifting in different directions. Carol walked to the back storage area for inventory. She spent ninety minutes figuring out what needed to be ordered in juniors tops and shorts, then grabbed the empty circular metal racks for the sundresses she had to organize.

The dresses were in every bright color you could imagine, and Carol debated whether to design the racks by color or by style. There were short dresses, long ones, knee-length styles, with sleeves, without, low-cut, medium-cut. She liked to think like a vacationer and she imagined if she was going to the beach somewhere she would first look by color, so she started organizing all of the blues, in descending order darkest to lightest and according to sizes.

As she worked, her mind drifted back to Friday night and how carefree she had felt sitting down to watch the eleven o'clock news. She had been tired but happy at the end of a workweek, cozy in their den, enjoying her popcorn and cranberry juice and expecting nothing but a normal TV-watching experience. How was it that everything could be upended so suddenly? Her favorite meteorologist murdered, her niece mixed up in it in a strange way? Names on a weird list?

Carol moved from blues to yellows and had started arranging those on the rack from dark to very light when her phone buzzed in her pocket. Kohl's employees were not allowed to have their phones when they were on the floor, but in back like this it was fine. Thinking it might be Olivia needing something, Carol fished it out quickly and looked down.

It wasn't a call at all. It was another breaking-news alert from Channel 9. Without hesitation, Carol clicked on it to see if this was anything related to Faith.

BREAKING: MEDICAL EXAMINER CONFIRMS FAITH RICHARDS WAS SIX WEEKS PREGNANT. CHANNEL 9 STARTING A SCHOLARSHIP IN HER NAME. CLICK HERE TO CONTRIBUTE.

"Oh my God, no," said Carol, and the blues and yellows of the sundresses all started to swirl in front of her eyes. Faith *was* pregnant, after all, just as that strange guy Steve had said. The one who was on the list. Thoughts came stomping into her head all at once, knocking into each other like bumper cars. *Could he have killed her over some dispute and murdered his own child too? But would Steve really have been Faith's boyfriend in the first place? He was just so odd. Or did someone else do it, maybe in a jealous rage or who knows what?*

Reaching out to steady herself, she held the cool metal rack where the dresses were as tears started to pop into her eyes. A baby gone too. Not just one life but two. Faith would have been such a good mother. Carol could only imagine how cute her son or daughter would have been, and Carol would have bet the house that Faith would have shared a lot about the baby on her videos, so this was a lost opportunity for the whole community to follow along on her mom journey.

Carol's phone buzzed again, a different type of buzz indicating an alert but not from Channel 9. She looked down to see Facebook Messenger with a notification. She clicked on the app to open the message.

> Carol, it's Heather from the vigil yesterday. I just got a breaking news alert about Faith being pregnant and I'm absolutely sick. Chloe and I were already discussing a scholarship. Now that Channel 9 is doing one we thought the FWFFC could try and be the biggest donor. We're getting a big group together after work tonight to discuss it. Would you be able to attend?

Carol knew her answer almost immediately. Whereas before she thought Heather was level-jumping, now this was a different story. Heather was working with Chloe, so this clearly wasn't a "hey, let's get together just the two of us" situation, and there was a baby to consider, for God's sake. It changed the dynamic of everything. Not to mention . . . Steve. Maybe that weird guy would be there and Carol could keep an eye on him and look for clues.

> When and where are you meeting?

Heather said 5:30 at a coffee shop that was just a little out of the way of Carol's usual route home. Carol confirmed she would be there. She knew she had to help out. It was another way to honor Faith, and now the baby. She would donate money, solicit others, do whatever was needed to bring justice for Faith. And she wouldn't tell a soul about what Olivia had found out. That would stay secret. Between the two of them they had three suspects cased out. Olivia could watch Matthew and Laura, and Carol could watch Steve. If they could figure out who Kelly was, they'd be in really good shape.

It was a start. Carol had a laser eye on Steve now. She would be watching him very, very closely.

CHAPTER TWENTY-TWO

Laura

June 4

She pulled into the parking lot at Channel 9 at 2:30 PM, the usual time for the start of her night shift. But Laura had to sit in her car collecting herself before going in. Her eyes were burning from lack of sleep, and her mind was a pinball machine stuck at some warp speed, the ball zinging back and forth uncontrollably. She was thinking of so many things: Faith's death, Perry and his latest shenanigans to get ratings, Elliott being out of town so much, and, of course, Quinn. Her baby would always be her top priority and at the forefront of her mind.

Quinn had been up and fussy a lot the night before. But at least his mood seemed to match Laura's. She was up and fussy too. She rocked and rocked him and put him on the breast so many times her nipples were sore. It was the evening following the vigil and she thought Quinn would be exhausted from the event she had to drag him to, but instead he was wired, arching his back and crying when she put him back in the crib. At one point she literally begged him to sleep, and finally resorted to lying on the floor of Quinn's room on the rug decorated in rocket ships under the crib, curled in a fetal position, trying to will herself even an hour of slumber.

While she dealt with Quinn, Elliott slumbered in the other room soundly. He had arrived home from his guys' camping weekend later than he said he would. He never took a phone with him on these weekends and she had been waiting all day to tell him about Faith's death, and as soon as she heard his car in the garage, she ran out to share this horrific series of events he missed while gone.

Breathlessly, she recounted the details, from Friday night when she went to the weather office and Faith wasn't there to how they had to call Matthew in to do the show, to the call from Perry Saturday morning that Faith was dead, to the vigil and having to bring Quinn and speak at it. Her words tumbled over themselves.

Elliott stood stock-still next to the car listening, the tent he had taken from the trunk in his hand. When she finished he said, "Wow, that was definitely not what I expected to hear. Are you doing OK?"

She nodded, but it was a lie. She was not OK and was hoping Elliott would drop the tent, rush to her, and envelop her in his arms, smothering her with affection, but that did not seem to be his plan. He put the tent up in its spot on a rack in the garage before turning her way again.

"I hate to say this, honey, but Faith being gone does solve one problem for us. No one will be waking us up in the middle of the night anymore. Well, except for Quinn." He chuckled a bit. Then he came over for a hug and a kiss.

"Missed you, babe," he said. "What's for dinner tonight?"

Laura had a hard time reconciling Elliott's words. They were, in fact, true on some level. Faith wouldn't be calling anymore but also she was *dead* and that was a horrible thing. Laura wasn't sure how to respond, so she focused on just the last part of his question.

"I was pretty beat from the vigil so I just ordered Chinese. There's plenty for you."

After dinner, Laura asked Elliott to help with the baby's bath.

"Honey, there's a game on I really wanted to watch, I've been thinking about it all weekend. Can't he go without a bath for one night?" Elliott asked.

"No, he can't go without a bath." Anger surged in Laura. "It's an important part of his bedtime routine and helps to calm him down. That's what all of the baby books say. Also, you haven't seen him in days. Don't you want to spend time with your son?"

"Of course I do but I'm just beat from being off the grid all weekend. It takes a lot out of you. I really just wanted to unwind with this game."

Laura sighed heavily, hoping he'd catch her tone. "Fine, I'll give him his bath."

She got Quinn's little plastic tub out and warmed the water to just the right temperature, then strapped him in and squirted water on his legs and arms with the little plastic animals they had. He giggled and kicked and stuck his fist into his mouth, looking adorable, but she couldn't even enjoy it. She was resentful thinking of Elliott.

Now it was Monday and she had to be at work and see Perry. Another person she was angry at. Perry had told her at the vigil that Faith was six weeks pregnant but that it was a secret and that the station had asked the medical examiner to redact the info. Apparently, it wasn't a secret anymore. She had gotten the push alert from Channel 9 on her phone along with the rest of humanity that morning. Why would managers change their minds and tell everyone now? She had a pretty good guess: ratings. It would drive up viewership for the prime-time special Perry had planned.

Sighing, Laura grabbed her purse and a mug of extra-strong tea she had prepared at home. She made her way to the newsroom. Perry was talking with some other managers by the assignment desk, and he waved her over as soon as she walked in.

"Laura, perfect timing. I was just going to explain our push alert and tell you all a few other things. Come with us to the conference room."

He led the way and they all sat down around the table, looking at him expectantly. Laura wondered if others were as flummoxed by the pregnancy push alert as she was.

"So I told a few of you yesterday that Faith was pregnant. The ME had given us that info on Saturday but we asked him to redact it before the report went out to the public. We wanted to protect Faith's privacy. However, I got a call from Faith's sister today. She had also seen the ME's report and knew about the pregnancy and she asked me to go public. She said it was important that everyone know. She also said that Faith's body has already been cremated."

Laura grimaced, as did several other people around the table.

"So," Perry went on, "I want you to know we only did this with the blessing of Faith's next of kin. It does change our prime-time special, however. I'm thinking of calling it *The Faith Richards Tragedy: Two Lives Lost.* We'll need to reinterview some viewers so they can speak about the baby in addition to Faith. I have several crews working on that. And we started a scholarship in Faith's name. In just a few short hours we've raised almost ten thousand dollars. That's incredible! I've never seen anything like it. I was contacted by the president of the Fair-Weather Friends

Fan Club too, Chloe something, and they're planning to contribute in a big way, so this is all looking great right now."

Looking great? Those words were hard for Laura to digest when it came to a murder. She stared at the floor.

"One more thing. You may be wondering about the investigation. I have been in touch with our police chief and they have crews working round the clock. I can't divulge too much but they already have talked to some suspects and will be looking to get to some more. Any questions?"

Laura glanced up. Everyone else at the table looked as sullen as she felt, and they all shook their heads.

"OK then, back to work," Perry said. "But Laura, can you stay a moment, please?"

Laura felt the eyes of others on her, wondering why she was being chosen to stay. She was as baffled as they were. Maybe Perry wanted her to supervise the prime-time special.

The others filed out and Perry shut the door. He turned to Laura with that piercing gaze of his.

"Laura, I have something very serious to talk to you about."

Based on his tone, she gulped, her mind suddenly pole-vaulting backward to figure out what she had done wrong. Did she get a fact wrong in a script?

"Yes, sir, what is it?"

"Laura, this must stay between us. I mean that—this is a police matter and confidentiality can't be broken."

"Of course, whatever you say stays just with me." Good gracious, what could it be?

"Faith apparently wrote some kind of note with a list of names on it the night she died. The police want to talk to all of these people, as the note seems fishy. Laura, I don't know how to say this so I just will—your name was on it along with your husband's, and one other person in this station and their significant other who shall go unnamed."

Laura wanted to form words but they wouldn't come. Her mouth fell open and all she could do was stare at Perry.

"I can see that you're shocked by this, as was I. I told them I had complete confidence in you and my other employee but they won't be deterred. They need to speak with you today. I am trying my best to keep this confidential so I told them I would send you to the police station as soon as you came in for work rather than them coming here. You and your husband both need to go there now. I will cover for you in the newsroom. I'll tell everyone I sent you on an errand."

"I . . . uh . . . I'm sorry, what? My name? Elliott? The police station?" Her mind could not compute this information, and the pinball machine in her head added about ten silver balls.

"Yes, District 3. Head there now please." He gave her a further icy stare, and she could feel a bit of suspicion seeping off him despite his proclamation that he had complete confidence in her.

She stood up in a trancelike state, left the conference room, and moved through the newsroom to the back door, trying to keep her face from looking like a complete mess. A few people glanced up, but no one said anything. People were coming and going in a busy newsroom all the time.

When she got to the safety of the car and shut the door, she had a moment of panic that she might faint right there and someone would find her passed out in her car.

Calm, Laura, calm, she told herself, and pressed her right thumb into the webbing of her left hand in an acupressure stress relief point she had learned about. After a few minutes she was at least OK to drive. She was about to pick up the phone and call Elliott when he beat her to it.

"Laura—my boss just pulled me aside and said I had to meet you at the District 3 police station. What is going on? Is Quinn OK?"

"He's fine, he's at day care. Elliott, this is crazy. We're going to be asked about Faith's death."

"*What?*"

"I guess she had some note with names on it. No one knows why or what it means but they could be asking people on the list for alibis and such. I don't know. I was only told they want to talk to us. Both of our names were on it."

"That fucking bitch," he muttered. "That little conniving bitch. I can't believe she would stoop to this."

"I wonder how many people she had on the list," Laura mused. "I mean, we had our problems, she and I, but I can't believe she would do this either. At least you and I both have alibis. I was working and you were with your friends camping."

He was very silent and Laura thought the connection might be lost.

"Elliott? Are you still there?"

"Yeah."

"Did you hear what I said? We both have airtight alibis. We would never hurt Faith. We couldn't have. We were both in a place with other people."

Elliott let out a long low sigh before speaking again.

"Laura?" His tone was odd and Laura felt a prickle at the back of her neck.

"Elliott? What? You were camping and I was at work."

"Honey, I . . . I . . . I'll have to be honest with the police so I better start with you."

Laura's hand gripped the phone tightly and her insides turned into a tiny, mushy swamp. Her next words came out in a whisper.

"You were camping, right, Elliott?"

"Of course I was, but . . . the truth is, I went alone Friday. The guys weren't going until Saturday. I just needed an extra night away. I'm sorry. Being a parent is a shit-ton of work, especially with you working nights. I just needed a break, that's all. So I wasn't actually around anyone Friday but don't worry, I still have an alibi. They can check the campsite registry if they want, I was there. I went fishing alone before dark and made a campfire, had a few beers, hung out, listened to the Tigers game on the radio, and went to sleep. The next day the guys joined me."

"You . . . lied to me?" Her voice got stronger. "You actually lied to me about camping?"

"I didn't think you'd want me out there alone but I needed that night, Laura, I needed it. I'm falling apart here trying to juggle everything. I don't want to hate being a parent. I want to love it but some days I hate it and I don't know what to do."

"And you think I'm not falling apart?" Laura could feel her voice seething with resentment. "I'm the one nursing Quinn all night and giving him baths and tummy time and taking care of him every morning and getting him to day care and still working full-time at my crazy job. We're supposed to be partners in this."

Tears stung at the corners of her eyes. They were both quiet, and a long moment passed.

"I fucked up, OK, Laura? I fucked up. So sue me."

"I don't want to *sue* you, Elliott. I just want you to be a better dad . . . and husband."

The tears started coming now and she couldn't stop a couple of sobs. He said nothing.

She was just about to tell him to meet her at the police station and they would talk more later when her phone pinged with a text. Looking down, she saw it was from Perry.

When you get back from the
police station, come to my office
right away. Something else is
happening that I need you to
know about.

CHAPTER TWENTY-THREE

Carol

June 4

The Fair-Weather Friends Fan Club had taken over a back room at the coffee shop. Someone pushed together about a dozen little tables to form a long rectangle. When Carol got there, more than twenty people were already milling about with mugs of coffee, plastic cups of smoothies, or other drinks in hand. Chloe was at the head of one side of the tables, wearing a bright yellow shirt and a pair of "jet stream" earrings that were giant swooshes.

Carol glanced around and saw two other people she recognized right away: Steve, Faith's alleged boyfriend, and Heather, the woman who had glommed on to Carol at the vigil. She was thrilled to see Steve so she could snoop.

Heather spotted Carol and waved her arm enthusiastically, yelling out, "Carol! Hi!"

Carol gave only a slight smile and a less-than-enthused lift of her hand in return, but Heather was beelining Carol's way as fast as she could with her slight limp. Carol had that weird feeling again of being penned in by this person she barely knew.

Eyeing Heather warily, Carol noticed Heather was once again

carrying Mr. Bojangles, her emotional-support teddy bear, and she was wearing the funky earrings with bright colors and little mirrors.

"I'm so glad you came," Heather gushed, reaching out and putting her hand on Carol's arm. Carol pulled it away. *Remember why you're here,* Carol told herself. For Faith and the baby. And Steve. She wanted to spy on him. Her eyes wandered past Heather to scan the room. Steve was standing in the corner, rocking back and forth like the slowest speed on a metronome. He seemed to be the only one without a beverage in hand.

"Do you want to sit together?" Heather asked in her irritatingly nasal voice, and Carol tried to scramble for an excuse.

"Oh, I can only stay for a bit so I'll probably sit near the door so I don't make a scene. Thanks, though."

"I don't mind being by the door," Heather responded with a big grin, and Carol wished she could build a brick wall between the two of them. She couldn't figure out why this woman felt so attached to her when they were relative strangers.

Heather pulled two chairs back and plopped down in one, patting her hand on the other and smiling up at Carol. Warily, Carol lowered herself into it, knowing that walking away now would be rude. Heather placed the teddy bear on the table.

"Watch this," Heather said, squeezing the bear's paw. The bear started to make a noise that sounded like a heartbeat. "I made him at Build-A-Bear. You get to choose a sound to be installed. I like the heartbeat. It calms me down when I feel anxious."

"Isn't that nice?" asked Carol. And it would have been, in the arms of a child, but since Heather was a fully grown woman Carol started to move her back into the "nutjob" category.

People were still milling about and the meeting hadn't started yet. Steve continued his painstakingly slow rocking. Carol knew if she wanted to play amateur detective she would need to make the first move. Turning back to Heather, she said, "Excuse me, I'm going to mix and mingle before we get started."

"OK, I'll save your seat for you!" Heather replied.

Carol tried to push Heather out of her head as she stood up and walked toward Steve. Talking to another mildly crazy person was not what she necessarily wanted to do, but it had to be done. For Faith. For the baby. Carol and Olivia had to suss out these suspects.

When she got to Steve, he looked at her uneasily.

"Hello," she said in what she hoped was a soothing voice. "I recognize you from the vigil yesterday. Steve, right? Faith's boyfriend?"

At the word *boyfriend* he stood a little taller and said, "Yeah, that's me."

"I'm so very, very sorry for your loss," Carol responded, adding a tinge of sadness to her voice to sound sincere. "May I ask, when was the last time you saw Faith?"

It was the first question in what she hoped would be a revealing chat with Steve that might yield insights she could report back to Olivia.

"Friday night," said Steve. "We met during her dinner break. She was pregnant, you know. I told all of you that and now you know it's true. She asked me to meet up with her and get some food. She wasn't feeling great so I was there to make sure she was OK. You know how ladies get when they're pregnant, like they want to puke or something."

Carol was carefully studying Steve as he spoke. He didn't seem to have the emotions a boyfriend would have if he had just lost his girlfriend and their baby to strangulation. Steve spoke very matter-of-factly and didn't appear upset at all. Carol thought of the photo he had produced that was so clearly photoshopped. But she wasn't here to determine if he was truly Faith's boyfriend, she was here to figure out if he did something to Faith, boyfriend or not.

"Oh, how kind of you to meet up with her," Carol replied, hoping by lobbing a few compliments his way she might warm him up. "Where did you go for dinner? I only ask because I'm such a *huge* fan and it would be nice to picture what Faith did on her last night."

"Applebee's," he said. "But then I had to go home and she went back to the station and then, you know, something happened somewhere along the way. I dunno what happened."

His monotone style was hard to place. Carol was trying to figure out whether he was a psychopath and killed Faith, or a clueless nerd making up stories. She tried again.

"Steve, your loss is unimaginable. My deepest condolences. And then you went home? Did you ever hear from her again that night?"

He opened his mouth to respond but before he could a loud clinking sound came from behind Carol and startled both her and Steve. It was Chloe banging a fork aggressively against a glass cup.

"FAIR-WEATHER FRIENDS," she called in a loud bellow that wasn't really necessary given the space they were in. "Please come sit so we can get started. We have a lot to talk about."

Reluctantly Carol moved back to the chair next to Heather's. She wanted to spend more time grilling Steve but he slunk back into a chair that wasn't even in the main rectangle.

Chloe started talking about the baby and the unthinkable loss of two lives. Carol noticed that Steve looked at the floor and wiped his hands on his jean shorts multiple times. Chloe then turned to the scholarship the station was starting.

"As her number-one fan club, we must step up," Chloe said. "My partner and I are donating two hundred dollars. Please give what you can. I have the station Venmo account here. If we raise more money than any other fan group in town, their news director told me they'd put our names on a wall of donors they're creating. Isn't that neat? Who's in?"

Carol shot her hand up and so did everyone else, including Heather and Steve. Chloe's eyes widened and she grinned.

"You all are the best. Although we've lost Faith, look what we've gained in getting to know one another. It's truly the best community I've ever been in. Let's all get our phones out and Venmo at the same time. The station will be blown away!"

People fumbled for their phones, saying things like, "How do I do this again?" Heather leaned over toward Carol and Carol thought she was going to ask her something about Venmo. Carol barely knew how to operate her own and didn't want to teach someone else, so she faked that she didn't notice Heather getting closer to her by keeping her eyes on her own phone.

"Carol, did you say your niece met Faith?" Heather whispered. "I heard a rumor that Faith gave an intern some piece of paper. Was that *your* niece, by chance?"

Carol's head snapped toward Heather. How would this woman know that bit of info?

"Where did that rumor come from?" she asked, suddenly worried sick for Olivia if this got around.

"From Chloe," hissed Heather, nodding toward Chloe, who was helping an elderly couple who didn't have Venmo and wanted to donate cash. "She knows a lot of things."

"Well, it was not my niece. Must have been some other intern."

Carol was going to protect Olivia at all costs. No way she was divulging info to this teddy-bear-toting, weird-earring-wearing, glomming-on woman.

"Oh, OK, I just wondered 'cause you know, we're all looking for justice for Faith. That's all we want. If it was your niece, your secret is safe with me. I mean, if she told you anything, anything at all that could bring justice, we could all work together to do so."

What an odd thing to say, Carol thought. Why would Heather press her in this manner and say "your secret is safe with me"? Did Heather not believe her?

"Well, it wasn't my niece," said Carol firmly.

"Cool beans," replied Heather. Carol glanced around again and wondered if she could slide over to an open chair without being rude. Chloe started talking loudly again.

"Venmo time is over but if you need tech help I will stay after this meeting. Next I want to talk about Faith's . . . you know . . . her . . . her baby." Chloe's voice cracked at the last word, and she paused to compose herself. "I've been thinking of ways to honor him or her. What about a community baby shower where we all get diapers and wipes and formula and things for those less fortunate? Or does anyone have any other ideas?"

For a few minutes they went back and forth on thoughts, Chloe writing them all down and nodding vigorously at each one. Steve raised his hand.

"Yes, Steve?" called out Chloe.

"We were gonna name the baby Zeus, it was a boy," he said.

Heather leaned over and whispered in Carol's ear.

"No way you can tell that at six weeks."

Chloe smiled in that appeasing way toward Steve and said, "Thank you for sharing. Anyone else?"

Another woman raised her hand and started talking about a day care that really needed donations and maybe they should zero in on that.

Carol heard a ping of a phone and thought it was hers. Others seemed to as well, as a few people near her fumbled in their pockets or bags for their phones. But as she glanced down at her phone Carol saw that it had nothing new on it.

Heather was reaching into her purse for her phone. She pulled it out and clearly it had been her phone making the noise as she pushed something on the screen to read whatever the text or alert was.

Heather's mouth dropped open. She shoved the phone back into her purse and stood up hastily. Her whole demeanor seemed to change. Her face looked stricken and her eyes sort of wild. She snatched the teddy bear off the table and shoved it into her purse.

"I need to go," she declared. "Sorry."

Heather bolted out of the room, startling the rest of the members of the FWFFC, who all looked after her quizzically. Carol watched Heather practically run through the coffee shop toward the parking lot.

"Well, oh-kaaay then, we certainly hope everything is all right," said Chloe. "Listen, some great ideas here. Let's wrap for the night and I'll post on the Facebook page what our Venmo total was. We should be very proud, Faith would be very proud. This has been a super meeting."

People began standing and collecting their items, chatting with each other and shaking hands. Carol wanted to try and pin down Steve for more info. She walked back over to him.

"We were interrupted," she said. "I think I was asking if you ever heard from Faith again Friday night."

"No, I didn't," he said. "But Faith and I were in love, deep love. Look . . ."

He took a string bag off his back and pulled it open, reaching in and producing two pieces of paper.

"I brought these to prove it to all of you."

Glancing down, she saw an autographed photo of Faith, exactly like the picture Olivia had procured for Carol, and a handwritten note. Reading both, Carol was surprised to see that Faith had said some rather nice, and very flirty, things to Steve. Maybe they were boyfriend and girlfriend. But then something caught Carol's eye. She squinted and said, "May I see these more closely, Steve?"

"Sure." He shoved them her way and Carol looked each over carefully. The thing that stood out, as obvious as could be, was that the handwriting was not the same as the writing on the autographed picture of Faith Olivia had given Carol. Not even close. Whereas the writing on Carol's autograph was tall, bold, and easy to read, this was slanted and very curlicued. The signature was not close either. The one Carol had utilized a giant *F* and smaller *a, i, t,* and *h*. This one was almost the opposite. The *F* was small and the other letters seemed to get larger with each one. Carol wondered if Steve had written this himself or gotten someone else to write it. She wasn't sure, but she figured it wouldn't hurt to show this to Olivia. Quickly, she scrambled for an idea.

"Steve, these are so beautiful, the most beautiful things I've ever seen. I'm such a huge fan of Faith's. Would you mind if I took pictures of these just to have and hold on to, to remind myself how special she was?"

Carol looked at him expectantly. Steve didn't respond at first and had an uncertain look on his face, so Carol doubled down with a comment she had a feeling might resonate with him.

"This would remind me of the incredible love you and Faith shared, and of your devastating loss. No one has suffered a loss quite like yours."

With that he nodded and said she could take a picture. Carol put the picture and note on the table closest to them and quickly snapped two photos, then handed the items back.

"Thank you," she said. "I will cherish these. Have a good day now. And thank you for loving Faith so much."

"Yeah, OK, see you," Steve replied.

Carol walked out. She felt good that she had donated fifty dollars, the most she felt she and Jim could afford right now, and she felt good that the FWFFC was finding ways to honor that poor precious and innocent baby. She had new info to share with Olivia about one of the possible suspects plus his weird autographed photo and letter.

But as she got to her car a different thought came into her head: the moment when Heather had stood up and thrown Mr. Bojangles into her purse, dashing off so hastily for reasons only she knew. Heather had seemed to morph into a very different-looking, and -sounding, person. Her voice got deeper and stronger and was just *different* from the other times she had spoken. The nasal tone was gone. It was like an entirely new being overtook her. Heather's shoulders were back and not hunched, her eyes had an intensity

Carol had not seen. Her stride as she hustled to the parking lot looked different from the way she had walked with a slight limp before. In fact, the limp seemed entirely gone. It was as if whatever text Heather got had zapped her into a new human being, and it felt unsettling in a way Carol could not properly place.

CHAPTER TWENTY-FOUR

Olivia

June 4

Olivia was back at her internship Monday trying simultaneously to be the head-down, focused intern that Channel 9 expected her to be, and to spy on Laura and Matthew to see if she could pick up any clues about why Faith would have put the two of them in her note to Tom.

Laura was gone for a chunk of the afternoon, and when she returned she went straight to Perry's office and shut the door. Matthew was milling about the newsroom telling various people how unfair it was that he had to work seven days in a row.

Olivia was trying to focus on another bump she had been assigned to write, but it was hard not to have her attention diverted thinking of Laura and Matthew. While both seemed so normal, Faith could have known another side of them. Could either be up to no good, even a killer? It made Olivia shiver, and she wrapped her cardigan around her even more tightly as she tried not to be obvious about peeking at Matthew as he whined to yet another person about how he was constantly taken advantage of.

Olivia thought his demeanor was inappropriate given that the news of the baby had just come out and that he was covering for someone who had passed away. Show a little respect. She would have worked seven days in a row in her future career. Wasn't that just a part of TV news? Olivia's professor had told the class she once worked a month straight for the Super Bowl and two weeks straight for political conventions. True, the professor had also said the crazy hours eventually drove her from the news, but Olivia was just getting started in her career. Crazy hours didn't scare her, and other than Gizmo she had no obligations.

Perry and Laura came out of Perry's office about four, and Olivia saw Laura walk to the five o'clock producer and whisper something in his ear. He looked surprised, and a little annoyed, but nodded. He then leaned over to the associate producer and whispered something to her. They both started typing furiously on their rundowns. It looked like they were making some sort of change, but their computers were too far away for Olivia to clearly see.

Laura walked over to Olivia. Olivia stiffened but tried to act normal. A nervous smile was all she could muster and she felt her eyes darting around. Could Laura be a killer disguised as a new mother? Olivia's nerve endings seemed to stand straight up at attention.

"Olivia, I'm running behind today because I had to do something this afternoon. Can you please go to the weather center and ask Matthew if he needs more than his usual two minutes, thirty seconds tonight in any of the shows? I saw it's possible we might get some thunderstorms. Thanks."

"Uh, OK, sure," Olivia said, and her nerve endings went from standing on edge to being lit on fire. She was being sent from one possible suspect to another, and Matthew would likely be alone in the weather office. It was one thing to converse with Laura out here in the middle of a busy newsroom, but to have to do so with Matthew in a quiet weather office made Olivia a little uneasy. She gulped. Laura was looking at her, waiting for her to stand, but Olivia's entire body felt encased in cement. She truly wasn't sure if she'd be able to rise at that moment.

"Please go now, Olivia. We need to know if Matthew requires more time in the show," said Laura with a tinge of annoyance in her voice.

Olivia stood up as if in a trance, her arms and feet not even feeling attached to her body. She moved through the newsroom like a sleepwalker.

The weather-office door was closed. Stopping in front of the door, she took several deep breaths and wiped her brow before tapping lightly. No response. She tapped again, harder. Nothing. Trying the handle, she discovered it was unlocked and gingerly pulled it open just a bit, peeking around.

Matthew was sitting at the main desk, looking over some printed maps. He had earbuds in and was bopping his head around. Glancing up at Olivia, he pulled his earbuds out without a smile.

"Yes?" he said.

Olivia summoned all of her courage, reminded herself of her spying duties, also reminded herself that the newsroom was just steps behind her and she could run if he tried anything, and stepped in.

The door closed behind her with a menacing click.

"Yes?" he said again. Matthew was looking at her with an annoyed expression, as if being interrupted was the worst thing that could have happened to him.

"Umm, hi, I'm Olivia, an intern. Laura—the executive producer—oh wait, you probably knew that, that was dumb of me. OK, well, Laura sent me over to ask if you need extra time for weather tonight."

Olivia felt herself wringing her hands as she spoke. And while her forehead was sweaty, her palms were clammy.

"Tell her I could use twenty," Matthew said coolly.

"Twenty minutes?" Olivia responded, shocked. She was thinking that it would eat up most of the show.

"Twenty *seconds,*" Matthew replied as if she were a complete idiot, and she guessed she was.

"Oh, OK, right," she said with a nervous laugh. She glanced around the weather office and saw Faith's spot, looking so totally normal. There were shoeboxes and some shoes under it, things pinned to a corkboard, and items scattered about the top of the desk. Olivia shivered again. How could Faith just be gone, vanished from this earth?

"Anything else?" asked Matthew, clearly eager to get back to his maps.

"No, that's all," said Olivia, but as she turned away she thought of the "wicked" nickname her mom had given her, and of the mischievous ways she was known for. Was she really going to leave this office without trying to get some nugget of info from Matthew? Something that could break the case? Olivia had a flash of herself and Aunt Carol being hailed as heroes by the mayor, given a key to the city and honored at a banquet. Or maybe they'd be on the cover of *People* magazine, or interviewed on *Inside Edition.* Her career could really take off then, her name would be known everywhere. She had to at least try, right? Renewed courage came into Olivia's body and she turned back around.

"Actually, there is one more thing. I've only been here for one week but I'm still so brokenhearted about Faith. I saw the push alert today that she was pregnant. I know you were close to her and I loved your remarks on the news Saturday night. Did you . . . um . . . did you know she was expecting?"

Olivia held her breath. No one would kill a pregnant woman, would they? She looked at him, trying to read his face as she waited for an answer.

Matthew's jawline tightened.

"No one knew," he said. "She kept it a secret."

"Oh, OK . . . you must be so upset. You all seem so close back here."

"Yup, I'm devastated," said Matthew. "Now if you'll excuse me, I have to start working on the forecast. Please tell Laura I need twenty—*seconds, that is.*"

Olivia nodded and went out through the door, simultaneously relieved to be gone from Matthew and the weather office and wishing she had more time to grill him. She hadn't really gotten much info. She would have to keep trying.

Back in the newsroom, she walked to Laura and told her that Matthew needed twenty more seconds. Laura nodded and instructed Olivia to keep working on writing the bump.

Olivia resumed her seat and snuck a side-eye glance at Laura. It was hard to believe Laura would do something to Faith. A nice person, a new mom, the executive producer of the show. Olivia sighed. It was all so much to think about.

One temple was starting to throb, and she rubbed at it as she looked back at the bump. This one was teasing a story about how families could save money on vacations and cruises over the summer. Olivia tried to remember what Laura and the producer had taught her: Less is more, don't give it all away, have a play on words.

"Parents, we have some great vacation tips that will save you boatloads of money, after the break," she wrote. She was a little scared to show it directly to the eleven PM producer. Maybe one of the talent would look at it first so she wouldn't have to get criticized by the producer. Olivia glanced over at Tom's desk. He was the nicest of the anchors, the one who called her "dear." Maybe he would help. But Tom wasn't in his spot. Veronica was in hers, yet Olivia still wasn't sure whether to trust her or not. She just didn't seem as nice as Tom.

Olivia decided to wait five minutes. Maybe Tom was just in the restroom. Rubbing her temple some more, she snuck some Tylenol from her purse and downed it with a chug of water. She looked at the wording on the bump at least five more times, and kept her eyes out for Tom.

"Olivia, do you have that bump written yet?" Kyle, the producer, asked.

"Yes, I thought I might show it to Tom to see what he thought, then show it to you. Is that OK?" Olivia asked.

"Just show it to me," said Kyle. "Tom called in sick today. Super late callout too. Laura told me and we had to change the rundowns from a two-anchor show to a one-anchor show. Total pain in the butt. It involves recoding a bunch of stuff and reformatting things. An earlier heads-up from talent would be nice every once in a goddamn while."

Olivia didn't know how to respond, so she said nothing. Kyle walked to her desk and looked at her computer over her shoulder.

"This is your bump?" he asked.

"Yes." She sucked in her breath in anticipation. Having someone evaluate your writing was so nerve-racking.

"That's perfect, good job. Put it in the rundown," Kyle said, and Olivia felt like doing a cartwheel. A flood of gratitude and a glow from being recognized for good work overtook her. She smiled. Genuinely. For the first time that day.

"I gotta do a bunch more stuff before the show, all thanks to Tom suddenly deciding he was sick," said Kyle. "Freaking talent. They never give us producers the respect we deserve."

He walked back to his desk muttering. Olivia was surprised Tom was calling out sick so late. It seemed out of character for him from the little she knew. He must be really, really ill to do so.

CHAPTER TWENTY-FIVE

Matthew

June 4

When the damn intern finally left the weather office, Matthew reached for both Tums and ibuprofen. He wondered if that had been the intern who had been handed the note from Faith, but Channel 9 had so many interns, who knew? More importantly, he wondered how he would ever get through this seven-day work week. Having to continually lie about his feelings regarding Faith and fake grief was awful enough. Now there was panic added in about what he and Tara had done.

He didn't want to ruminate about the night it had all started but he couldn't keep himself from thinking back on it. If only he had put the kibosh on the whole thing then.

He shut his eyes and leaned back in his chair, and the image of Tara and him at the Sky Lounge came to mind.

They were having drinks on the top floor of a skyscraper downtown. The place was dimly lit, with velvet-covered booths, dark wood tables, and little white Christmas lights strung all over the ceiling year-round, giving it the effect of stars above your head. A jazz band trio played in the corner.

Tara was sipping a bright pink cocktail that cost Matthew twenty-four dollars. It was a perfect example of why he felt he needed his salary to maintain or even go up. If he left the week-end job now he'd likely either have to move down in market size and make significantly less or find some PR job that sounded like the march of death to him. He and Tara had a fun lifestyle and he wanted to keep it. They chatted for a while about other things, but then the conversation turned to Faith, as it often did.

"So . . . she has a stalker, right?" Tara asked.

"Yes, several I think," Matthew had replied. "But this dude Steve is the worst. He leaves messages on the weather-office voicemail all the time. I've seen letters he's sent her, crazy shit about how much he loves her. Ha! If only he knew her."

"Can you get your hands on any of these letters?"

"Sure . . . why?"

"I'll tell you in a minute. You're sure you can get them?"

"Yeah, we've been told by HR not to ever throw away those kinds of letters just in case we need them as evidence, so we keep everything, with the envelopes and return addresses too, and they all go into the PC file, it's just a drawer in the office."

"The PC file?" Tara asked.

"Yeah, it stands for Psychos and Crazies. Jack named it that before he retired and it stuck. He had some female stalker who would write in asking him if he wanted to walk backward with her. Jack used to joke that if he ever met this woman in person he'd run away screaming."

Tara laughed, and Matthew did too, but he was wondering why he himself had never had a stalker. Although parts of it seemed like a true pain in the rear, it also would show that some woman found him so attractive that she was obsessed with him, which might not be all bad. It bothered him that he was one of the only TV people he knew who had never encountered such a person. It also bothered him that despite being on TV in Detroit for a decade he rarely got recognized in public.

"OK, this is sooo perfect," Tara said, taking a long sip of her drink. The lights of the city twinkled in the background. "You also have access to her promo pictures, right?"

"Sure, there's a stack for each of us in the office. We take them out on remotes and to festivals and sign them for fans."

The photos were done professionally every few years, using a studio space the station had set up in a back room. They lit it well and brought in photographers who did the whole "chin up, chin down, slightly less teeth, more teeth, no teeth at all" thing while snapping away hundreds of shots and angles. One would be the winner each time and would come to the talent in a giant stack of eight-by-tens, their name and the station logo stamped across the bottom. Of course Faith's also had to have "Your Fair-Weather Friend" and the info for the fan club on hers. Matthew's, Faith's, Abby's, and Chuck's were all side by side on a shelf in the office.

"Here's what I need," Tara said, lowering her voice to a whisper and glancing around the bar to make sure no one could hear them, but the jazz trio was in a long riff and there was no way anyone could have overheard. "Get me a few of the stalker Steve's letters with his return address, and bring me a few of her promo photos. I'll handle the rest."

"What are you going to do? Are you going to write to him?" Matthew whispered back. He felt an equal amount of titillation and trepidation. These were dangerous waters, more dangerous than hiding a lipstick for a few days. Tara was unpredictable.

"Yup . . . just a little fun. I have that female handwriting."

"But what if he writes back or leaves another voicemail thanking her for her letter?" Matthew asked. Nerves crept into his stomach. Tara could be just thinking she was having fun, but it was his career and their future in jeopardy if he was somehow ever caught.

"Hmm . . . let me think about that," she said, looking down at her drink and slowly swirling it. She looked up with a Cheshire cat grin. "I'll just tell him not to, that management wouldn't like it if they knew I was corresponding with a fan that way but that he's so special I have to. I can keep him on the fishing line for a while."

"OK," Matthew said cautiously. He knew that when she got on a roll there really was no stopping her. "But what is our ultimate goal in this?"

"To make her life miserable, of course!" Tara cackled. "At some point we'll ramp it up with him and he'll start showing up everywhere she is—out at station appearances or wherever. She'll get so freaked out she'll quit and you'll be promoted!"

Matthew looked down at his own drink, a dark beer. He felt his stomach tighten. Didn't the old saying go "Don't play with fire if you don't want to get burned"?

But if he didn't do it Tara would think he was a pussy. And really her plan had some merit to it. Maybe Faith would get flustered and decide to leave. He knew her contract was coming up and she'd have a decision to make soon. So he looked back up and gave a smile and a nod.

"Woo-hoo! You're the best, honey!" she cried, lifting her drink for a toast. They clinked glasses and Matthew said he would deliver the goods to her after his next workday.

He knew getting them would be easy, and it was. He just waited until he was alone in the office, locked the door, and went to the PC file, where the number of letters from Steve dwarfed all others. There was one declaring that Faith was "three diamonds" but he could make her feel like "five diamonds."

Matthew knew Faith lived at the Three Diamonds apartment building and he paused for a moment, wondering if that was what Steve was referring to. But no, there was no way this guy could know her address. Matthew dismissed it as a coincidence.

He took that letter and several others, including one that asked if Faith remembered Steve from the Belle Isle Art Fair. Then he grabbed a few promo photos and put everything in a manila envelope, hiding it under some other things in his work bag.

Tara took over from there. She didn't even tell him about the first letter she sent out until after the fact.

"I did it, I sent letter number one to Steve yesterday," she announced a few days later.

Soon after, she began really ramping up the chatter with the stalker, to the point where Matthew found it extremely uncomfortable, but Tara thought it was fun. She set up a private email address and took a picture of herself in a bathrobe in the mirror, pretending she was Faith.

"The idiot has no idea it's not his lover girl," she said, laughing. "I told him we'll only take pictures of our bodies, not our faces, and he agreed."

For weeks she played this guy, taking a picture of her shoulder or leg or a bare foot or her cleavage. She took one in her underwear and a bra and she might have even gone further in stripping, Matthew wasn't sure. He did know that Steve reciprocated with photos of himself, usually in the exact same poses. Tara showed them to Matthew and they both made fun of Steve for everything from his awful looks to his puppy-dog eagerness.

At the R&B Music Festival one Saturday, Matthew was

standing next to Faith in what talent at Channel 9 jokingly called "the bride and groom receiving line" with viewers when he saw a dorky guy in jean shorts, white socks, and a cheap polo shirt that was too tight stop in front of Faith and start to say loudly that his name was Steve and that he was her boyfriend and they traded pictures.

Matthew's antennae went up. This had to be the guy Tara was conversing with. Although Matthew had never seen the guy's face, because all of Steve's photos were from the neck down, this *had* to be him.

Faith was completely clueless as she tried to appease this viewer in front of her, and Matthew felt a tinge of guilt. He also wondered if she noticed, as Matthew had, that Steve then stood under a tree not far away from them and watched for the entire rest of the time they were there. Matthew tried hard not to stare at him too much. Luckily, the meteorologists all got into the weather vehicle at the end and quickly took off.

He told Tara about it that night, and she checked the private email to see if Steve had written.

"Oh yeah, he's asking why she ignored him at the festival," Tara said. "Don't worry, I got this. I'll tell him I was trying to keep it secret from you and others."

Her fingers flew over the keys and she smiled in satisfaction as she hit send. But when Steve responded, he asked for an in-person date again. He had been doing this for a while now.

"How long can you keep this guy at bay?" Matthew asked, leaning over her shoulder at the laptop to read Steve's email.

"A while. I have a great idea," Tara replied. "I'm going to ask him to follow me home and to other stuff instead. Can you get me Faith's calendar from the shared one you all have for events? I'll ask him to show up at all of these. This is when Faith will get unnerved by this guy and it will make her want to leave Detroit. Then operation 'Matthew to the main met chair' will be fully complete. When she leaves the city I'll write to Steve one more time pretending to be Faith saying 'I'm so sorry I got transferred to another city and our love will never have a chance to grow' and then he'll be out of her hair for good and she'll be out of ours. It's just soooo perfect."

Matthew had never felt fully on board with all of this manipulation, and he certainly didn't like his girlfriend sending sexy pictures to another man, even if she never showed her face. But Tara was unstoppable. There was really no way of stemming the tide now, he knew that. Tara was having too much fun. The whole thing seemed to excite her.

He let out a deep sigh and told her not to go too overboard. She turned her head toward him and gave him one of the more passionate kisses he could remember in a while, and he was jelly for her, as usual.

But just a month later Faith was dead, strangled in her car. Was it possible Steve had followed her on her dinner break and done this? Or was he as heartbroken as the rest of humanity seemed to be and he was innocent, nothing more than a clueless fool?

Now Matthew sat in the office and ruminated over not only the course of events with Steve the stalker but also just the whirlwind past few days. It had been nonstop since Perry had called Saturday morning to tell Matthew the news. He had to wake Tara and tell her, and she screamed and even cried a little. They both had looked at each other with trepidation and Matthew said aloud what he was sure they were both contemplating: "You don't think? Not the stalker? It can't be, right?"

"I don't know," Tara replied, her face whiter than he had ever seen it. "Let's not even let our minds go there."

He had always been nervous that somehow their little game could be traced. Even if Steve was not responsible for Faith's death in any way—and God, he hoped not—Matthew could be fired if this *ever* came to light.

It could go any number of ways. The police might never bother them again and they'd be scot-free for life, or the complete opposite: they could be accomplices to a murder. Or perhaps a middle ground. He could be fired for harassing a fellow employee. With the amount of harassment training they had to do at work, he knew there was a zero tolerance level for anything like that.

Two of the three options were very, very bad things for their future, and his bowels seemed to shift. He felt like he might have diarrhea coming on.

Why oh why had he ever let it get this far? He should have stopped it long ago. This kind of game-playing wasn't worth it, and it hadn't had the desired effect. It didn't make Faith just turn and run away to another city, it made her dead.

CHAPTER TWENTY-SIX

Laura

June 4

Laura returned from the police station pissed off and ready for battle. She had answered all of the questions from detectives honestly. Elliott answered his too, she hoped honestly, but how could she tell? If he had lied to Laura about camping with buddies, who knew what he was capable of? That was the pissed-off part of her. Well, that and being on some hit list from Faith. What had Laura ever done to deserve being on a list like that? It was so unfair. Yet Faith was dead, so it was hard to be mad at her for too long.

Laura needed to direct her rage toward someone living and breathing, and right now that was Elliott. He might be her husband, but she would do anything to protect herself and Quinn, and if she needed to give Elliott an ultimatum about being a better parent or losing her, she would.

Meanwhile, Perry had asked her to come to his office when she returned, so she beelined there. The newsroom was busy at this hour and she hoped no one would ask where she had been when she came out of her chat with Perry.

Perry was on the phone but motioned for her to come in and shut the door.

"I gotta go. Talk to you later," he said to whoever was on the other end of the line. Hanging up, he gave her a look she couldn't place; it was like the glare of a disappointed father mixed with pity.

"How did it go with the police?" he asked.

"Just fine. Elliott and I answered every question. Of course we had nothing to do with this. We're as shocked and devastated as the rest of Detroit. Faith and I were close, as you know."

He nodded. Laura remembered that someone else at the station was on the list. She scrolled through a flip-book of coworkers' faces in her mind, wondering who in the world it could be and whether they also had to be in Perry's office answering questions.

"I'm glad to hear that, Laura," he said. "Listen, as I told you, there's something new. Again, I tell you these things in complete confidence. Can I trust you to not tell anyone else, not even your husband?"

Laura nodded vigorously. Perry didn't need to know that right now she didn't trust Elliott with anything, so that wouldn't be a problem at all.

"OK, we may have a problem on our hands."

A "problem" in TV news could be anything: a technical difficulty, an error they made on the air that needed correcting, someone suing them, an issue between coworkers in the newsroom. Or was this problem somehow related to Faith? If so, Laura had no idea what Perry might say next.

"What is it?" she asked, trying not to sound too panicky. It had all been so much lately. She almost couldn't compute another issue to deal with.

"Well." He paused and took a drink from a water bottle that had the station logo on it. "You know how we sent out another push alert this morning that Faith was pregnant?"

"Yes."

"And people have already started donating?"

"Yes."

Laura was confused about where this was going. What could the problem be? This was everything Perry would ever want.

"So . . ." He looked down at his lap.

"What is it?"

"I got a call from the assistant medical examiner today after she saw the push alert. She said the pregnancy part might not be accurate."

Laura's eyes widened and she leaned forward in her chair.

"What do you mean? They told you she was pregnant."

"I know, it was on the ME's report. I told her that and she said she needed to speak with the ME. She said she would like to examine the body herself but Faith's sister already had it removed and taken to a funeral home for cremation, so she would talk to the ME and get back to me."

"But they can't make a mistake like that. Wouldn't they know for sure if she was pregnant?"

"That's what I thought," said Perry. "Listen, no one knows this right now and I mean no one. It's just a massive headache for us if she wasn't pregnant. How do we put that genie back in the bottle? People are now mourning for two. I had the title of the special changed already and we're reshooting interviews. The whole world thinks she was. If she wasn't . . . it's just awkward to retract that."

"But it's not our fault if she wasn't. We can just blame the medical examiner's office," Laura said, her mind doing flips like an Olympic gymnast. It was quite a one-eighty to go from pregnant to not pregnant to maybe pregnant. She tried to put on her executive-producer hat, though, and think about how to help the station.

Perry sighed. "Yes, but it still makes us look bad, like we pushed it too soon or don't know our people, or were just doing it for profit."

Laura bit her lip. She didn't want to say that she thought Perry had been pushing the special just for profit, so she stayed quiet.

"Anyway, we'll cross that bridge when we come to it. I just wanted you to know," said Perry. He ran his hand through his hair. "What a mess this whole thing is. I've never dealt with something like this in my decades in this business. I've only had one other talent die while actively on the air and that was from cancer in my first market. This . . . this is unprecedented. Murder, Jesus Christ. I'm doing my best." He sighed and rubbed his eyes.

"You're doing a good job," Laura said, trying to make her boss feel better. "The vigil was everything Faith would have wanted."

He nodded and they sat in silence for another moment before Laura added, "I'll get back to the newsroom now. Thank you for entrusting me with this information. I won't tell anyone, but I'll start to think of the wording in case we need a retraction. Oh, and thank you for believing me that I would never hurt a fly, let alone Faith. I will do anything to find her killer."

"You're welcome. I knew it couldn't be you," he said. "As for the other person from the station on the list, we'll see. But I will do anything to find her killer too, Laura. We at least owe her that."

CHAPTER TWENTY-SEVEN

Steve

June 4

Was Faith really pregnant with Steve's child? Were they madly in love?

Steve couldn't be 100 percent sure. Sometimes reality and fantasy conflated in his mind. He thought about things so deeply that he could make himself positive they were true. But he did occasionally make things up too. The picture of him and Faith on the beach. OK fine, it wasn't real. He photoshopped their heads on two bodies, but he just knew that some sort of trip like that was in their future so why not do it now? The name of their daughter being Charity if the baby was a girl? He read in that magazine article about Faith coming to Channel 9 that she had a sister named Charity who died at age three. He figured she would probably like to honor her sister. He was proud of himself for being so thoughtful.

And the night she died, he had been on duty to follow her for her dinner break. So what had gone wrong? He thought he lost sight of her car but he couldn't really remember. Or maybe he had gotten into the passenger seat of her vehicle on a backcountry road with the intent to talk, and maybe she said she wanted to cut things off, and maybe he went a little nuts. He's really, truly not sure. He has images of things in his mind. Different things, different scenarios. In one, she was going very fast and he couldn't keep up with her and her car was gone, and in the other he wrapped his hands around her perfect neck and she begged him to stop and he wanted to but he couldn't. And then she went limp and he scrambled back to his car and raced home.

Where was the truth? He wished he knew. And when the police shocked him by knocking on his door the night of the vigil and he had to sit on the couch between his mom and dad, his mother shaking uncontrollably, he was forced to tell an outright lie to protect himself. He couldn't divulge to the cops about his full, deep relationship with Faith or he might be a prime suspect. How did they even know he had anything to do with Faith? He couldn't figure it out.

So he said he went to the casino for the night as an alibi (it's only later when he realizes they can probably check security cameras) and he says that yes, while he and Faith corresponded at times, it was nothing unusual or important. He is hoping against hope they won't find the emails between him and Faith.

When the police finally left after a bazillion questions, his father turned to him sternly. "Stephen, what is going on here?"

"It's nothing, Dad, no big deal. Must be some kinda mix-up."

"Stevie, I just can't believe you're wrapped up in this," cried his mother, still shaking.

"Ma, don't worry about it. Cops make mistakes all the time."

Then he bolted up from the couch, grabbed the laptop from the desk in the dining room, went to his room, and called up the email exchange between him and Faith. He printed a few things to keep forever, but as much as it pained him to do so, he deleted every flirty email and photo the two of them shared. How he wished he could keep them all, but it was too dangerous. Instead he committed them to memory and lay down on his twin bed, letting some tears finally come—for Faith, for himself now caught in some kind of weird thing with the cops, for his parents and their worried looks, but most of all for what he and Faith almost had and now lost that she was gone. He knew he would never find another love like her, ever.

CHAPTER TWENTY-EIGHT

Carol

June 4

Carol was proud of herself for her detective work at the FWFFC meeting, and she couldn't wait to share the information with Olivia. In fact, she texted as soon as she got to the car in the coffee shop parking lot.

> Olivia—I've got something. I don't know how important it is but it's very interesting. It's about Steve, the guy from the list. Can you call me ASAP?

Olivia called immediately, saying she was on dinner break. "What is it, Aunt C?"

Carol laid it out for Olivia, how Steve had shown her the photo with the autograph and the handwritten note and how they hadn't matched the writing or signature from the autograph Carol got.

"Well, I saw Faith sign the photo for you, Aunt C, right in front of me, so I guarantee the one you have is her signature. The one this guy Steve has, do you think he faked it? He sounds like a weirdo."

"Yeah, I thought about him faking it but it looked like a woman's handwriting for sure, just different from Faith's. Very different. I don't know, it all felt fishy. Steve seems to really think they were in love, though. Did you get to sniff around with Matthew or that woman Laura?"

"Yeah, a little. Laura, I just don't see it. She has a newborn, photos of her baby all over her desk, she takes breaks to pump breast milk. Not that a mother can't be a killer but it also doesn't work because she was at the station all night Friday. But Matthew . . . I don't like him. He made a snide comment to me when I asked him if he needed more time for the show. I thought he meant minutes and he said it was seconds but he said it in a really mean way. I just didn't know, I'm new."

Carol's dislike and distrust of Matthew grew exponentially. She narrowed her eyes.

"That's horrible," she said. "You're an intern. Of course you're learning. If Matthew has a mean streak in him maybe we should focus on him."

"That's kind of what I was thinking," said Olivia. "Let me think of some other ways I can poke around or get more info on him. Can you imagine if we broke this case open? We'd be heroes."

"But Liv, you have to be careful, so careful, for your safety and for your job."

"Of course I will!" But Carol could tell that Olivia was excited for the process of snooping. It likely appealed to her mischievous side.

When they hung up, Carol thought about Jim. She had told Olivia she wouldn't be telling Jim about their mini detective agency yet. She knew it would worry him, and she didn't want anything stopping the forward momentum, but the time felt right to bring him into the fold. Jim was smart, maybe he would have some ideas of what to do, and she liked the thought of her husband being in protective mode for the two women. Not that anything bad was going to happen, but if it did, Jim would be there to help. When she got home he had dinner ready and the table set and she felt a surge of love and warmth toward him.

"I knew you'd be hungry, so I got everything ready," he said with a smile. It was true. She was starving after going to the coffee shop right after work. She sat gratefully across from him. He asked about the meeting and she told him about the Venmo donations and the ideas for how to honor the baby. Then she took a deep breath.

"Jim, honey, there's something else you should know. Olivia told me something yesterday that we have to keep a secret, for her own safety if nothing else. She feels terrible but . . . she actually decided to look at that note that Faith gave her to give to Tom. She opened it in the restroom."

Jim's eyes grew wide and he stopped in midchew.

"I know, I know, honey," Carol went on. "Don't get mad at Olivia. She feels awful enough. Here's the thing. The note listed names. No one knows what it means but what if poor Faith knew something bad was going to happen? But there's more . . ."

"More?" Jim said through his mouthful of food, nearly choking on it.

"Yes, the names were Steve, the guy who said he was Faith's boyfriend; some woman named Kelly with some guy Joel; Laura, who is one of the bosses at Channel 9 and who Olivia knows;

and . . . get ready for this one . . . Matthew, the weekend weather guy, along with his fiancée."

Jim put his fork down, swallowed hard, and stared at Carol.

"Only Olivia, me, and now you know this outside of Tom and maybe the police if Tom shared it with them. So Olivia and I decided to do a little snooping just in case these names actually meant something."

"What are you talking about, Carol? You're doing *what*? You're snooping around for a killer? Are you crazy? This is a police matter is what it is."

"Jim, I need your support. We're not doing anything bad. I saw Steve at the coffee shop and Liv saw Laura and Matthew at work. They don't know we're snooping. We're just asking a few extra questions."

Jim leaned back in his chair and pushed his plate away.

"I don't know what to say. What has come over you, Carol? Do you think you're going to uncover something the cops don't? Why not just call the cops?"

"Because they probably already have the same info we have. Sometimes citizens can uncover more than police. We see it on *20/20* or *Dateline*. Maybe we can help the police. We owe that to Faith. It's the very least we can do."

Jim stared at her. She knew it would take a bit to warm him up but she knew he eventually would come around. He wouldn't leave his wife and his niece out to dry, he loved them both too much. And Jim liked to solve puzzles and close loops too. Unfinished business never sat well with him. It was part of the reason he enjoyed roofing. It was a clear, delineated process that involved a team of people working together, and it yielded almost immediate and very satisfying results.

Jim was quiet that evening as they watched TV and got ready for bed. But when he looped his arm over her hip in their sleep position he said, "Honey, I support you and Olivia, you know that. I've been thinking hard on it all night and I actually have an idea. Something we learned on *48 Hours* a few months ago . . ."

CHAPTER TWENTY-NINE

Olivia

June 5

The first thing Olivia saw when she woke up was a text from Aunt Carol.

> Jim is looped in on everything.
> He actually had a crazy idea last
> night. Call us as soon as you can.

She didn't waste time even getting up to use the bathroom or to brush her teeth. Olivia called right away. Carol answered and put it on speaker.

"All right, hear me out," said Jim. "At first I was against this whole thing but I know how you two are when you get a notion in your heads about something so I knew I wouldn't be able to persuade you or especially my better half over here. So then I got to thinking about something you both could do other than just asking questions. I started to ponder about the incredible access to the station you have, Liv. If you really want to try to get info, I have a tool for you."

"A tool?" Olivia was picturing one of Jim's hammers or saws. What would she do with that?

"Yup, I got up out of bed last night and ordered it on Amazon. It's already here at the house. That crazy fast delivery they have."

"But . . . what is it?"

"I got you a pen with a camera hidden on the side. You can record anything. Super clear audio and video and you can download their app to watch. Has a long battery life and only needs recharging every once in a while. I thought you could plant it in the weather office so you can see what Matthew is up to when no one else is around. Maybe hear his phone conversations, things like that. No one would notice a single pen on a desk, right? And Michigan is a one-party consent state so you are allowed to record things without the other person's knowledge."

Olivia gulped, her mind starting to race.

"Geez, Uncle Jim, that's quite an idea. I don't know what to say. Aunt C, what do you think?"

"I'll be honest, sweetie. At first I thought your uncle had smoked something funny but then he reminded me of a *48 Hours* episode where a civilian cracked the case using just this item. I don't know, Liv, I worry about your safety but you do have more access than anyone else and I think we all suspect Matthew most of all, right?"

"As of now, yes," said Olivia. Her temple was starting to throb.

"We'll leave it up to you. As Jim said, the pen is here if you want to use it. We actually both stayed up so late talking about this that we called in sick today so we're home. We needed the rest anyway after the whirlwind few days we've had. So if you want to look at it or play around with it, you can come over before your internship starts today."

"Let me think on this," said Olivia. "It's quite the idea, Uncle Jim. I just need time to digest it all."

They hung up and Olivia let out a low whistle. Her uncle and aunt were encouraging her to plant a spy device in the weather office to try and record and potentially frame the weekend meteorologist. And she was just an intern in her second week. It was bananas. The whole world had gone upside down. She curled into a ball and pulled the covers over her head. Part of her wanted to call in sick too, to hide under these blankets all day.

She could feel Gizmo walking up the blanket, and he let out a soft meow. She pulled her head out and said, "Giz . . . what would you do if you were me?"

He nuzzled his head into her hair. She reached out to pet him and he started to purr.

Olivia lay there for a good ten minutes stroking Gizmo and listening to his deep motor noise. The very sound of him soothed her. She had read that a cat's purr was known to lower blood pressure, and she felt it doing it for her. Her mind started to slowly rake back and forth over people and possible scenarios. She thought of Faith. She thought of her mom and wished she had her advice. She thought of Carol and Jim, of Laura the executive producer, of Steve the weirdo, of this mystery woman Kelly. She thought of her career just starting and what would happen to it if she were caught spying on someone, but also what would happen if she turned in a killer and was a hero.

After ten minutes, one thought was dominating all others. There was a saying, "Well-behaved women seldom make history." She couldn't just sit by and be well-behaved when a person had been murdered.

The rascal side of her started to rise and the scared part was falling. She had to plant that pen. And she knew it wouldn't be that hard either. Faith's desk had a cup full of pens sitting on it. Olivia could wait until Matthew was on dinner break that night and then wander into the closed-door office unseen and slip the pen in. Whether or not it would yield something on the video was unknown but she would do her part. And no one would ever figure that it was her. Even if someone found the pen they'd likely think Faith had planted it before her death.

She remembered reading about the civil rights activist John Lewis in a class the previous semester. His famous quote stuck with her: "Get in good trouble." She was ready to do so.

Grabbing her phone, she texted her aunt and uncle back.

> I'll be over in an hour to pick
> up the pen

CHAPTER THIRTY

Olivia

June 5

Matthew was taking longer dinner breaks, so Olivia knew she had time to get into the weather office and be alone while he was out. Plus, if he returned and saw her there, she could fake that she had a question about something, something stupid that an intern wouldn't know.

She watched him walk through the newsroom after the 6:30 show, heading to the parking lot. Waiting until many others had also left for dinner, she took her time casually strolling toward the weather office so she would look completely normal. The door was unlocked. She slipped in.

The first order of business was to plant the hidden-cam pen. That was easy. Every meteorologist had a cup full of pens on their desk. She walked to Faith's and slipped in the pen, turning it on and rotating it so the lens would be facing out toward the main area. She checked the app on her phone to make sure it was working.

Standing at Faith's desk she scanned the items strewn across and under it for a quick moment. Who would come and pack all of this up? Probably HR. They'd send it to Faith's family, she figured. Olivia felt a tiny sting of tears in her eyes. It was so unnerving to be looking at a desk preserved in time. Faith had gone out for dinner and never returned and her desk was still there but Faith wasn't. Olivia had a hard time making her brain believe it all.

Before she could even help herself, her fingers traveled to the drawers of the desk and she gently pulled each one open. She just wanted to feel Faith's life for a moment, be a little closer to her. Several drawers were jammed with all kinds of office supplies and quickie junk food, but one had newspaper clippings and magazines with articles about Faith or pictures of her.

THE EARRING QUEEN said one headline.

THE BEST OF DETROIT . . . screamed another.

CHANNEL 9 ON CLOUD 9 WITH RICHARDS BOOSTING RATINGS read a third.

Olivia lifted them out and glanced over them. She was about to put everything away when her eyes spotted what looked like a leather journal under it all. Gently, she extracted it from the drawer, cocking her head and listening carefully to make sure she didn't hear any sign of Matthew returning. She was ready to stuff everything back and act natural if she did. It was all silent in the hallway.

Flipping the journal open, she saw pages of writing in the same cursive script she recognized from Faith signing the auto-graph for Aunt Carol. Olivia couldn't help herself. She started to read. It was almost like a diary format but not with dates, just with random musings.

Today has been excruciating, the anniversary of Charity's death. Thirty years later and I can't get over that I let go of her hand, that I turned my little eight-year-old attention away. Dad told Hope that he trusted me. I had to take two sleeping pills last night to try and sleep and I'm so groggy today I can barely go on air. Charity, sweet Charity. My little sister. I can't forgive myself. Can you forgive me wherever you are? I was only a kid, I didn't know what I was doing. I have lived with this pain in my heart every day since. I'm sorry, I'm so sorry. I would trade places with you in an instant.

Olivia kept reading. There were more entries like that, all talking about a little sister and something that happened at a Lake Michigan beach all those years ago. It was obvious how painful this was for Faith, and that pain caused Olivia to feel a heaviness settle into her own chest. Wow. This was a side of Faith she would never have guessed about. Knowing this about one of the most popular talents in the entire city was a very weird feeling. Olivia wondered if others also had a clue. It made Faith actually human, it made her a sad and regretful person dealing with demons, not just a happy face on the news.

Glancing at her watch, Olivia saw that she had better wrap it up to be sure she wasn't caught by Matthew. She replaced the journal and everything else in the drawer, closed it, double-checked the pen, and left the office. She needn't have worried. Matthew didn't return for another forty-five minutes. When he did, Olivia glared at his back after he passed her in the news-room. Knowing this new information about Faith made her that much more likable, and him more of a target than ever. If he did something to Faith, Olivia was going to help convict him. She would check the hidden-cam pen app that night and every night to see if she could find anything.

CHAPTER THIRTY-ONE

Matthew

June 5 and 6

He was in an absolutely foul mood, likely due to not sleeping. He couldn't shut his brain off at night and then had to work all day and act natural on the air, plus pretend he was the grieving coworker. It was all too much. He was living off caffeine, having downed three Diet Cokes that day already.

After dinner he came back to the office and felt like he was going to explode. He paced the office, tried a few push-ups and jumping jacks, and when that didn't help, finally called Tara. He still had a wiretapping situation in the back of his mind, but the police hadn't bothered them since they were interviewed Sunday, so he figured that wasn't likely, plus he was so pent-up with emotions he just had to talk to her, and she was the only one who knew what was bothering him or could commiserate.

"I'm going crazy here," he told her. "I'm filled with . . . I don't know, regret? Guilt? Worry? Every time I look at her desk I think about what we did. We were stupid. We could jeopardize everything we've worked for."

"I'm a mess too," she said. "I was so lost in thought during a meeting at work today that coworkers made fun of me for being a space cadet. I had to laugh it off and say I'm just thinking about the wedding. But honey, I'm keeping my eye on the prize: You have made it to Jack's spot as the main met. I would think Perry would offer you a new contract soon to stay there."

"Yeah, hopefully a new contract and much more money will make this all worth it. Maybe someday you and I can move on and forget—as long as we don't get caught, of course. People will eventually turn their attention to other things, right?"

"Of course they will. Hang in there, honey. No one knows anything. It's going to be OK."

"OK, I'm trying to act normal. I love you."

"I love you too. We'll be married in a few months and you'll be working Monday through Friday like we always wanted and we can buy a new condo, maybe down at the river with a view of Canada. Remember, this too shall pass."

"I'll try to keep my eye on the wedding and a new condo we can finally afford. I'll try to stop thinking about what happened and about Faith's death. We lied to the police once and they seemed to buy it. They haven't been back around so I think we're in the clear."

When he hung up he turned his attention to work and getting his forecast ready. He knew tons of fans were writing to the weather email or leaving messages begging for someone to pick up the earring forecast or to do something similar, but he wasn't going to stoop to some gimmick. He was a hardcore meteorologist with science to back him. Viewers would just have to adjust to his style.

That night after he got home from work following the show, he fell asleep faster than any previous night since Faith had died. When he woke up Wednesday, Tara had already left for work and there was a text on his phone from an unfamiliar number.

> Hey Matthew, it's Tom. I need to talk to you about something confidential. Can you meet me at Ford Park? I'll ping you the exact spot. There's a quiet parking place down by the lagoon where no one goes where I like to take walks. 12:15 before work?

Matthew sat up in bed. He and Tom were not super close, but they had been coworkers for many years and had gone out socially a few times. Curiosity poked at Matthew. What was so confidential that they had to meet at a secluded park? But if one of the main anchors wants to see you, you do it, especially if you're trying to get in good with the Monday-through-Friday team. He texted back right away that he would be there. Then he texted Tara about it, went on the treadmill for twenty minutes, took a shower, ate a big breakfast, and put on some casual clothing for the meeting. He would pick up a bunch of suits from the dry cleaner after his Tom meeting and wear one of those later on the air.

Tara texted back that she thought this was a good sign. Tom wanting to confide in him, Tom wanting to get closer to him. It likely meant Tom would put in a good word with Perry.

Matthew drove over to Ford Park feeling optimistic and starting to relax just a touch. Maybe everything was really going to be OK.

The spot that Tom had pinged him about was set way back from the main parking lot. Matthew saw just one car on the road, going the other way. Other than that there was nothing but nature.

Unrolling the windows, he listened to the wind and the birds as he went along. It felt so refreshing to be somewhat calm for a change. He would chat up Tom, see what he wanted to talk about and have plenty of time to grab lunch before getting to work for the afternoon editorial meeting.

At the lagoon he saw Tom's Lexus parked in the corner of the small lot, facing the water. Matthew pulled up next to it and glanced over to wave. He didn't see Tom. Maybe Tom had stepped out to use the bathroom. Matthew looked around for a porta-potty but none were nearby. Would Tom be the kind of guy to take a piss in the woods? It was hard to imagine the buttoned-up main anchor doing that, but certainly anything was possible. Matthew turned off his ignition and unbuckled his seat belt. A few ducks were swimming in the lagoon, and he watched them circle and quack at each other for a moment. A bird sang from a tree somewhere above his head. Matthew reached for his phone to see if he had any new messages. Scrolling, he saw nothing of major importance.

Yawning, he looked around again. If Tom had gone off to pee in the woods he certainly was taking a long time to return. Matthew stepped out of the car. Walking toward Tom's vehicle, his sneakers crunching the gravel of the parking lot, he thought he might just glance in the driver's-side window to see if Tom's phone or wallet was in there, a sure sign Tom had just stepped away for a moment.

The peace of Mother Nature was suddenly punctuated by a wail of sirens in the distance. Matthew noticed the bird who had been singing turn its head. Even the ducks seemed to cock their beaks a tiny bit. The sirens were getting closer. That was weird. Something must be going on in another part of the park.

Matthew reached the driver's side of the Lexus and looked into the window to ascertain what Tom might have left behind.

That was when he saw Tom, slumped to his side so that his shoulder and head were in the passenger seat. He was wearing a polo shirt and gray shorts like one might don at a golf course.

"Tom! Oh my God, no!" Matthew cried out, and he grabbed the handle on the driver's door. Thankfully, it was unlocked. He reached for Tom, trying to tell what was happening—it must be a heart attack or a stroke. Tom was in a very unnatural position so Matthew knew immediately it was a medical emergency and not a nap. The sirens got louder.

"Tom!" He tried to turn Tom's body so that he could see his face but it was too hard at that angle and too far to reach across. Running to the passenger side, he pulled that door open, also unlocked. Using all of his strength, he pushed Tom's shoulder back and twisted Tom's body as best he could. Tom's eyes were wide open and vacant. A thick line of a very foamy saliva was coming out of his mouth. There were no other obvious signs of trauma, but Matthew knew immediately and unequivocally: Tom was dead.

"Tom, nooooo, Tom!" he cried as the sirens became so loud he realized they were headed right to that small parking lot. Tom must have called 911 before he keeled over.

Matthew thought about attempting CPR, but a police car and an ambulance pulled to a stop and he was grateful to defer to the professionals. Plus, he knew deep in his soul that Tom was gone and that no amount of CPR would bring him back.

As the EMS workers and an officer jumped out of their

vehicles, Matthew glanced at the floor of Tom's car and noticed two Channel 9 water bottles.

One had a sticker from the Detroit Pistons on its side.

It looked exactly like Matthew's own water bottle, the one that had been stolen from the weather office.

"What the heck?" he said aloud as the EMS workers pushed him out of the way and started dragging Tom from the car, laying him on the ground and attempting CPR. As Matthew had predicted, there was not an ounce of life left in the man. Matthew watched it all in horror. His brain was not ready to compute what he was seeing. It was like watching a movie, and he could only stare.

The police officer stepped forward.

"Sir, I need your name and ID, please."

"Of course, Officer. I'm Matthew Hayes." He dug into his back pocket for his wallet. The officer took his driver's license and looked at it.

"I need you to get into the back of the squad car."

"OK, but why? I just got here right before you. I came upon the scene. What happened? Did he have a heart attack? Did he call you guys for help?"

"Get into the squad car," said the officer with such force that Matthew just complied. The officer stayed outside the car and moved a little away, talking into the radio strapped to his vest. The EMS workers were putting Tom on a stretcher. Matthew looked at them through the window and wondered if anyone had realized yet that this was Tom Archer, main anchor for Channel 9. The reality began to hit Matthew. Who would tell Perry? Tom's wife? Veronica? How could the station lose two of their main talent in a week? This was unfathomable. He began to feel nauseous.

The officer came back to the car just as Matthew heard more sirens coming their way.

"I'm taking you down to the station, you have a lot to talk to investigators about," said the officer.

"What do you mean? I told you I just got here. I got a text from Tom asking me to meet him and when I got here I came upon this scene."

"Tell it to the detectives," said the officer. "It sounds like they were planning to contact you today for other things and then this."

"Other things?" Matthew's mind began to race. He thought of Steve the stalker and the emails Tara had sent, and his nausea reached new depths. Was this his worst-case scenario coming true? But that was only one thing. What did the officer mean by other things?

"I'm not saying anything else," said the officer sternly. He turned on his own siren. As soon as the other squad cars arrived, they took off through the park headed for the police station. Matthew had no way of contacting Tara or anyone else. His phone was still in the console between the driver's seat and passenger seat in his own car.

He sat paralyzed with fear as the squad car sped toward District 3.

CHAPTER THIRTY-TWO

Laura

June 6 and 7

At first everyone thought Tom was just out sick again, but that he had not bothered to call in this time. The producers were complaining. Then Perry brought Laura into a meeting with HR, the GM, and three other top newsroom managers. Perry's eyes were so red you could hardly see a trace of white. His voice was only a small octave above a whisper. At first they all just stared at him as if in a trance. What he was saying did not compute.

He had gotten a call from the police, he told the group. Tom was found dead in his car in a remote spot at Ford Park, poisoned. Next to him were two water bottles with the remnants of champagne in them. One had been laced with cyanide. And Matthew was there when police rolled up, telling them a story about Tom texting him and Matthew just coming upon the scene. Matthew was now being questioned at District 3.

One of the news managers started to sob. Another cried out, "Fuck noooo." Laura was having an out-of-body experience and truly felt as if she were floating above the scene. How could another main anchor for Channel 9 be dead? What would they tell the public? How would they pull off another vigil and remembrance? What was happening that anchors were being killed? Were they *all* in danger?

Perry asked them not to talk about it in the newsroom, but places like that were notorious for whispers and rumors and soon the whole newsroom was aware. Veronica had to solo-anchor the shows and they called in Chuck to fill in for Matthew. They hadn't told the public yet but it was coming soon. HR was arranging counselors for staff, and PR was figuring out what to say and when.

That night after the 6:30 PM news Perry ushered them back into his office.

"Team, Matthew has been arrested. His water bottle with his DNA on it was in Tom's car. It looks as if they were having champagne together for some reason and Matthew put poison into Tom's drink. But there's more. A rock-solid police source tells me they scoured Matthew and his girlfriend's computers and found Google searches about poison plus an email address where Matthew's girlfriend sent pictures of herself pretending to be Faith. She sent them to a stalker, a guy named Steve that Faith had reported to HR some time ago. It looks like Matthew and Tara were setting up Faith. Finally, the source tells me someone sent footage from a pen camera to the police anonymously and it recorded Matthew basically admitting to killing Faith. In fact, my source even sent me the verbatim so that I would believe it was true."

Perry looked down at his phone and started to read:

"'I'm filled with . . . I don't know, regret? Guilt? Worry? Every time I look at her desk I think about what we did. We were stupid. We could jeopardize everything we've worked for. Yeah, hopefully a new contract and much more money will make this all worth it. Maybe someday you and I can move on and forget—as long as we don't get caught, of course. People will eventually turn their attention to other things, right? OK, I'm trying to act normal. I love you. I'll try to keep my eye on the wedding and a new condo we can finally afford. I'll try to stop thinking about what happened and about Faith's death. We lied to the police once and they seemed to buy it. They haven't been back around so I think we're in the clear.'"

Perry looked up at them. No one said a word.

"I'm so sorry to be the one delivering this shocking news. We are all in complete disbelief but we do need to let the judicial process play out and we need to honor Tom. I will be putting out a push alert later tonight. We'll do a second vigil this weekend."

PART THREE

CHARITY

———

CHAPTER THIRTY-THREE

Hope

The truth was I felt horribly guilty about it. About the way Charity
died, yes, but also how I pinned it on Faith for all of these years.
Faith still didn't know the truth. It was too late now. You can't
walk up to your sister more than thirty years after a tragedy and
say, "Oh by the way, I've been lying to you all of these decades.
It wasn't actually your fault."

And Faith thinking it was her fault had been to my great advantage. Faith was indebted to me for life because of the way I
twisted the truth. Sometimes at night I would lie awake staring
at the ceiling and feeling as if the universe was sure to punish me
soon. But oddly it never did. Other than me having sucky jobs,
of course. Not like my famous sister who had somehow become
Detroit royalty. But no lightning bolts had hit me on the head,
no close calls had befallen me as I crossed the street, no diseases
ravaged my body. I had escaped retribution and I felt like I had
a horseshoe tucked up my ass.

One thing was for sure—I still had trouble being on beach
boardwalks and avoided them at all costs. The smell of hot dogs

and kettle corn, the sound of children laughing and playing, the feel of the wood planks beneath my feet, the sight of so many kitschy tourist shops with their T-shirts and kites and snow globes and fudge and beach toys. It all reminded me of that day with Charity. Of what Faith did, or rather what I did.

I couldn't stop replaying every detail and over, even decades later.

It had been late afternoon in our quiet corner of the beach and Mom and Dad decided it was time to go home. Charity was sure to sleep the whole way, especially after being our water hauler for most of the afternoon. Faith and I might actually snooze too. The sun and wind had taken the energy out of us and we looked at each other with drowsy eyes. But first we wanted ice cream. We begged for it, pleaded.

Mom thought it would ruin our dinner but Dad overruled her and said we'd stop for one scoop on the boardwalk. He was in a better mood than I had seen him in in a while and we all tried to take advantage of it, hugging and kissing him and saying "Thank you, Daddy" over and over.

When we got to the boardwalk, the line at the ice cream shop was long. Faith and I were trying to teach Charity how to say "ice cream," but it was a lost cause. She was doing her best, but other syllables would come out.

There was an arcade nearby with bright lights emanating from the space and the alluring sounds of beeps and buzzes. It was irresistible to me and Faith. Our eyes kept looking that way, as it was just a few storefronts down from the ice cream shop.

"Mommy, Daddy, can we go to the arcade for one game?" Faith begged. "Just one? Pleeaasse."

I saw Mom and Dad glance at each other before Dad shrugged and reached into his pocket, drawing out four quarters.

"Once these are gone, you're done," he said. "We should be at the front of the line by then."

"*Thank you, thank you, thank you!*" I cried out, surprised by his generosity. As the eldest I took control of the quarters, holding the precious metals in my hand as Faith looked at me with eagerness. We started to turn away but Charity reached for us and began crying. She knew we were leaving her and didn't want to miss out on the fun.

"Charity wants to come too!" said Faith, laughing. I saw Mom's eyes dart to the arcade, back to the ice cream line, and back to the arcade, assessing.

"Let her go," said Dad. "They'll only be gone a hot minute."

Faith took Charity's hand and our little sister's face went from sad to thrilled in an instant. The two of them started walking toward the arcade and I was about to follow when Dad clamped a hand on my shoulder.

"Hope, you're the oldest. Keep an eye on your little sister. Don't let her out of your sight."

"I won't," I said, and I meant it.

But something happened in the chaos of the arcade, something I've tried to piece together for thirty years. I have trouble remembering exactly how long we were in there. It couldn't have been more than ten or fifteen minutes. Faith held Charity's hand as we walked around. I lifted Charity up to see what one of the race car games looked like. We watched two boys play on a golf simulator before getting bored and moving on. Then Faith and I spotted side-by-side *Ms. Pac-Man* games and we went running over, Charity's little feet following us.

I don't remember why we were so absorbed in the game but we knew we had only four quarters and we had to make them count. Faith and I were both focusing intently on the screens in

front of us, trying to steer Ms. Pac-Man to gobble up every ob-
stacle in her way and avoid the ghost characters coming at her. I
know I thought Charity was just standing behind us.

But when our last Ms. Pac-Man died with that sound that's
like something spiraling and splattering, I turned around and
Charity was nowhere to be found.

"Charity?" I called out, sure that she was nearby, maybe at a
game just out of eyesight.

Faith whipped her head around too.

"Chair?" she yelled. There was no response.

We looked at each other with a sudden sense of fear and took
off running through the aisles of the place, yelling her name.

The guys at the golf simulator were still at it; other people
were camped out at various games, seemingly having a blast,
oblivious to our plight. The arcade, which had been a dream
destination for Faith and me just minutes prior, now felt like
a haunted house. There was darkness and weird lighting everywhere. The games seemed to mock us, clown faces and aliens
on pinball machines, and we ran, yelling her name, looking behind and next to every machine. She was so small she could have
wedged herself in any number of places. We were getting frantic
and we were both panting. We stopped near the entrance back
to the boardwalk, putting our hands on our knees. We had no
idea what to do. There didn't seem to be any employees, security
guards, or even adults in the arcade. It was filled with kids, preteens, and teens.

"Maybe she went back to Mom and Dad," Faith suggested,
and I thought that it was as good a suggestion as any but I also
felt a huge pit in my stomach. What if she hadn't? Then it would
be the moment of reckoning for us.

We decided to do one more sweep of the arcade but saw nothing. We looked up and down the boardwalk. Plenty of people were walking about in the late-afternoon sunlight, smiling and chatting, but there was no sign of a little strawberry-blond girl.

I saw Mom and Dad heading our way with three ice cream cones in their hands. Charity was not with them. And I knew. I knew this was very, very bad. A feeling of dread like I had never felt came over me.

Everything is a blur after that. Mom dropping the ice cream cone she had in her hand and running into the arcade, screaming Charity's name as loud as she could. Dad bolting over to a security guard who was leaning casually against a railing. Dad dumping the other two ice cream cones in the garbage can as he and the security guard took off down the boardwalk. Mom coming out of the arcade in hysterics, and people on the boardwalk beginning to notice and ask if they could help.

I have a gap in my memory after that. My next major recollection is being in the car with Aunt June, who had come to pick us up. Aunt June's car smelled like cigarettes and I didn't like it. She said nothing all the way home as Faith and I each just stared out our respective windows. We were hungry as it was well past dinner now but we didn't ask for food. When we got home Aunt June told us to go straight to bed and we did so, even though it was still early.

From her twin bed across the room from mine, Faith whispered, "What do you think happened?," and that's when the lie came out of my mouth so easily it shocked me.

"I don't know but it's your fault. Remember when you started walking to the arcade holding Charity's hand? Dad told me he trusted you to watch Charity, that you were even more responsible than me. He told me to have fun playing the games because you would be in charge of Charity. You lost her. It's your fault."

Faith was very quiet but then a sob came out, then another, and she was heaving and crying harder than anyone I had ever heard. I felt bad and I thought about going over to her bed to comfort her but something stopped me, I don't know what. Instead, I stayed in my bed but I said, "Faith, I will never tell anyone how you screwed up, OK? It's our secret."

She cried even harder but thanked me over and over.

They found Charity's body three days later in a remote part of the state park that bordered the beach. For a full year, there were no suspects. Then another little girl went missing from the arcade but someone spotted a guy in the parking lot trying to push the girl into his car while covering her mouth. That girl was saved. It turns out an arcade worker lured both with lollipops to his office in the back. I couldn't help but wonder if Charity's had been grape—her favorite flavor. The office had a second door that led to the parking lot and he would get them to his car quickly. I couldn't stand the thought of little Charity being pushed into the car. I sometimes have to throw up when I think of it even now. I guess if there was any consolation, he never sexually assaulted her. He confessed to having a fascination with just strangling little kids.

Our family was shattered. Faith and I both had to go on antidepressant meds. Faith would get wired, almost manic, on hers and she became this wildly big personality that I knew wasn't truly her. I had the opposite reaction, becoming more sullen and preferring to be alone. Dad burrowed deeper into his own demons and I think he took out his grief on us for the rest of the time we lived at home. Mom just got despondent and by the time we both finished college she spent most of her time in their bedroom. Dad was especially cold to me after that fateful day on the beach, but I didn't want Faith to notice that, so when Faith would get home from being out somewhere I would make up little lies about fun things Dad and I did together.

Faith could never get past her remorse, shame, and guilt. At least once per year she would break down and say to me, "Please, please, please promise me you'll never tell anyone what I did. I don't think I can take it." And I would promise, even as I felt my own guilt at continuing to dupe her.

Even as adults Faith would tell me she felt she owed me bigtime for keeping her secret safe. After all, she couldn't be the famous Faith Richards if people knew how she neglected her little sister, causing her death, right?

So when I started to run into money problems I leaned on Faith for a little here and there. She was on TV; she had to be making better money than me, even in the smaller markets. And she always helped out. I tried to stand on my own two feet, I really did, but I just couldn't find a job or a boss I respected, and I drifted around a lot.

I was trying to figure out my next move, feeling poor and down in the dumps, when Faith called. It was Charity's birthday. Faith cried on the phone and said she was close to a nervous breakdown at work and in her personal life. She had a stalker following her, she was snapping at people for no reason, she didn't get along with her coworkers, she had no boyfriend and no life other than going to work and coming home, she was tired of being on TV and being recognized, she couldn't stop thinking about Charity. The list went on and on. I told her about my crappy life and how I really could use a break and a fresh start. She said she felt the same.

Then a week later she told me about her conversation with Tom, the idea he gave her. She was unsure, but I wasn't. This was the escape we both needed—no, deserved actually after so many problems in our lives. She hesitated. I couldn't stand it any longer so I had to push the envelope. I told her if she didn't do this I would tell everyone the truth about her not looking after Charity. I knew if I did she would confess; I could see how tormented she had been, she told me she journaled about it constantly and thought about it all the time.

My ultimatum was mean, one final twist of the knife that had already resided in her heart for decades, but she had to be pushed. We both needed this change in the worst possible way and Tom's idea was brilliant.

CHAPTER THIRTY-FOUR

Faith

July 1

Her calves hurt and she had trouble catching her breath but a run had never felt so good. The weather was pristine. If she had been doing a television forecast, she would have worn her "Perfect 10" earrings that had a "1" on the right ear and a "0" on the left. Viewers knew that meant it couldn't get any better.

Faith had really pushed herself, earbuds in, pumping hard rap music to give her a beat to run to. She was wearing a short wig and a baseball cap, plus her sunglasses, of course, to hide her eyes. It had been one month since she was found "dead," strangled in her car near the TV station. Although no one in Door County, Wisconsin, would likely recognize her, she still had to be very, very careful.

Faith had worn a wig on air ever since coming back to Detroit because her natural hair had been thinning so much. Her eyes were always too pale a blue, she thought, so the colored contacts really helped her eye color to pop on the air. Now the contacts were gone, her eyes reverting from a striking blue to the boring light cornflower she was born with.

A huge collection of wigs had awaited her in the Airbnb when she arrived, left there by Hope. Wearing a wig for disguise instead of to impress viewers was a strange concept, but she liked the comfort of one on her head. With that, her thick glasses on, plus a dowdy way of dressing, she was fairly certain she would just blend in. Not to mention that hardly any tourists in Door County came up this far along the Wisconsin peninsula compared to the other vacation towns of Fish Creek, Ephraim, and Sister Bay, which were always teeming with people from Milwaukee and Chicago.

It was why she and Hope picked this out-of-the-way dot on the map as their starting spot after the disappearance. Hope did the research and found the long-term rental on the far tip of the county: Gills Rock, unincorporated. Everyone there kept to themselves. Hope said there were a lot of artists and writers, and so many people lived a quiet, indoor life. The owners of the house Faith and Hope rented were an older couple who proudly told Hope they didn't even own a TV in their own house but provided one in the rental. It felt like extra insurance to the women that the couple would not recognize Faith, even though they only got signals from TV stations in Green Bay and, on a clear day, Michigan's Upper Peninsula. Certainly not from Detroit.

Gills Rock had a single restaurant, the Shoreview, and it was open only on Thursday, Friday, and Saturday evenings due to staffing shortages. The rest of the tiny hamlet consisted of a maritime museum also with limited hours, three small gift shops for the few tourists or locals who took the ferry across to Washington Island, a playground that always seemed deserted, a smoked-fish store, and one motel that perennially had the VACANCY sign out, although the *Y* had been rubbed almost invisible for years. Nature was everywhere. There were so many deer in the wooded areas peeking around trees Faith would sometimes distract herself by counting them. The wind in the tree provided the only soundtrack most days. Raccoons, squirrels, and chipmunks abounded.

Hope did their grocery shopping ten minutes down the road at a tiny country place called the Frontier Store in Ellison Bay that closed every night by six PM so the owners could retire to their apartment above the store. Faith joined Hope there once, as a litmus test to be sure she wasn't recognized. Faith kept her eyes low and the brim of her cap pulled down and she never spoke. Still, she was weak with worry the whole time. The few townies getting their milk, eggs, and meat only nodded at the sisters in that friendly Midwestern way, and when Hope and Faith walked out the heavy front door with the bell jangling on top and made their way back to their car, Faith had collapsed into the front seat with relief.

The sisters hoped to do something way more adventurous than Gills Rock at some point, but this was home base until they figured out their next move. The rental house was set well back from the road and hidden by a huge grove of mature oak trees. The living room and upstairs master bedroom overlooked a bay and they marveled at mesmerizing sunsets that came with facing west. In the backyard a fire pit was set up along with a hammock, a picnic table, and several lounge and camping chairs.

Hope used part of the money she got from selling Kelly's jewelry to pay for the rental. Soon the life insurance would be rolling in—thanks to Faith naming Hope as beneficiary—and they would really be set. A few months and they might be ready to head somewhere else. They didn't have a fake passport for Faith and were too scared to try and procure one, so they limited their options to the United States.

At night the duo sat in the backyard with a crackling fire in the fire pit and a bottle of wine on the table between them, and they looked at a map. Maine? The Oregon coast? Myrtle Beach? Arizona? There were so many options. They would have to drive, but that was OK.

Discussions went well into the night about how to use the money to allow them both to live their best lives for decades. Hope would be the front man now and Faith the quiet sidekick, so different from how they grew up, but when you've faked your own death, you have to retreat and morph into someone new. It was worth it to Faith.

Faith knew she could never use her credit cards, ID, anything. But with Hope by her side, she felt she could manage just fine. They planned to get Faith a fake identity—Lord knew there were plenty of ways to do so on the dark web. Hope would also provide Faith with prepaid credit cards.

It was exactly what Faith had been dreaming about for years. The chance to escape her life as a TV star, but with dignity and the love of the community rather than shame if she just quit. It had been a treat to watch the vigil through the nanny-cam teddy bear Hope brought along, pretending it was her emotional-support animal. They named it Mr. Bojangles after a favorite cat they had as children. So many people showed up to honor Faith at the memorial, and hearing the tributes from her ex-colleagues had actually made her tear up. After all, doesn't everyone want to attend their own funeral?

The medical examiner had asked Faith how she wanted to die—he could fake anything on the report—and she had hesitated for only a moment before whispering, "Strangulation."

He had no idea how personal the idea of strangulation was

to Faith. It seemed the only fitting way for her to die in light of what she had done to Charity.

"Ugly way to go but it also makes sense if someone got you in your car," the ME said flippantly.

Hope suggested Faith also tell the ME to fake that Faith was pregnant. It would make her all the more the fallen hero in everyone's eyes. So they did so, but after they learned that Channel 9 had unexpectedly held back the pregnancy part, Hope had to call Perry and say that as Faith's next of kin she wanted the information out. That pushed Perry to release it.

Yes, it had been expensive to pay the medical examiner for this whole ruse—$100,000, plus another $50,000 split between two police officers to write a false report that they had come upon the scene. They promised to pay off any ambulance drivers needed to complete the fictitious tale. But they were the only ones who knew. Except for Tom, of course. And that was another $50,000.

Faith remembered the night she told Tom she couldn't take it anymore: the fans who recognized her everywhere she went, the pressure of being perfect on TV; the stalker, Steve, who not only sent letters but had started following her home and beeping his horn when she turned in to the parking garage. He was even showing up at events now.

Then there were the coworkers who hated her, thinking she faked calling in sick all the time when the truth was she needed a lot of mental health days and was scared to admit it. She had a doctor's note that only Perry and HR knew about for the FMLA accommodation.

Faith couldn't stomach parades, because the anxiety of such large crowds of people all staring at her nearly crippled her. In her mind someone in the crowd would know the truth about

Charity and would be glaring at her. It was ridiculous, of course, but she couldn't get it out of her head.

Perfect Faith Richards should not require mental health help. Perfect Faith Richards should not be so tense at in-person events that she could barely function at times, saying "Thanks for watching Channel 9" to everyone as she counted the moments until she could leave. Perfect Faith Richards was confident, filled with grace and poise. But the real Faith Richards was a mess, and Faith Richards knew it. She often had pounding headaches, even as she smiled on air.

Sure the money was great, but she started to feel so stressed coming to work that her hand would shake as she reached for her key card to let herself into the newsroom. Having such a huge following on social media was what she thought she wanted, but when she got it, the reality was crushing. The station pushed her for more and more. More appearances in front of the public, more videos, more earring ideas. She had become a brand instead of herself. And she couldn't think of an escape valve that would keep her reputation intact, give her even more money, and allow her to find her true self again away from TV.

She didn't like anything at that point: not her job, her co-workers, or really any aspect of her life. Matthew hated her and had played multiple tricks, starting with the missing lipstick. Faith knew that from that same nanny-cam teddy bear Hope had taken to the vigil. Back when Faith first bought it she put it on her desk, suspecting that Matthew might be up to no good. When the lipstick disappeared she rewound the video the nanny cam recorded and saw Matthew going into her makeup bag and pulling out her favorite red lipstick, hiding it among her shoeboxes. She wasn't shocked. She had a feeling he would pull some crap like that at some point. She had watched and heard him through the nanny cam for years, as he talked to Tara, his fiancée, on the phone in the weather office when he was alone. She had winced at the names he called Faith and the many ways he made fun of her.

When she saw him take the lipstick, she decided not to say anything. Let him think he got away with it. Although she hated the pink shade she had to wear on air that night, it also was a "win" for him. Ha. She knew she'd have the last laugh, stealing his precious signed baseball and throwing it in the dumpster behind her apartment building. It might have been worth something, she didn't know, but there was an incredible satisfaction to seeing it in the garbage. She took his water bottle too. At first just to piss him off, but then she realized it could come in handy if she ever wanted to frame him for anything. His DNA was on it.

Next, the nanny-cam teddy bear showed him swiping publicity photos of her and going into the Psychos and Crazies drawer, taking letters from a stalker out. At first it wasn't clear to Faith what he was doing, but when some weirdo named Steve came up to her at a festival and said he was her boyfriend and that they traded photos, she began to theorize. She noticed the same guy in her rearview mirror following her home and honking, and showing up randomly at obscure events they hadn't even advertised on TV. Only the meteorologists would have access to that full calendar of events, not the public. So Matthew had to be behind it. She knew it couldn't be Abby or Chuck.

It was Tom who came up with the idea to bribe the medical examiner. Tom had listened quietly to her concerns about being on television and the pressure that came with it from all sides. He nodded and said sympathetic things and gave her a hug, but it wasn't until that weekend that he asked her to take a drive out to the country with him. He had an idea, he said, but it required complete privacy and discretion. Given how famous they both were, they needed to be away from any prying eyes or ears.

On a quiet dead-end country road, Tom parked and turned to look at Faith.

"Hear me out," he said. "I'm friends with the medical examiner and I know he's going through a very messy divorce right now and could use some extra money. I also know quite a few police officers who would jump at the chance to get cash. If you truly want to disappear, and I mean truly, as in forever, I have a way for you to do so . . ."

He laid out his plan. It all seemed so complex and yet so simple. They would pick a night where Faith would act totally normal all day but then go on her dinner break and not return. Everyone in the world would believe the medical examiner when he said she was strangled. The medical examiner was the coroner, the official arbiter for any death. The medical examiner would have to inspect the body and write a report. He could claim he released the body to family—Hope—right away and Hope could claim she had it cremated.

"Oh my, this is . . . extreme," Faith had said as a mix of excitement and trepidation started to fill her. But as she pondered it over the coming weeks it seemed to make more and more sense. Tom laid out the price for her freedom: what the ME would want, the police officers, and himself for coordinating.

It was a lot of money but Hope was already the life insurance beneficiary for Faith. Faith had taken out a large policy many years ago in case some crazy stalker ever got her. So they knew money would come flowing back pretty quickly and no one would suspect Faith in the way they might have if she had just taken out the policy recently.

Hope was always up for anything that helped her pay the

bills. She had drifted around to various jobs but always got mad at her boss and wound up quitting and asking Faith for money. So when Faith hesitantly approached Hope with the idea, Hope was giddy.

"Let the insurance company pay for our retirements!" She squealed and she came up with even more plans, from the Airbnb in Wisconsin to bringing the teddy bear to the funeral and any meetings of the FWFFC, to the idea that Faith could take a big jab at some of her enemies on her way out.

"What if you wrote a note with a list of names on it? Something cryptic the police are sure to look into. One final F-you on your way out the door, a mic drop, so to speak. Give the note to Tom to give to the police. That will cement your and his innocence even more too."

So they picked a date: a Friday night. Faith thought she would feel nostalgic as she did her final forecast ever with her sun earrings on, but instead she was almost giddy.

Before leaving on break she straightened up her desk a bit, wrote the note with names that included that weirdo Steve, Matthew the asshole and his fiancée, Laura for being a bitch to her, and Kelly her college roommate, plus their significant others. She felt bad about the Kelly one. After all, Faith and Hope had already colluded to steal Kelly's jewelry, Faith getting the intel at lunch, and Hope casing the house trying to figure out what excuse she would have to get inside. When she saw the electrician's truck and spied the electrician himself through an upstairs window, the idea of the assistant came to Hope and she showed up at their house less than a week later wearing a curly wig and glasses.

They needed the money from pawning it all to help pay off the people involved and to reserve the Airbnb. In Faith's eyes,

Kelly had not truly been a good friend to Faith, so Faith didn't feel that bad about the jewels. In college Faith always had the sense that Kelly thought Faith was overdramatic. Faith took a few things—true, yes, some credit cards—but she took nothing of consequence from Kelly, and she expected Kelly to stand up and defend her against the charges others were bringing against Faith at the dorm. Kelly didn't do that. Instead, Kelly watched Faith pack her things and said nothing when she was suspended. Years later, Faith thought Kelly would help her when she needed money for more overshopping, and while Kelly did loan her the money, she also went to Faith's mom and squealed, which caused a mess between Faith and her mom. It never got better between the two of them and when Faith's mom died, Faith was despondent to realize she would never be able to make amends, all thanks to Kelly. The cause of death for Faith and Hope's mom was listed as heart disease but the sisters truly believed it was the culmination of years of a broken heart over Charity. Their dad passed a few years later of cancer.

Hope had been worried about a lack of money to get to the incoming life insurance, and Faith had an idea. She decided to ask Kelly to lunch and try to see if Kelly still had her mom's and grandma's rare jewelry. Plus, Faith wanted to pump Kelly for innocent details to see if there was a time or a way to break into Kelly's house. Hope suggested Faith bring Kelly a jewelry box as a sign of goodwill, but really as an opening into asking about her jewelry. Hope and Faith found one on Etsy, and Hope had liked the earrings this kid named Emilio made so much she bought a pair of those too.

Faith and Kelly's lunch went better than Faith could ever have imagined. Not only did Kelly divulge that yes, she had the jewelry, but she also said that her boyfriend worked at home and that she had a new job at a high school. Faith even got Kelly to tell her the days and general times her boyfriend was on conference calls, and Faith and Hope planned Hope's arrival as the electrician's assistant as perfectly as they could, so that the boyfriend would let her in but then be distracted by his call.

The night of her disappearance, Faith wrote the note with names on it and folded it up into a tiny square. She looked for an envelope but couldn't find one in the weather office and didn't want to risk asking anyone in the newsroom. So she decided she'd give it to an intern to give to Tom. No intern was going to open the note.

Grabbing a few favorite curling irons, her makeup mirror, and the nanny-cam teddy bear, she was going to put them all in her car and go back inside to try to find an intern when one happened to be right there in the parking lot. It was the girl who had asked Faith to autograph a photo for her aunt. Faith recalled the aunt's name for some reason but couldn't remember the intern's, so she asked her and then asked her to take the note to Tom.

The note was preplanned by Faith and Tom. It meant that the operation was a go, and it was a way for Faith to send suspects down the river with police. At the very least they'd be questioned and made to feel uncomfortable. Tom hadn't known who would be on the list, only that one was coming.

Faith got into her car and started to steer away from Channel 9 for the final time. At the main road she saw that nutjob, Steve, again in his car, leering at her. Of course he turned to follow her, as he always did. Could she have called the police on Steve and asked for a restraining order? She probably could have if she was choosing to stay in her old life, but she was shedding it like lizard skin.

She peeled away from Steve going so fast he couldn't keep

up and turning at a place she normally didn't to get away from him. Then she changed her wig quickly and drove to the designated meetup spot with Hope to switch cars and pick up her burner phone, along with cash for gas and food. She handed Hope the nanny-cam teddy bear and Matthew's water bottle and took off, all the way to Door County, Wisconsin. Faith had none of her clothes from the apartment, not even her toothbrush. Everything had to seem normal to investigators. Hope took Faith's car to the secluded spot where she was allegedly strangled so the car would be towed and inspected as part of the investigation, and then Tom picked her up and dropped her at her apartment. He was back with plenty of time for the eleven o'clock news.

Around Gary, Indiana, Faith called Hope on the burner phone to compare more notes. She told her about meeting the intern in the parking lot and handing the intern the note. Hope said it was all good except for one thing: not having an envelope.

"Incredibly stupid, Faith," Hope said. "Who was this intern? What if she looked at the note?"

"No intern is going to disobey the orders of talent," Faith reassured Hope. "No way in hell. She's just a baby-faced college kid. Don't worry. Plus, she wouldn't have a clue what it meant even if she did."

"I am worried, that was reckless of you," said Hope. "We have to think ten steps ahead for the rest of our lives. I think we'll need to keep tabs on this intern. What's her name?"

"Uh . . . Olivia, I think."

"Uh . . . Olivia, I think? That's your answer? You have to pay attention to damn details, Faith. This is *your* disappearance and I'm wrapped up in it too, so is Tom, so are two policemen, possibly an ambulance driver, and the medical examiner. Don't play games and don't be foolish. What the hell else do we know about this intern who you just handed a very weird piece of paper?"

"Wait, I remember," said Faith, not liking the feeling of being admonished by her older sister as she had been so many times as a child. "Yes, it was definitely Olivia and she told me she had an aunt who is a major fan of mine and is in the Fair-Weather Friends Fan Club. Carol Henning was the aunt's name. I remember because Olivia had me autograph a picture for her and Carol's husband, Jim. I also remember that Olivia said she tells her aunt everything and that they're super close."

"Well, now we're getting somewhere," said Hope. "I'm going to google Carol Henning, Detroit, and see if I can find any pictures of her, like maybe from wherever she works or something. Then I'll go to the vigil they are sure to plan in your honor and look for this woman. If she's there I'll cozy up to her and try to get some info. I can tell when people are lying so I should be good at this. You'll see it all through the teddy bear camera. Sound good?"

"Sounds good."

"You have to be way more careful, Faith. We have everything on the line here."

"I know . . ."

Faith hung up but felt angry. No intern was going to look at a note, it just wasn't going to happen. Even if the intern did, what was the worst that could come of it? It was all good.

And it seemed to be. Faith drove all night, arriving just as the sun was starting to rise in Gills Rock. She checked to see if there was anything official out in the world about her, but other than a "Where's Faith?" Reddit and some speculation on X there was nothing. She fell into bed and slept more deeply than she had in months. When she woke, news of her "death" was just getting out. Smiling as she made a simple breakfast with ingredients Hope had stocked up the previous week, she took a mug of coffee outside and sat overlooking the bay, thinking, *It's done, it's all done now. I am a free woman.* Hope was going to plan the fake funeral for family and say that she had Faith's body cremated immediately.

It was all going perfectly.

For two days.

But then Tom began to gum up the plans.

It started that Monday night after the disappearance. Faith's burner phone rang as she came out of the shower. She had left it on the side of the sink. She jumped, thinking it was Hope. But the number was Tom's.

"Hey, everything OK?" she asked, grabbing for a towel as she juggled the phone against one ear.

"Yes. Are things good for you in Gills Rock?"

"It's like heaven here, the most beautiful little house in the woods on a cliff that overlooks the water. A big backyard, a fire pit. It's amazing."

"Sounds like paradise. How's it going for Hope? She's still here in Detroit, right, keeping an eye on things?"

"Yes, all good for Hope. She's headed to a Fair-Weather Friends Fan Club meeting tonight. She'll take a teddy bear with a camera in it so I can see what's going on if I want to, and she'll keep using her fake name of Heather and changing her voice and posture so no one can ever put two and two together. She connected with the aunt of this intern who handed you a piece of paper. Are you absolutely sure the intern didn't seem like she read it?"

"No way, she was just a kid delivering something. Nothing to worry about there."

"Thank God. So what else do I need to know? I saw the pregnancy push alert earlier."

"Yeah, that's blowing up, great idea as sympathy is absolutely pouring in. Listen, Faith, I do have something important to talk to you about, though."

"What is it?"

"Honestly . . . this is awkward . . . so I'll just come out and say it. This whole thing is a lot more than I bargained for."

His voice had shifted, taking on a stronger and darker tone. Her throat tightened up.

"I wanted to help you, as a friend and a colleague. I really did, Faith. And I did my part. I did everything but, quite frankly, the stress of this has been overwhelming. More so than I envisioned. I actually had to take a sick day today."

"I'm sorry to hear that," she said. "Is there anything else?" Not that she didn't care that he was stressed out, but she had paid him a lot of money, and there was no way he was more stressed than her. She wanted to be sure there was nothing else he needed to talk about, nothing that more directly impacted her.

"Everything is going all right with the whole ruse, but I lost my entire weekend between interviews about you and the vigil. I'm not sleeping, I'm worried. It's all been *a lot*. I'm calling because I think I deserve another fifty thousand . . . for my troubles. I went in too low. The ME got a hundred thousand and I think I should too. I am asking you and Hope to wire me more money."

Faith's hands turned so cold she wondered if a person could get frostbite indoors in the summer.

"Are you kidding me? You're kidding, right?"

"I think you know me well enough to know that I'm not

the type of person to joke about something like this. I'm dead serious."

Faith was stunned into silence. Her friend was trying to milk her for more money. She opened her mouth to form words but nothing came out.

"Faith? Are you still there?"

She had to clear her throat. Her fingers remained ice.

"I'm here."

"I trust Hope will take care of it by tomorrow? Since she's still in Detroit it should be an easy wire transfer. You have my account number. I would like it by noon."

Anger started to bubble up from every corner of Faith's belly. Who the *hell* did Tom think he was?

"This is insane, Tom. We agreed on a price. Hope and I can't just give you fifty thousand more. Money is tight. We have to live within our means. I know it's stressful but you are one hundred percent in the clear. I'm not giving you more money and there's no debating."

Silence. Faith could feel the anger coming from his end too.

"Faith, you realize I'm in the driver's seat here, right? I am one of only four people outside of Hope who know you're alive. What if I went to the police?"

Faith thought of all of the things she had told Tom during this conversation alone: the fake name Hope had used, the nanny-cam teddy bear, Hope's attendance at the FWFFC meeting at the coffee shop that night. What if he'd recorded it?

"Are you *blackmailing* me? You would be implicated too. Lose your job, your reputation, the ME's job and reputation ruined, the police officers, are you insane? You can't be doing this. You were in on it as much as me."

"I hold all of the cards, Faith. I don't have to implicate myself or anyone else but I could make your life very miserable."

"Oh yeah, how?"

"For starters, watch me play around with your pregnancy rumor. The station pushed it out today and you're getting mountains of goodwill. I know the assistant ME very well too. I might just put in a call and slide her a little cash to cast some doubt on the report. Just enough to get everyone rattled."

Tears came into Faith's eyes. She was so tired of people doing this sort of thing to her. Taking advantage of her, pushing her in ways she didn't want to be pushed. Tom, who had suggested this whole thing. Tom, who had been a friend, or so she thought. It went back to her dad pushing her around, punishing her with clothes.

"No," she whispered, a sob threatening her throat. At least her fingers were regaining some normal warmth. "Just stop this, Tom."

"Fifty K by tomorrow at noon, Faith. That's all I'm asking. I know you both have plenty of money now from that jewelry heist and a lot more coming from insurance. Tell Hope."

He hung up on her. Faith let herself cry for several minutes, and then she screamed until she had nothing left. Curling into a ball on the bed, she felt sorry for herself for a while, lost in pity, but then started thinking.

Hope would go ballistic. Money was everything to her, and they didn't have 50K just lying around. Yet their lives would be ruined if Tom ever went to the police with the real story.

Slowly a solution started to form. It was not a perfect plan, but it was as close as she could get. Glancing at the clock, she realized that Hope would be in the middle of the FWFFC event. Faith turned on her nanny-cam app and peeked at the meeting through the teddy bear's stomach camera, but it seemed rather boring, as they were all just talking about where to give donations in honor of the baby.

She had to text Hope right then what was happening and the plan she came up with. Tom wanted his money by noon Tuesday, but she was fairly confident she could hold him off at least a day and put the wheels in motion.

Sending the text to Hope, she watched through the nanny cam. The camera went sideways and upside down, and then showed nothing but black. Faith knew Hope had likely thrown the bear into her purse and rushed out. She waited for her sister to call, and Hope did about forty-five seconds later.

"I just got to the car," Hope said, panting. "That jerk-off Tom is asking us for more money? Are you frickin' serious?"

"Yes, but don't worry. I have a plan. It took me all afternoon but I came up with something that gets us even more in the clear."

"Do tell, Sis, do tell."

As Faith laid it out, Hope muttered "Aha" and "Yes" and "Wow." Then she said, "I'm on it. I'll tell Tom we're good to go with the money but I'll say to meet in person at a private place for the handoff. Then I'll bring three water bottles: Matthew's and two other Channel 9 ones you've given me over the years. I'll put champagne in all of them and keep Matthew's in my purse. I'll tell Tom we're going to toast our good fortune—we're both rich, after all. His will have cyanide in it. A pharmacist friend once told me how to order it on the web. It can be shipped as fast as any Amazon product. I can get it overnight. I'll drink from my bottle. Tom will die shortly after drinking from his. I'll put Matthew's bottle in the console. Earlier I will have texted Matthew to meet me at this remote parking spot at 12:15. Then right after Tom keels over I'll call the police anonymously on a burner phone and tip them off to a man dying in his car by the lagoon. Then I'll take off. Police and paramedics should arrive just after Matthew. It will look very, very bad for him. Matthew should be up the river without a paddle. Oh, by the way, I tried to sniff around with good ol' Aunt Carol again tonight at the meeting. I lied to her and told her I heard a rumor that Chloe said you gave an intern some piece of paper. I'm just trying to break her down for some info. She hasn't given up the goods yet but it sounds like we won't need it now anyway. Tom won't be squealing anything to anyone soon. That asshole doesn't know who he's messing with."

CHAPTER THIRTY-FIVE

Faith and Hope

December
Las Vegas

Channel 9's ratings plummeted soon after Tom's death was announced. Of the four original anchors, only Roger the sports guy was left. Veronica took a leave of absence due to stress and just two weeks later told the station she was retiring.

Abby was given the main meteorologist job, but she was no Faith. Abby tried delivering the earring forecast but it fell flat, and the station got so many complaints from people who thought they wanted someone to take on Faith's gimmick but realized they didn't that Abby stopped doing it. The daily videos Faith had been known for never revived under Abby either, and the special spot on the website with the password went away. So did the Fair-Weather Friends Fan Club Facebook page, retired by Chloe.

The vigil for Tom was less well attended than Faith's, mostly because people were so in shock at two anchor deaths and because everyone was glued to what would happen with Matthew after his arrest. The station had to report on the trial of its own meteorologist.

Matthew was convicted in Tom's murder due to DNA on the cup. As for Faith's death, video from a pen camera in the weather office showed Matthew essentially confessing to it and he was found to have googled poison and "how to kill a coworker and get away with it." But the rest of the evidence just wasn't there, and his lawyers argued vehemently that you couldn't convict on circumstantial evidence.

A lot of people still thought he was guilty. They theorized he was so jealous of Faith he couldn't take it and had strangled her between dinner with Tara and coming in to the station to do the eleven PM weathercast. Even Sergio, the waiter, testified that the couple left the restaurant with plenty of time for Matthew to perhaps meet Faith near the station and for Matthew to then kill her. It didn't matter in the end. He already had life in prison for killing Tom.

Tara confessed to falsely representing herself as someone else with the emails and pictures she sent Steve, and she got probation, but was fired from her job.

Channel 9 constructed two small memorials outside of its front door with two plaques, one with Faith's face and one with Tom's. For months viewers would drop off cards and flowers, but after some time that pretty much stopped. Even the most loyal Channel 9 viewers, like Carol, began to move rapidly to other stations. Carol found a new meteorologist she liked, a young woman who made graphics with fun things like the "honey-do-list forecast" for wives to decide if their husbands would accomplish chores indoors or outside that day. This wasn't Faith and the earring-cast but it was still a little something to make Carol smile.

Olivia finished out her internship that summer. The newsroom was in complete shock and disarray and frankly, Olivia couldn't wait to be done. No one ever knew that it was Olivia who had turned over the pen-camera video to the police. When she, Carol, and Jim had heard and seen what Matthew said on the phone in the office that night, they raced to download the footage onto a thumb drive and dropped it in the mail for District 3 with a short typed note explaining what it was and also talking of the signature discrepancies on the autographed photos from Faith to Steve, just in case that was helpful to the investigation.

Police later found the pen in the cup of pens on Faith's desk; they had no idea who had placed it there. In the end, Olivia and Carol decided not to try and be the public heroes. Jim convinced them it was better to do this anonymously. Help investigators but stay low-profile, he counseled. It would be better for Olivia's career and it would also help keep both of the women he loved safe. They would simply live with the quiet satisfaction that they got justice for Faith.

Perry took a job as a news director in Chicago, happy to escape Detroit and all of the turmoil there. Laura was contemplating looking for a PR job with better hours and more pay. That way she could also be home with Quinn at night. She and Elliott remained together, but she had a gut feeling it might not be for the long haul.

Kelly and Joel were able to reconcile, and after couples counseling and rebuilding trust, Kelly felt a true proposal might be forthcoming, maybe even for New Year's Eve.

Steve found a new love: a female sportscaster on a different station. He started emailing, writing, and leaving messages for her. He showed up to every event he knew she would be at. He was still waiting for her to reciprocate, but he knew it was coming. They were in love. He felt it when he shook her hand at a public appearance. He had plans to follow her home from the station and see where she lived.

Faith watched Channel 9's downfall from afar and laughed. It had all worked out so perfectly. Matthew convicted of her and Hope's crimes. Her other enemies sucked into the vortex.

She cackled in delight as she walked the streets of Vegas as her new self, free from obligations and pressures. Her headaches were gone, and there was more money in Hope's bank account than they knew what to do with. They spent most of it on clothes, scouring the boutiques embedded in nearly every casino and along the Strip and feeling revenge on their father every time they bought something fun and cool.

Faith had a new name and ID off the dark web. After contemplating every city and state in the US, Faith and Hope decided that there was no better place than Sin City to blend in. Faith could change wigs and looks as often as she wanted and no one would care. She had plans to use some of the massive insurance money to get work done on her face from a high-end "plastic surgeon to the stars" place so that she really would look different. And she put on a bit of weight, not feeling the stress of being tiny on TV anymore. Between those changes and the wigs, she was sure no one would recognize her.

One of Faith's favorite things to do at night was to sit off to the side by the Bellagio hotel watching their famous fountains and thinking of all that transpired. It was ironic, she mused, that Steve's psychosis, Matthew's anger, Laura's turning against her, and Kelly's naivete had all played a part in getting Faith to this point. In their own ways they had either driven her to fake her own death or helped her to complete the fictitious story to take the money and run.

Now she didn't have to work at all. Hope bought a condo near the Strip and they had fun all day, every day, lying by the pool reading fashion magazines in the afternoon and going to shows at night. Plus, shopping, of course. Lots and lots of shopping.

The old password to the website to get to her videos, "Cloud 9," came to mind. Viewers had thought they were on cloud nine back then, and the TV station had too. All because of her driving up ratings. Now Faith was truly living on cloud nine, and she was loving every single second of it.

One warm night Hope came over to join Faith at the fountains, two margaritas from a nearby stand in Hope's hands. One was lime green and the other neon orange. The sisters sat shoulder to shoulder. Hope was going to meet up with a guy she found on a dating app, but Faith wasn't ready for that scene yet and was headed home soon. She didn't want to push dating until she had plastic surgery. Her wig, natural eye color, and different clothing style were enough to keep her anonymous in a crowd, but she couldn't change her voice and didn't want to be overheard talking in a restaurant or bar.

That night she wasn't wearing her glasses for the first time. She had accidentally sat on them at the condo and they were bent awkwardly. She would have to get them fixed. She had in regular contacts but she wasn't worried. In all of these months no one had so much as given her a second glance in Vegas.

"How are you feeling tonight?" Hope asked, taking a long, slow slurp of her margarita.

Faith looked around at the ever-moving tide of humanity, the street musicians playing a variety of tunes, Jimmy Buffett music pumping from a speaker at the margarita stand, women in bikinis with giant peacock feathers on their backs drawing every glance, Chippendales men in tight white pants and matching white vests flirting and taking pictures with tourists. She smiled.

"I'm good. Really, really good," she said. "How are you, sis?"

"The best," replied Hope. And she was. She felt as happy as she'd ever been, all of those low-level jobs of her life behind her. She never had to work again.

"You don't miss being on TV at all?" Hope went on, taking another sip.

"Nope. Thought I might but I don't. I'm as free as a bird."

"And you're still OK with being the one to come up with the idea for Tom's death? And Matthew rotting in jail for it despite being innocent?"

"I had to do it," Faith replied, looking at the fountains as they went through their nightly dance with music and colored lights. There was a strong smell of marijuana mixed with cologne in the air. "What choice did I have? When someone wrongs you, you have every right to retaliate. That's how the world works. An eye for an eye. I couldn't just sit by like a patsy. For once I wasn't the puppet but the puppet master and it felt so good to be in charge."

Hope held her drink up for a toast.

"Amen to that, sister."

"Amen to that," Faith repeated, and the women clinked glasses. They both took a long drink and dissolved into giggles.

CHAPTER THIRTY-SIX

Carol, Jim, and Olivia

December
Las Vegas

The trio had just left a Barry Manilow concert and stepped out into the warmth of the night when Carol spotted the margarita stand. Two workers in costumes, one dressed as a strawberry and one as a salt shaker, were dancing to Jimmy Buffett music and waving people over. The queue was long, but there were three cashiers wearing straw sombreros and the line was actually moving pretty fast.

"I'm parched. What do you two think about grabbing some margaritas and sitting by the Bellagio to watch the fountains before we go back to our hotel?" Carol asked.

"Sure, that sounds great," Olivia replied, and Jim nodded. He was happy to see his wife and niece so happy. This trip had been a surprise birthday gift for Carol, something to get all of their minds off Faith and all that happened. It was not the kind of adventure Jim and Carol usually went on. Neither had ever been to Vegas, but he knew Carol would cherish the opportunity to see Barry Manilow one time in her life, so he'd gone ahead and purchased the tickets, plus hotel rooms for four nights and the flight, without her knowing. Olivia was in on the secret and thrilled to come along. It was winter break of her senior year. They were all having a blast.

At the margarita stand each customer got to choose the color of their drinks, and Jim and Carol both went with electric blue, while Olivia chose cherry red. The Bellagio fountains were minutes from starting, and people were crowding all along the low stone fencing, three or four deep in some cases.

"Can we find a spot to actually sit?" Carol asked. Her left hip was hurting. Jim glanced around.

"Over there to the side." He pointed. "There's a bench with two women on it but there's room for more. Maybe they'll let us in."

They started walking that way. The women at the bench were also holding margaritas, clinking glasses and laughing. Carol noted that one of their drinks was lime green and the other bright orange. That stand sure knew how to use food coloring, that was for certain, Carol thought. She decided she might make a comment about it to the women when they sat down on the bench, solidarity with strangers over giant, ridiculous margaritas.

They'd gotten about fifteen feet from the bench when both women turned their heads to gaze at the crowd. Carol froze, grabbing Jim's arm.

"Oh my God, look natural but take a hard right and keep walking," she said in a fierce whisper.

"What's going on?" he whispered back. Olivia leaned her head over to hear too.

"Tell you in a minute, just get away," Carol said, and they did as she had instructed, moving quickly from the bench and the women, falling back into the river of humans.

"That woman back there," said Carol when they had reached a

safe distance. "That was Heather, from the Fair-Weather Friends Fan Club. The one who brought Mr. Bojangles. Remember I told you about that strange lady with the emotional-support teddy bear?"

"Oh yeah," Jim said. "That was her?" He twisted his head to look back, but there were simply too many people to see the women on the bench anymore. "I thought the other woman looked kind of familiar," he said. "But I couldn't place her."

Olivia was thinking the same thing.

"I definitely do *not* want to run into Heather," Carol said with a laugh. "There was a screw loose with that lady. I really didn't like the way she glommed on to me. I can't believe she's in Vegas. What is she doing here?"

"Whatever it is, it looks like she found a new target," Jim mused. "She and that other woman were pretty giggly. Don't worry, you'll never have to see her again. Let's try to find a different place to sit. The fountains are supposed to start soon."

"I should go back and warn that woman to stay away from Heather!" Carol said, laughing.

They walked on, sipping their drinks and absorbing the sensory overload around them. A street magician was juggling fire off to the left while a breakdancer was twirling on a piece of cardboard to their right. Vendors with pushcarts of souvenirs yelled out, and people, people were everywhere, all ages and races, choking the sidewalk and making it difficult to maneuver at times.

Despite her hip flaring, Carol felt herself smile. This trip had been exactly what she and Jim needed, and she reached for his hand. "This has been fun, Jim. Thank you so much for this surprise."

"You're welcome. I'm glad you're enjoying it. I thought you

might really like the concert tonight. Liv, I know Barry Manilow is not in your wheelhouse so we really appreciate you coming along."

"No problem, Uncle Jim. It was actually not half bad, and hey, I got to see SZA last night on my own too."

"Right, a little too noisy for us," said Jim.

Olivia took a sip of her drink and thought about the women on the bench again. She was picturing the one woman's face. Not Heather but the other woman.

Suddenly, it hit her.

She stopped walking so quickly that a group of women wearing matching pink sashes for a bachelorette party behind them almost knocked into her.

"Hey! Look out!" cried one of the women.

"Liv, you're blocking traffic," Carol admonished.

"I, uh . . . You guys go on to the fountains. I was just thinking I might explore the other side of the Strip. I'll catch up with you at the hotel." Olivia knew she needed time alone to investigate for a moment.

"Are you sure?" Carol asked. "The fountains are about to start."

"Yeah, I'm sure. I'll text you if I need anything."

Olivia gave them a fast hug and took off with her drink still in hand, headed back in the direction of Heather and the other woman on the bench.

"Oh, to be young again and stay up late walking the Strip," Jim mused. "I couldn't do it. My dogs are barking from all of the walking we did earlier. I can't wait to hit the hotel."

"Me too," said Carol. "By the way, do you know what I was thinking about when Barry sang 'Can't Smile Without You'?"

"No, what?"

"I was thinking about Faith. I told you they played that at the vigil, right? Apparently Faith's sister told Channel 9 that Faith loved Barry Manilow. It's just one more reason why I admire and miss Faith so much."

"Faith was a special one," Jim summed up.

Carol sighed deeply and thought of the tribute she had created in their den back home. She asked Jim to make a shadow box in his basement workshop, with a large space for her to pin the autographed photo she got from Faith on one side and a smaller box to hang the cloud earrings on the other. Jim had put a light on the top of the shadow box so the whole thing could be illuminated. The box had a prime spot on their wall, displacing one of the generic impressionist art photos.

Even though Carol watched Channel 11 now, she would look at the mementos often and think about Faith, and she hoped Matthew would rot in prison, her anger at him so strong she could taste it.

"I just hope Faith is at peace," Carol added. "It breaks my heart that she'll never get to be in a place like Vegas. She should be enjoying the same things we are. She was young, she should be having fun. It's just not fair, Jim, it's not fair."

"Who ever said life was fair, hon?" He squeezed her hand again. "But we all do our best. We helped to put Matthew away and to get justice for Faith. She's in heaven now and I bet she knows what we did and thanks us, and Olivia. We did good work, sweetie. You should be proud."

"You too," said Carol as the fountains started shooting upward to the oohs and aahs of the crowd. Elvis Presley's "Viva Las Vegas" was the musical accompaniment. Jim and Carol stopped and turned to watch from the sidewalk. There clearly was no place to sit anymore, so Carol leaned her head into Jim's shoulder, taking a little pressure off her hip.

Tears came to her eyes as she watched the dancing fountains. Tears of happiness for being alive and for being there at that moment with Jim, and tears of sadness for Faith, who would never get to experience anything like this anymore.

I will always be in your Fair-Weather Friends Fan Club, Faith, Carol thought to herself. *Always.*

CHAPTER THIRTY-SEVEN

Olivia

Las Vegas

Beelining back to the area where the bench was, Olivia worried that the women might be gone, but the two of them were just standing up. Staying a safe distance away, Olivia studied their faces.

She didn't recognize Heather as her aunt Carol had done, of course, but she had the strangest feeling about the other woman. The hair was completely different, but . . .

Olivia shuddered. It couldn't be, could it? Faith was dead. Memorialized by an entire community, Matthew convicted of her murder. Faith couldn't be alive and well and walking the streets in Las Vegas. It had to be a coincidence.

The women gave each other a hug and started heading in different directions. Olivia followed the one she was suspicious of. And that's when she saw the way the woman walked. It was exactly what she remembered from Channel 9. That distinctive style: delicate, ballerina-like.

A ripple of pure shock went through Olivia's body. She thought of calling Jim and Carol, but something told her to handle this on her own.

Falling into the crowd, she followed the woman, who seemed to be making her way to a taxi stand on a side street. The crowd was not as thick there, but there were still a half dozen people in line for the cabs. Olivia wondered if she should get into one and follow this woman to wherever her destination was, but the woman walked instead to a Dunkin' Donuts, where she went in.

Staying at a distance but watching the woman through the big windows, Olivia saw her asking the cashier for something, maybe a bathroom. He pointed in one direction.

Olivia dumped her margarita in the garbage, no longer interested in it. She leaned against a tree in a darker spot off to the side, waiting for the woman to come out. Olivia's body was filled with adrenaline and also a sort of determination. She just had to see this person's full face a little closer.

After a few minutes, the woman was thanking the cashier and heading for the front door. Olivia stood taller and waited. This was it.

The woman pushed open the glass door and Olivia stepped forward from the tree to get a clear look. The nose, the chin, all the same as Faith. The eyes were a softer blue and the hair was way shorter and a different color but wow, this was her clone if it wasn't her.

"Excuse me, are you . . . ?" Olivia ventured, stepping toward the woman. "You look like someone I know."

The woman glanced at Olivia and her eyes grew wide and frantic. Her head whipped left and right and Olivia thought the woman might bolt.

"Wait! Don't run away," Olivia said, and lowered her voice.

"I'm Olivia, the Channel 9 intern. You have to be . . . You're Faith, right? Are you Faith?"

The woman opened her mouth to speak but her jaw just hung there and no words came out. She shook her head but still didn't speak. She turned quickly.

"Wait," Olivia said, and grabbed her elbow. "You really look like Faith. Are you sure you're not . . ."

Before she could finish her sentence, Olivia saw tears in the woman's eyes. That's when it was confirmed in Olivia's mind.

"Don't cry," Olivia said. "Please, come sit."

There was a bus shelter a few feet away. It had large advertisements for perfume and jewelry on the side, making the interior private, and no one was sitting there. Olivia gestured that way, but Faith shook her head.

"I'm not going to hurt you," Olivia said gently. "I just noticed you on the Strip and wanted to talk to you."

A single tear traveled down Faith's cheek.

Olivia pointed to the bus shelter again, and Faith followed in a robotic state, sitting stiffly on the hard bench and looking at the ground.

Everything felt surreal to Olivia, and yet she had a strange sense of calm. She knew she had to be the grown-up in this situation, not the eager intern anymore. She took a long breath.

"Faith, the most important question is . . . are you OK?"

Faith lifted her eyes to look at Olivia. For a moment she didn't say or do anything; then she nodded ever so slightly as more tears welled in her eyes.

"Did you . . . ? Did someone kidnap you? What's going on here? I'm so confused. I'm so happy to see you alive but I'm so confused."

Faith shook her head and stayed mute. Olivia sighed. This

was not going to be easy. She went for a different tactic, lowering her voice to a whisper.

"Faith, I told you I won't hurt you and I won't."

"Does anyone else know?" Faith finally said in a hoarse, ragged whisper.

"No," answered Olivia. "Only me. I noticed you on the Strip. Faith, I'm so happy you're alive! I just can't believe it!"

"Are you going to turn me in?" Faith asked warily.

"So you weren't kidnapped?"

There was a beat of silence before Faith answered.

"No."

Olivia thought about it. Was she going to turn Faith in? She could break the case wide open right here, right now. She could stand up and yell for cops, tackling Faith to the ground if she tried to run, screaming for help from the people in line for cabs, handing Faith over to the police triumphantly.

But then Olivia thought of the journal she had read, the life Faith led, the things Olivia and so many others had not known about the public version of Faith. The death of Faith's little sister, how that loss had reminded Olivia of what felt like the death of her own mother, who had now decided to live permanently in Paris.

Suddenly it was clear to Olivia that Faith must have, indeed, faked her own death. How? Olivia was not sure. Did it matter? Faith clearly needed to escape. And Olivia appeared to be the only human on earth who knew it.

"I read your journal, Faith. The one in the weather office. It breaks my heart about your little sister. I'm so, so sorry. That still has to be so hard."

"You read my . . . ?" Faith whispered as she wiped at the tears that were now making their way steadily down her cheeks. "How did you do that?"

"I had a few chances to poke around the weather office."

"Wow . . . you are a crafty one. You know, I almost took that journal with me but I figured all of my personal belongings would just go to Hope anyway and they did. They sent them all in a cardboard box."

There was silence for a few moments before Faith added, "You can't even imagine the pain of losing Charity. Honestly, I think about it every single day."

"Did you fake your death because you needed to escape?" Olivia asked softly. If that was the case, she felt empathy. Olivia had thought once or twice about dropping out of college when the workload became too hard. After her parents got divorced the pain was so raw she fantasized about having a rabbit hole to disappear into. She had even imagined taking her own life once or twice, mostly to envision the number of people at her funeral who would say nice things about her.

Faith was quiet for a moment but then looked directly at Olivia and said, "I haven't told anyone but my sister this. Yes, it was all too much, all of it. I just . . . I just didn't even want to be on TV anymore, can you even believe that?"

"I actually can," said Olivia. "After doing the internship all summer I see what you talent have to go through. Producers never get recognized, in some ways it's a lot easier being behind the scenes."

Faith took a long sniff and spoke again.

"Thank you for understanding that. Most people think talent like me have the best jobs in the world. But . . . you haven't fully answered my question, Olivia. Are you going to turn me in?

Everyone in Detroit thinks I'm . . . you know . . . Please don't turn me in."

Olivia looked at Faith, a shell of her former "Fair-Weather Friend" persona. She seemed like a small and very vulnerable woman. The psychology class Olivia took the semester before the internship came back to her, especially the part about childhood trauma and how that affects us our entire lives. The professor had said, "If you ever have a chance to help someone who has endured true childhood trauma, please do it. You will be a powerful force for good and change in the world. It's one of the deepest traumas a person can endure."

Olivia made up her mind. She shook her head.

"I'm not going to turn you in," she said.

Faith's face registered shock.

"You're not . . . but why?"

"After what you've been through, consider this an act of charity. And perhaps it's in honor of your sister Charity too. Go live your life, Faith."

Faith started crying so hard that Olivia had to hold her to keep her from toppling over. Olivia couldn't stop her own tears from flowing either and the two women held on to each other for a long time in the bus shelter.

"Thank you, oh thank you, thank you so much," said Faith when she caught her breath. "I will never forget this kindness, ever. I promise to pay it forward. You are amazing. I'm so indebted to you. What can I do for you? Do you want my money?"

Olivia recoiled. "No, I don't want your money."

"Do you want to get into the TV business? I can offer some advice. I would give you a reference but obviously that's not possible anymore."

"To be honest, after my internship I'm not even sure I want to be in TV anymore. Certainly not on air. Maybe a producer, like an investigative producer."

"You'd be pretty good at that." Faith chuckled through her tears, and they looked at each other. "I can't believe you recognized me. I tried so hard to hide. I should have worn my glasses tonight, even if they are broken. I'm so stupid."

"You're not stupid, Faith. If you want to know the truth, it was your walk. It's distinctive. Maybe practice a different gait."

"My walk . . ." Faith mused. "I hadn't even thought about that."

"Listen," said Olivia. "You're not the only one who's been hiding something. I actually have several confessions to make to you. Do you remember that note you gave me in the parking lot the day you disappeared? I feel awful, but something made me open it in the women's room on my way back to the newsroom. I then started looking to see if the people on the note were suspects. I feel terrible about opening it, though, and violating your orders. I should have just handed it to Tom."

"My sister . . . She was right about the note . . ." said Faith softly.

"What do you mean?"

"She worried all along that you read it. I told her I didn't think you had. You fooled me."

"I guess I was just a bad intern," said Olivia. "And, well, there is one more thing I did. I planted the pen cam in your office to try and gather evidence against Matthew when I thought he killed you."

"That was *you*?" Faith asked. Olivia nodded.

Faith grabbed Olivia's hand.

"Wow, you seem like a very feisty young woman, Olivia. I truly admire that. It took me a long while to find the courage to be one and here you are, just in your twenties. You'll be a great investigative producer, or whatever you want to do."

"Thank you," said Olivia as a gush of warmth filled her stomach.

"No, *thank you.*"

"Do you forgive me for opening the note?" asked Olivia. She was surprised at how much she felt she needed that closure.

"One thousand percent," said Faith. "Do you forgive me for not remembering your name in the parking lot that day? I should not have just called you 'intern.'"

"One thousand percent. And as long as we're opening up to each other, there is one more thing I want to say," said Olivia. "Remember how you told me 'Good luck at Channel 9' as you were leaving in the parking lot after you gave me the note?"

"Yes."

"It seemed a bit odd, almost like something you would say to someone when you know you're not going to see them again. I thought about that a lot after your supposed death. I dismissed it as a coincidence but it makes sense now. You knew you weren't going back that night, right?"

"Correct," said Faith softly. "Very good detective work. I guess I was too transparent. But I meant it. I wanted you to have a good experience there even if I didn't."

"You didn't?"

"I shouldn't say that. It was my childhood dream, my dad's favorite station, and he was the one who got me into meteorology. But the reality did not live up to it. I tried my best, you know, to connect with viewers, but I couldn't connect with coworkers much. And some viewers got out of hand and became stalkers. It was just . . . a lot. Being a public figure is an incredible amount of work. I needed to escape. Please promise you won't turn my sister and me in. We're not bad people. We're good people. We just wanted a fresh start."

"I promise, I told you that. Your secret is safe with me. Promise me you won't ever tell anyone I planted the pen cam or opened the note. I could get in a lot of trouble for the pen cam."

"I promise," said Faith. Her eyes filled with tears, and she squeezed Olivia's hand. The women stood up and looked at each other one more time, smiling. Wordlessly they nodded and walked out of the bus shelter. The line for cabs was down to just three people, and Faith stepped behind the others while giving Olivia a little wave. Olivia lifted her hand back, turning and walking toward the hotel.

As she made her way through the streets, she thought that it might have been nice to find out *how* Faith had done this. The mischievous part of Olivia wanted to know how one fakes one's own death and escapes. But she realized as she passed the Bellagio fountains, now quiet and waiting for their next show, that maybe in the end it was good if she didn't know. Some things were better left unsaid.

Back at the hotel, Olivia wondered if her aunt and uncle were asleep. The three of them had adjoining rooms with a door between the two. Kicking off her shoes, Olivia changed into sweatpants and a T-shirt and put her ear to the door. She could hear the TV and Jim's laughter. She knocked softly.

"Come in," called Carol, and Olivia opened the door. Carol and Jim were sitting up in bed in their pajamas, shoulders leaning into one another, watching one of the comedy shows. Their faces were glowing from the TV and from what felt to Olivia like an internal light of happiness. They both grinned at her.

"Hey late-nighter, how was your walk on the Strip?" asked Jim.

"Good," replied Olivia. "Believe it or not, I actually did an act of charity."

"Oh yeah, what?" asked Jim.

"I saw a woman near a bus shelter who needed help."

"What did you do?" asked Carol.

"I gave her the help she needed," Olivia said.

"Did she ask you for money?" Jim pressed.

Olivia hesitated for a moment, thinking how to respond. She decided that her aunt and uncle did not need to know that Faith had faked her own death. Sometimes a hero could remain just that. It would be Olivia's secret. And Faith was now a hero to Olivia in a different way. Aunt Carol could continue to eulogize the Faith she knew and loved.

"Something like that," Olivia responded. "I gave her what she needed to get back on her own two feet."

"What a sweetheart you are," said Carol. "That was awfully nice of you. I bet she really appreciated that."

"She did." Olivia nodded as a lump threatened her throat. "She really, really did."

"Want to hang out and watch some TV?" Jim asked.

Olivia could think of nothing she wanted more. She could only nod again, though, because the lump in her throat now prevented her from speaking. Carol patted the spot on the bed next to her.

"Plenty of room for you, hon."

Olivia crawled into bed next to her aunt and uncle and snuggled against Carol's side. Jim and Carol were more like Olivia's parents than her own mom and dad, and Olivia was grateful for them. In fact, it was hard to imagine life if they weren't in it.

The three of them stayed like that for a long time, laughing together. Olivia's thoughts drifted to the future. Just one more semester of college and she would be out in the real world. It was scary, but she also had a distinct feeling that she'd be OK; a feeling of confidence was in her that she had the skills to make her way successfully. She thought of Faith, saying she'd pay it forward after Olivia let her walk free. She wondered what Faith might do. Maybe something to help other women, or little kids.

Olivia went back to her own room forty-five minutes later. As she brushed her teeth and washed her face, she realized that she likely would never have all of the answers on Faith's disappearance, but she knew one thing to be true: Matthew had killed Tom and he was locked up, so justice had been served.

She didn't see any reason to further punish Faith or Faith's sister. They hadn't done anything like that. She recommitted to never telling anyone.

An act of charity had never been so satisfying.

CHAPTER THIRTY-EIGHT

Faith

Las Vegas

Faith was still in shock as she sat in the back of the taxi heading toward the condo. One of the interns had been in Vegas and somehow had recognized Faith despite Faith's best efforts. An intern!

Moreover, the intern could have turned her in but didn't. It had been petrifying sitting in that bus shelter wondering if the entire world she and Hope had built was about to crumble. Now that she had Olivia's promise, Faith felt much better but also a little wary. Promises were just that. What if Olivia changed her mind? Faith didn't know Olivia very well. Faith decided she needed to book that facelift *now*. The plastic-surgeon-to-the-stars place was so popular with the elite crowd that it took a long time to get an appointment.

Inhaling a ragged breath, Faith looked out the window as city lights gave way to suburban quiet. The cab was nearing their place, a nondescript condo that resembled all of the others in the complex, sandy colored with low, rugged shrubbery.

Hope would be on her date and likely out at the bars or

casinos for a while. Faith just wanted to collect herself and take a steamy, hot shower. Then she would look up the plastic surgeon place and book the earliest they had. It still might be months away.

Hope would be apocalyptic about this latest development with the intern recognizing Faith. Maybe Faith wouldn't even tell her, she'd just say that it was time to get the facelift done. Stupid, she was so stupid for not wearing her glasses that night and for never considering how her walk might be recognizable. She would be smarter moving forward.

The condo was dark, and Faith flipped on lights as she went. As she got to the kitchen and turned on the overhead, something caught her eye immediately.

An envelope was propped against the napkin holder on the table. On the outside was scrawled:

FAITH: READ THIS

It was Hope's handwriting. Faith furrowed her brow. Hope must have left this for Faith after Faith went to the Bellagio. Hope had said she needed more time to get ready for her date and would meet Faith there. Picking up the envelope, Faith saw that it was sealed and was thin, as if it held just one piece of paper inside.

She opened it and leaned against the counter.

Dear Sis,

We've been through so much together. From Charity to Dad to this. I love you and I thank you SO MUCH for what you did to gain us freedom, but I have decided that we need to live apart. It's not safe for either of us to continue to travel as a twosome. Therefore, I have taken my portion of the money and you won't see me again. I'm not really on a date. I'll be long gone by the time you read this. Don't try to find me. You won't. I'm sorry I won't ever see you again but trust me that I have given this a lot of thought and it's truly what's best for both of us. You have your fake ID, this condo, and a chance at a new life. I have that chance too. The money is in my name and I promise I will use it well. I left you enough to get by for a while. It's in your top dresser drawer.

Good luck and be well.

Love Always,
Hope

PS—don't try to mess with me. Remember what I asked you tonight at the Bellagio? I recorded our conversation. If you turn me in I'll turn you in and it will be way worse for you.

Faith dropped the paper.

She looked around wild-eyed.

This couldn't be happening.

It had to be a joke.

Yet, everything around her was normal. The kitchen was exactly as she had left it just a few hours ago, dishes in the dish rack, apples in a bowl, the spinning spice rack on the counter.

She took off running down the hallway to Hope's bedroom. The bed was made but there was nothing on the bedside table and usually Hope had her medications, a phone charger, her glasses, and a water cup there.

Yanking open the closet doors and dresser drawers in Hope's room, she found them all empty. In the bathroom, all of Hope's cosmetics and personal items were gone.

Faith wanted to scream, but she knew that if she disturbed the neighbors and police came this could get ugly fast.

Dashing into her own room, she pulled open the top dresser drawer. A wad of cash was there, hundred-dollar bills held together with rubber bands. It was definitely many thousands, but she also recognized right away that it wasn't enough to live on for very long. It might not even get her that facelift. Hope had millions pouring in from life insurance and she was leaving Faith this tiny amount?

"*Nooooo!*" Faith cried out. A pounding started in her head. "*Fucking bitch!*" she said as loud as she dared without the neighbors being disturbed. Running wildly through the house, she opened every drawer and moved each bit of furniture to see if there was more money anywhere. There wasn't.

Making her way to the kitchen, she slid to the floor, back against the stove, and rocked and moaned. Sobs came. She hadn't cried like this since Charity's death, since Hope had told her that she had been the one responsible.

Faith ripped her wig off and hurled it across the room, a visceral noise coming from so deep inside of her she surprised herself with its depth. She couldn't help it. *Please, neighbors,* she thought, *don't call the cops.*

This was her money. She had made it. She was the one on TV who had done everything needed, from the earring forecast to the videos. She built up equity in the community while Hope accomplished next to nothing. Always leaving her jobs because she hated her bosses, the hours, the duties, her coworkers, you name it. Always drifting around. Now that two-faced, conniving scumbag had Faith's money flowing to her and there was *nothing* Faith could do. Hope had her and had her good.

Faith's mind whipped back to the PS part of the note: Hope telling her not to go public and saying she had recorded their conversation. What had Faith actually said on the bench? It had all seemed so casual, two sisters sharing margaritas and laughs.

Now it came back to her. Hope's questions:

"You're still OK with being the one to come up with the idea for Tom's death? And Matthew rotting in jail for it despite being innocent?"

And Faith's answers:

"I had to do it. What choice did I have? When someone wrongs you, you have every right to retaliate. That's how the world works. An eye for an eye. I couldn't just sit by like a patsy. For once I wasn't the puppet but the puppet master and it felt so good to be in charge."

With a sickening revelation she realized she was not the puppet master. Again. She had never been in her life and never would. Hope had been the one pulling the strings all along.

Faith grabbed her purse and took her cell phone out. She pushed the button for Hope's number but knew already what she would hear, and did:

"We're sorry, the number you have dialed is no longer in service . . ."

Anger came like a tsunami but then took a sharp left turn to a deep, deep fear. She was on her own. Her best friend, her sister, gone.

Faith was by herself in Las Vegas and apparently still recognizable. Her only skill was being a television meteorologist, and that career was shot. She could stay in the condo, as it was paid off, but she couldn't sell it—it was in Hope's name.

She and Hope were supposed to live the high life now. They were supposed to be the dynamic duo, never working again but enjoying everything good in this world, from clothes to food to travel. And now Faith was going to be broke soon if she didn't start working on her own in Sin City, while Hope wined and dined in whatever place she was going to. On *Faith's money.* And Faith was powerless to stop it.

Hope, who had played the scolding, "do what I say," "I'm smarter than you," big-sister role for way too long, had outwitted the little sister in one final coup de grâce.

Faith ran to the bathroom and retched into the toilet, closing her eyes so she didn't have to see what was in the bowl. Flushing, she sank down to the floor and sat there for a long time.

She knew one thing. She *had* to change her appearance. If Olivia ever squealed or if anyone else ever recognized her, it was over. Her mind went from the high-end plastic surgery place to one at a strip mall nearby she had seen ads for.

Nose jobs, chin lifts, eye lifts. Cheap. In and out in just hours!

She would have to take her chances with some low-level doc whom she hoped had a license.

Her body remained weak from throwing up and felt like an empty sack, but her mind kept zooming ahead, thinking of the next steps to stay hidden.

She would get a job somewhere in Vegas off the Strip and away from tourists. Maybe as a waitress. It was something she had done in college, starting the semester she was kicked out for stealing.

At least she had a place to live. She could stay at the condo and save money with an eye on eventually getting out of town. It was not the path she had expected, but it was clear she would have to figure out an escape. Again. Where she might go, she had no idea. The maps she and Hope had pored over in Gills Rock came to mind. There were endless possibilities, sea to shining sea in this vast country, from coastal towns to farming communities to mountain enclaves to bustling cities to desert oases. Perhaps she could be a nomad and just try them all.

She thought of how she had promised Olivia she would pay it forward. Faith had meant it too, but that was also when she believed she had the means to do so. She wasn't sure what she could do to pay that debt now given that she had very little money. Then she realized that maybe she was already paying it forward in a different way.

Or, more accurately, she was paying it backward.

This had to be the world handing her one final punishment for Charity and what Faith had done to get her little sister abducted. In some ways Faith had known that her comeuppance would happen eventually. You can't lose your little sister and never get punished. She was repaying the universe now. A bill she had owed for thirty years.

Olivia had told Faith that she was letting her go in an act of charity. That was one of the most beautiful things anyone had ever said to her. But this betrayal from Hope was perhaps an act *because* of Charity. And strangely, Faith could already feel just a tiny bit of the long-burrowed guilt in her soul starting to lift. It was a debt she had needed to pay and if this was the way to do it, well, so be it.

She stood up from the bathroom floor and looked at herself in the mirror as she realized sharply that there was no one in her life anymore. Not one soul. No one she had to answer to, listen to, or be worried about. Gone was Hope. Forever, Faith knew that. Hope would always look out for Hope first and foremost. Gone were the coworkers at Channel 9. Gone was Steve the stalker and all guys like him. She would never be on TV again and put herself in that kind of position with celebrity-obsessed people. It was time to stand on her own two feet and not rely on anyone else. It might bring loneliness, sure, at least until she made new friends under her new identity. It might be tricky with money for a bit, yes, but it would also bring power in a way she had never fully had.

It was a jarring revelation.

When she had first opened Hope's letter in the kitchen, shock, fury, betrayal, fear, and sadness had all rolled through her in various waves. Now, a different emotion began to dominate.

She leaned closer to her image and looked deeply into her own eyes and she was surprised to realize that despite everything, all of the losses and all of the changes, the new emotion she felt was actually . . . a tiny bit of excitement. She hadn't expected that, and she had to accept it and make room for it.

In one night, she had lost Hope but actually gained hope. She lost Charity decades ago but had also been handed unexpected charity by Olivia. She had almost lost the true Faith over the years by becoming a larger-than-life TV personality, a caricature, just a name, but now the real Faith was back, as was her faith in her own smarts to figure it out. There was simply too much living to do to give up.

A small smile began to play at the corners of her mouth. Faith's eyes started to glow and her cheeks flushed pink. She looked at herself for a long time, until that hint of a smile became an actual grin.

Turning, she walked quickly back to the kitchen and grabbed Hope's letter. The first tear was so gratifying. Ripping it up into the tiniest pieces she could, she watched with immense satisfaction as each one fluttered into the garbage can.

"Goodbye and good luck, bitch," she said aloud when the last piece fell. She would miss her sister, of course, but it was so incredibly freeing to realize that she would never have to be under Hope's influence again.

It might not have happened in the way Faith would have ever imagined or envisioned, but the reality was that Faith was now the puppet master of her own life. Finally. Every decision, every outcome was entirely hers.

And she couldn't wait to get started.

ACKNOWLEDGMENTS

My first thank-you goes to my editor, Jen Enderlin, who helped brainstorm this book and improved it at every step of the way. Eternal gratitude to my two agents, Meg Ruley and Logan Harper, for their creative ideas, mentorship, and advocacy. Thank you also to the incredible team at St. Martin's Press: Katie Bassel, Erica Martirano, Brant Janeway, Kejana Ayala, Lisa Senz, Christina Lopez, Mike Storrings, and Anne Marie Tallberg; and at the Jane Rotrosen Agency, Allison Hufford. I couldn't do it without you all.

My husband, Paul, listened to me reading chapters aloud and helped kick around many, many ideas. It's not every partner who will indulge you as you hash over devilish plot points and complex character sketches, and I am so thankful for his support. Our two sons, Jake and Charlie, have gotten used to their mom being immersed in her latest thriller and they just laugh at my odd habits and what they call my "bizarre mind." Thanks to my mother, Judy, and stepfather, Howard, for always being sounding boards for my fiction as well as everything else in life. A shout-out to the general manager at my TV station,

Anne Brown, and our company, Weigel Broadcasting, for their encouragement. And a tip of the hat to my coworker, meteorologist Michael Schlesinger, who asked what I was writing next. When he found out it was about Detroit and weather he said, "Do you want some weather stats to go in the book?" Of course I said yes. You can find them in chapter 4.

Deep appreciation to everyone who read my first thriller, *The Business Trip*, and/or this one. Going from a blank page on my computer screen to a book is quite the process, and I will never take it for granted.

ABOUT THE AUTHOR

Henry Jorgenson

Jessie Garcia is an award-winning journalist who has risen through the ranks in television news first as an anchor/reporter, then to newsroom management. She is the news director at the CBS affiliate in Milwaukee. Her nonfiction books *My Life with the Green and Gold: Tales from 20 Years of Sportscasting* and *Going for Wisconsin Gold: Stories of Our State Olympians* won Midwest Book Awards, and her documentary *Leaps and Bounds: The Men Who Changed Track and Field* was featured in more than a dozen film festivals. She has also taught journalism at four universities. A native of Madison, Wisconsin, Jessie has two adult sons and resides in Milwaukee with her husband, as well as a dog who stole their hearts at the Humane Society and a cat who wandered into their front yard one day and never left.